OLD FLAME: DANTE'S STORY

(MORELLI FAMILY, #8)

SAM MARIANO

This is a work of fiction. Names, characters, businesses, places, events and incidents are either the products of the author's imagination, or used fictitiously. Any resemblance to actual persons, living or dead, or actual events is purely coincidental.

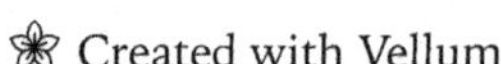
Created with Vellum

AUTHOR'S NOTE:

Warning: This is dark romance with a bad guy hero.

This is also only *sort of* a standalone. While this is Dante's whole story, this spin-off book is really only intended for existing Morelli family series readers, as a lot of things tie into the original series. If you haven't read those books yet, you won't know some of the characters, dynamics, or histories. This book will also spoil *major* things that happen in the Morelli series and ruin a lot of the magic of that journey. In short, this story really flows better if you're already exposed to and all caught up on the Morelli way of life. :)

Accidental Witness is where the Morelli family story begins, and that's where new readers should begin—not with Dante's book.

1

DANTE

THERE'S a lot of shit that goes through your head the night before your soulmate is supposed to marry someone else.

First, there's all the good times you had together. Flashes of holding her in your arms in Greece, not a foot away from the rough sea, feeling every slight movement of her body as she sighs and marvels at what an incredible view it is. It *is* an incredible view, but she's all you really want to look at. Fuck the great architecture all around us, fuck the choppy waves of a moody sea. Her blue eyes are the only sea I want to get lost in, her lips and her curves the only architecture I want to explore.

A calm moment, almost insignificant in the great scheme of things, but the kind of moment that plants itself deep inside you because it's the moment you know: this woman is my home. This is the woman I'm going to spend the rest of my life with, and there's no point looking at anyone else anymore.

Then you think about the bad times. There weren't even that many, it's just that when things get bad in my family, they can't just be normal bad—they're fucking traumatizing. Lives are ruined, people die, the course going forward is forever changed, even if it isn't my fucking doing.

Even if someone else's sins are the main reason I lost her, I know I could have handled it better. Could have been a little softer, a little more fucking understanding. She was upset and I could have been there for her, could have reassured her, but I was more focused on cleaning up a goddamn mess. My pride was scratched besides that, so instead of doing the thing she needed me to do, instead of controlling the fucking situation and fixing it so she eventually got over it, I let it get out of hand. I let her imagination run away with her. I let *her* run away.

I didn't know just how much I would fucking miss her.

A pit of emptiness inside me seems to hollow out even more. I'm used to it being there, but damn, if I can't feel it more acutely tonight. There's something about knowing beyond a shadow of a doubt that the only woman for you is perfectly content to walk down the aisle with some other bastard—that knowledge can't go down smoothly, no matter how much Scotch you imbibe to try and ease the passage.

Usually I sip on and savor my favorite Scotch, but on the eve before Colette's fucking wedding, I'm making an exception. There's not much left in my glass now. I throw the rest back, then wave down the waitress so I can get a refill. I'm at the strip club I own with my brothers, but I don't give a fuck about the gyrations of the half-naked woman on the pole a few feet in front of me. I don't give a fuck about anything tonight.

The waitress comes over, glancing at my empty glass, then briefly looking me over. My pain is laced with rage tonight and I feel like it must be plain to see, but I know it's not. I'm a consummate fucking professional. I might be torn up inside, but my exterior won't show any signs of it.

"I need another drink," I inform her, my words thick as they tumble out of my mouth.

Her gaze shoots back to my face. As a cocktail waitress, she has seen enough men in my state to know she should cut me off, but given who I am, she offers an obedient smile instead. "Of course, Mr. Morelli. Can I get you anything else?"

Before I can answer her, I catch sight of my younger brother heading my way, his dark brow furrowed in disapproval.

"Ah, Christ," I mutter, sitting up a little straighter.

Alec stops beside the waitress and stares at me. "What are you still doing here? I cut you off and told you to go home an hour ago."

I sit forward, grabbing the glass and holding it out for the waitress. "You did, but turns out you're not my fucking boss," I tell him. Turning my dark gaze back on the waitress, I tell her, "I don't have all night, honey."

She grabs the glass and turns, heading to the bar to get me a refill.

Alec turns to stare at her in mild disbelief, then he looks back at me. "This is it, Dante. This is your last drink. You're fucking hammered and enough is enough."

"No, I'm not," I mutter.

Alec is the second youngest in our family, and the absolute youngest of the children produced by both of my parents. By the time our mom and dad created Alec, I guess me and my older brother had already soaked up all the dysfunction their gene pairing had to offer. To be fair, Mateo and I definitely took more than our allotted shares.

Whatever the reason, Alec is normally a pretty laid-back guy, but right now he's agitated and impatient with me.

"Yes, you are, and this is fucking stupid." Sighing, he drops onto the booth next to me and meets my gaze. "Just go talk to her. Give her a chance to change her mind. Maybe she's thinking about you, too. Maybe she's having doubts about this whole thing. Maybe you showing up tonight is exactly what she needs. Maybe she would call off the wedding and come back voluntarily."

There are a whole lot of maybes in there, and they're all bullshit. Colette has had plenty of time to back out and change her mind if she wanted to. Me showing up tonight like some fucking sad sack piece of shit wouldn't change a goddamned thing—not for the better, anyway.

"If she's having doubts, she doesn't marry some other asshole tomorrow," I tell him. "That's not a thing you do when you have doubts, Alec."

"Maybe it's gone too far for her to back out without a reason. Go give her one."

I shake my head. "It's too late for that."

Besides, I *did* try to talk to her. After I found out Colette was engaged, I finally broke my own fucking rule and went to the flower shop to see her. To tell her she was making a mistake and I wanted her to leave this stupid asshole and come back home. She didn't want to hear it then, and there's no reason to think she'd want to hear it the night before she plans to marry the sorry bastard.

She doesn't *want* to come back to me, that's the problem. Colette Fontaine is exactly where she wants to be tonight—she's just not where *I* want her.

No point telling Alec that, though. He wouldn't approve and it's none of his fucking business anyway.

"It is *not* too late," Alec insists. "*Tomorrow* it will be too late. If you go through with this, Dante... she may hate you forever. You might really lose her. You may *never* get her back."

"Fuck that," I mutter. I know Colette. She was made for me. I know she might resist initially, but she can't hate me forever. Only for a time, then it will pass and she'll be mine again, like she always should have been.

I'm relieved at the sight of the waitress. She brings my drink over, but I don't even let it hit the table before I snatch it and take another gulp, trying in vain to numb the pain gnawing away at my insides. Trying to numb the trace of paralyzing fear, too. The fear that Alec could be right and *I* could be wrong, that Colette might hate me forever for what I'm about to do. That I may really *never* get her back, even I give her no choice but to be with me.

I picture Colette in her room right now, gazing dreamily at the puffy white wedding dress hanging on her mirror. I know it's hanging on her mirror because I couldn't keep from checking on her and I saw the goddamn thing. It's easy to imagine her running her hands along the delicate fabric, envisioning herself in it when she marries the new man of her dreams.

Fucking bullshit. How can *he* be the man she wants to marry when it used to be me? How can you just change your mind about something like that?

Not for the first time, the thought passes through my mind that maybe I was just wrong about her. I was a few years younger then, greener than I am now, even if I didn't know it at the time. Maybe she doesn't love hard enough to be with me and I'm remembering her wrong. Maybe she left because she truly isn't capable of sticking it out with me and maybe forcing her to come back to me won't change that. Maybe nothing will.

Nah, fuck that, too. Just like I do every other time the thought blows across my mind, I stomp on it until it's gone. I know what Colette and I can have together. I know she's it for me, and if I'm not it for her, well, that'll just have to change. Colette Fontaine is mine, and nobody is going to stop me from claiming what's mine.

Not Colette.

Not her fiancé.

Nobody.

I take another gulp. I'm gonna need another refill in a minute, so the waitress hasn't even bothered to walk away. Alec is going to be so pissed when she goes to get me a refill again after he expressly told her not to, but she'll do it, anyway. This one wants my dick, and if she thinks ruffling Alec's feathers to obey me instead of him will finally get it done, she won't hesitate.

It's a waste of her fucking time, but I don't mind wasting her time.

The glass is empty again, so I hand it back to her. I don't bother saying anything this time. She knows what I want, so she promptly heads back toward the bar to get it.

Alec calls after her, "For Christ's sake, at least make this one on the rocks."

"Neat," I call after her more forcefully, though it's probably an unnecessary reminder. I expect she would've brought it the way she knows I like it regardless of Alec's interference.

"First Mateo, now *you* just can't keep from ruining your own fucking life." Alec sighs next to me, massaging the bridge of his nose. "Why am I the only man in this goddamned family with any common sense when it comes to women?"

"Restraint," I offer, even drunk off my ass. "I have plenty of common sense, it's restraint you have more of than me, and only with this one. Someday maybe you'll find someone who makes you fucking crazy."

"God, I hope not. If I ever start acting like you self-sabotaging assholes, you have my blessing to shoot me in the face—save the poor girl and put me out of my misery in one fell swoop."

I nearly crack a rare smile, but he's not wrong. Love *is* fucking misery—at least, once you've lost the only woman you want but you can't stop craving her, it sure is. I've only ever loved Colette, so I can't say what it's like for anyone else.

"I should take her tonight," I mutter, getting lost in thoughts about how nice it would be to hold her. To touch her again, to feel her sigh against my lips as I kiss her.

"You should talk to her," Alec says again. "I'm serious. It doesn't even matter that you're drunk. I can drive you or you can call Adrian for a ride, but go to her tonight, tell her you still have all these feelings for her and you don't want her to marry this other guy. Just *tell* her that and give her a chance to change her mind."

Ha, put myself out there so she can tell me no again. Over my dead body. I ignore his shit advice and take another drink. "I'll pass," I tell him, easily. "I don't need advice or a shoulder to cry on, Alec. I've got the situation under control."

"I tried to stop Mateo and he didn't fucking listen to me. Look how well it worked out for him," Alec says, shaking his head as he stands. "You'd think you assholes could learn from each other's mistakes, I swear to God."

"I'm not Mateo, and I'm not making a mistake," I assure him, my gaze on the amber liquid in the glass.

"Yes, you are," he says seriously, watching me for another moment. "And once it's done, it's done. There's no taking this back, Dante."

Looking away from the alcohol in my glass, I meet my little brother's concerned gaze. His words irritate me more than they should. It's too late to change paths now, but since the only alternative is giving up on Colette, I wouldn't even if I could. Alec has more sympathy than the rest of us, so I'm sure he feels bad for the poor asshole who mistakenly thinks I'm gonna let him marry my woman tomorrow.

Me, I don't feel bad for anyone who's that fucking stupid. He should have known he'd never take what's mine without a little bloodshed, and his stomach's too weak for that kind of fight. It's fucking astounding that Colette went from *me* to some lily-livered desk jockey who probably doesn't even know how to throw a fucking punch.

If anyone is going to rip Colette away from me, it won't be without a fight. It won't be while blood still flows through my veins, while my heart is still pumping. The only way anyone is taking Colette away from me is if they take her out of my cold, dead arms.

I won't feel bad about prying her out of his cold, dead arms instead. Knowing who I am, any man with even a little bit of sense would know that's the price he'd pay for putting his hands on my property.

I don't need to convince Alec that this is what has to be done, but I do need to believe my own words, because I've bet absolutely everything on this hand. If Alec is right and it goes bad, I lose everything that really matters.

Alec can't be right.

I'm right.

I know I am.

Clutching that belief as tightly as my glass of Scotch, I assure my brother, "I will *never* want to take this back."

2

COLETTE

YOUR WEDDING DAY is supposed to be the happiest day of your life.

I've imagined mine lots of times—usually with a different groom, a different dress, a different guest list… a different everything. I wanted a simple wedding on a beach in Greece, not a Catholic ceremony in a big, beautiful cathedral. I wanted the only guests to be a few criminals in casual wear—my future husband's immediate family, of course. I wasn't even sure I'd invite what's left of my own, because Dante is like a beautiful, seductive natural disaster; he meets you, likes you, erodes the landscape of your life until he can change it to suit him, and before you know it, you become less of who you used to be and more of who he wants you to be. His will is greater than anyone I've ever met, *everyone* I've met. By the time I was ready to marry him, I was so hopelessly lost under his current, it wouldn't have even occurred to me to object if he told me no one in my family was invited to my own wedding.

Brutally hypnotic, that was Dante Morelli. I didn't know it was happening as it did because it wasn't hard or painful; it was easy, like falling into the pages of a well-woven fairytale. Anyone who suggested he was too good to be true wasn't long for my life anyway, and the damndest thing is, I barely noticed.

I barely noticed a lot of things until ignoring the harsh, scary reality all around me became impossible. Until I woke up and realized my fantasy was a nightmare, my prince was a monster, and I needed to escape if he'd let me and never look back.

I guess I'm the fool for believing he actually let me go.

I *didn't* believe it at first. I was paranoid, always looking over my shoulder. I was on edge every time the bell rang at my shop, alerting me to a new customer. Each time a well-dressed man walked through the front door, my stomach would sink and I would think that was the day Dante had come back for me.

For years I lived like a fugitive on the run from him. Then, finally, I allowed myself to move on. *Finally,* I recovered from him enough to let someone else into my life, into my heart. Finally, I let myself have some comfort instead of the self-imposed loneliness that resulted from constantly running from a monster who wasn't even chasing me.

I convinced myself that I had been overly dramatic all that time, overestimating my importance to him. Monster or not, Dante Morelli has a *lot* to offer a woman, and there was never a shortage of women who noticed. Surely Dante had picked out another one once the bruise on his ego faded. Surely he didn't even think of me anymore. Surely by then I had become just one more woman in his past—at least, that's what Declan assured me on the nights when fear would overtake me, when something innocuous like the wind blowing a branch against the window terrified me, when I couldn't focus on what we were doing, when I became unhinged in my mission to double check all the locks and look out each window to make sure he wasn't outside. To make sure he hadn't come for me.

When I was with Dante, he was my fairytale.

After I left him, he became my nightmare.

The line between the two is much thinner than people think. For me, it was so thin I couldn't even see it until I accidentally stepped over it.

Today, on my wedding day, I feel like the last character alive at the brutal end of a ghastly horror film, almost numb as I look around at all the destruction I have wrought.

Because make no mistake, *I* wrought this destruction.

Deep in my heart, I knew Dante wouldn't leave me alone. Deep in my heart, I knew he would never be done with me, but I let clueless people who didn't understand that life convince me otherwise. I'm so helplessly angry at them for feeding me that reassuring bullshit, but I'm angrier at myself for listening. Those people didn't know Dante. They meant well. They believed all their reassuring, stupid, wrong words.

But I knew better.

I knew him.

This is all my fault.

I dared run away from the devil and start a life without him, and now he's going to burn me for that unforgivable sin.

FIVE YEARS AGO

FIVE YEARS AGO

Colette

I smiled up at Dante as he opened the car door, offering his big, strong hand to help me out. I didn't need help, but I craved that man so much I seldom passed up a chance to touch him. Once I emerged from the car, his arm moved around my back and came to settle on my hip in a casually possessive gesture that reassured me he felt the same way.

"I like this dress on you," he murmured in my ear.

I leaned closer and wrapped my arm around his waist, nestling into his side. "I'm glad."

"I'll like it even better later, when I'm taking it off you."

Biting down on my bottom lip, I offered him a devilish smile. "You think that now. Wait until you see how many buttons it has down the back."

Cocking a dark eyebrow, he slid me a look of mild displeasure. "You know I don't have the patience for buttons."

"It was on sale," I told him, in defense of my purchase. "And it's so pretty," I added, running a hand down my hip.

"I'm gonna destroy it later," he stated, and I knew he wasn't just saying it the way some men would. I knew he meant it. "Enjoy those pretty buttons while they're still attached."

He's such an obstinate brute, *I thought. The mental image filled my head of him jerking my beautiful dress open, ruining the poor thing in his haste to get to my naked body… I couldn't seem to muster much sympathy for the dress.*

My stomach sank with anticipation and I bent my head to check his watch. Knowing what I had coming later, it seemed like dinner would take a million years.

Every Sunday we went to family dinner at his older brother's house. The first time Dante brought me for family dinner I thought it might be awkward, given my history with his brother, Mateo. It was hardly a great love affair, but Mateo met me first. He was the first Morelli to set my heart to fluttering and my stomach to sinking. Before Dante's dark eyes burned a hole right through me, Mateo's did. His were the first hands that traveled the curves of my body, the first lips to brush mine in a darkened corner. Even though Dante ended up being the one to sweep me off my feet, I still had a soft spot for Mateo, and I was terrified my extremely possessive boyfriend might notice and take issue.

All my worrying was for nothing, though. Mateo was far from hung up on me, and shortly thereafter, he met Beth. Once he had a girlfriend of his own at the table, I no longer had to worry about Dante watching too closely and making a big deal out of nothing.

We were early to dinner that week, but I needed to see Beth anyway. Two purses dangled from my arm—a cute, black one that belonged to me, and a smaller silver one I needed to return to her. I borrowed it a few weeks earlier and kept forgetting to return it. Beth had been supremely unmotivated the past few Sundays anyway, so getting there early allowed me a chance to go upstairs and find her, maybe perk her up before we got dinner started.

I knew she and Mateo were having problems, but I also knew Mateo had no intention of letting her go, so the best thing I could do for her was try to get her excited about him again.

Given I had spent some time pulled under the spell of Mateo Morelli myself, it shouldn't have been hard to remind his struggling girlfriend of all the really wonderful things about him. Even if I had never liked Mateo, I had plenty of practice handling my own high-maintenance Morelli.

Mateo is more difficult than Dante, though. As the oldest of the Morelli children, a lot of responsibility fell on Mateo's shoulders at a young age. I don't know the grisly details about his childhood, but I know there are plenty. Really, you need only meet him to figure he must have a fucked up past. The man is a puppet master, pulling the strings of his loved ones like we're all here to perform a show just for him.

Given all that, I could understand why Beth was feeling a little burnt out. Mateo must be a very demanding man to love. Beth knew what she was signing up for, though. I'm sure he warned her like he warned me. Didn't do much good for me, either, so I understand why she didn't listen. It's hard to focus on the underlying truth of a warning like that when it's falling from such sensual lips.

Beth more than ignored the warning, though, she threw herself into the deep end. She treated their relationship like a race, and she needed to hurry up and win the gold before anything changed and she lost her chance. Only a few months into dating, Beth turned up pregnant. I think she assumed she was landing herself a whale, but what she got instead was a cage—gilded, and with a handsome, powerful captor, but a cage nonetheless.

It gained her a beautiful baby girl and the love of the most ruthless man in Chicago. It wouldn't have been such a bad hand for the right woman, but Beth's increasingly desperate disinterest in Mateo made me worry… maybe she wasn't.

Still, since she was well and truly stuck, I considered it my duty as her almost sister-in-law to try and help her see the silver lining.

When we finally approached the front door of Morelli mansion, Dante opened it with the comfortable familiarity of someone who still lived there, even though he had moved out earlier that year.

"Was it strange growing up in such an enormous house?" I asked him casually, as we strolled inside.

Dante's gaze flickered to me. "No. It was a normal house to me."

Normal isn't the word that comes to mind when looking around the palatial residence. It's a home fit for royalty, and it suits Dante's family because sometimes it feels like they are *a royal family—just with stolen crowns, ruling over a city that shouldn't belong to them.*

We were no more than through the front door and a little blonde maid came hustling into the foyer. Her blue eyes were wide and uncharacteristically haunted. Before I could ask what was wrong, a man with scars on the left side of his face came following after her.

"I told you—" Adrian stopped dead and stared at Dante. "What are you doing here?"

Dante's gaze flickered from the maid to the man who works for his family, generally cleaning up messes. Adrian is also an old friend of Mateo's, so it wasn't unusual for him to be at family dinner, even though he isn't technically family. "What do you mean, what am I doing here? It's Sunday. We're here for dinner."

Adrian sighed, closed his eyes, and pinched the bridge of his nose. "Ah, Christ."

Dante's voice hardened, his next words snapping like rubber bands. "What's wrong?"

I stiffened at his tone, but it was nothing I hadn't witnessed before. I was more distracted by Adrian's clear dismay. In my limited interactions with the man, I had never seen an unguarded expression on his face. In that moment he was clearly alarmed, so I knew it must be bad.

Adrian's distrustful gaze drifted to me before returning to Dante. "I need to talk to you in the study."

Away from me. I wasn't offended. I knew the traditional Morelli men were raised to keep the women out of business matters, and I wasn't interested in those, anyway.

Glancing back at me, Dante told me, "Wait here."

Touching Dante's arm, I nodded. We didn't exchange any words; we didn't have to.

I felt bereft as soon as my fingertips left his well-muscled arm. Ordinarily I always felt insulated from the worst parts of their lifestyle, but with Adrian's urgency, I had to wonder if there was danger lurking. Was it even safe to be there? I figured it must be. It was hard to imagine anywhere safer than Morelli mansion, with its gates and surveillance, not to mention the army of capable, merciless men either living there or visiting for Sunday night dinner. I always felt safe at Dante's house knowing he would protect me, but I was probably even safer at Morelli mansion.

The maid rushed down the hall away from us. Adrian looked after her, but since Dante stood there waiting to be debriefed, Adrian didn't chase her.

My mind raced with what could be wrong, but I told myself I'd know soon. Or I wouldn't, but Dante would, and I'd be able to tell just being near him if the situation was under control or something worth worrying about.

All alone in the foyer, I considered taking a seat on the upholstered bench, but then my gaze drifted to the ornate double staircase. Imagining the men would be in the study for a while, I thought about going to find Beth so I could give her purse back. Beth was Mateo's live-in girlfriend, the mother of his baby girl. If there was a threat, he was bound to make sure she and Isabella were safer than any of us.

Decision made, I cast a glance back at the study before heading up the stairs. Dante did tell me to stay put, but he knew I was bringing Beth's purse back, so if he came out of the study before I made it back, he'd know where to find me.

It was a long walk to Mateo's wing of the house. An errant wave of unease moved through me as I approached his closed bedroom door, but I wasn't sure why. I paused outside and knocked lightly. No one called from the other side, but I figured Beth could be in the master bathroom or the walk-in closet getting dressed for dinner. She might not have heard me. Turning the knob, I pushed the door and eased it open slowly enough for someone to protest if I wasn't invited—and slowly enough that, just in case Mateo had come upstairs for a pre-dinner fuck, I would hear them and be able to flee with no one the wiser.

No sex noises, no sharp warning not to come in, so I peeked my head inside. My gaze searched the room for Beth and promptly found her. In bed? It was nearly dinner time, what was she doing in bed? I didn't want to wake her so I almost turned around and left, but before I could pull the door closed, I saw him.

Directly across from me, Mateo Morelli sat on the floor. I had never seen Mateo sit on the floor before and that alone jarred me, but everything *about the sight before me was unsettling. Mateo always stands tall with broad shoulders that can easily carry the weight of the whole Morelli world—and it sure can be a heavy one. He is always well put-together in a stylish-without-trying suit. He always oozes an aura of capability and command with never so much as a whisper of vulnerability.*

So it was an incredibly foreign sight, him sitting on the ground looking lost and disheveled. He was still wearing the black slacks and snowy white shirt he must have been wearing with his put-together suit, but his tie was gone, the top button of his shirt popped open and a little wrinkled, his sleeves rolled up to his elbows. His head was leaned back against the wall, his dark hair mussed like he'd run his fingers through it too many times, and there was an almost vacant look in his deep brown eyes. He was staring straight at me, but I felt like he couldn't even see me.

"Mateo?" I could hear the concern in my own voice. I was too far out of my element to mask it. I let go of the door and took a hesitant step forward.

At the sound of his name on my lips, his dark gaze focused more clearly on mine, but he didn't speak. The emptiness I saw in his eyes only a moment earlier seemed to dissipate and I saw a storm brewing in its wake. My heart galloped in my chest. I swallowed, ignoring my prickled instincts and reassuring myself, there's no danger here.

I took in his scattered appearance again, then I took a closer look at Beth on the bed.

The bedding was an absolute mess. Blankets hanging half on the floor, a bunched up bedsheet, pillows thrown everywhere. It was a disaster. Beth often left the bed messy, but this was next level, even for her. It looked like a fight or a fuck took place. Knowing Mateo, I assumed it was the latter. Maybe they had a round of particularly rough, exhausting sex and she was recovering. Maybe he was having a crisis, realizing their relationship wasn't fulfilling him no matter how hard he tried to force it.

Maybe I should have kept the purse and stayed downstairs.

Whatever was going on, I supposed I should be there for him. He was practically family. I cleared my throat and took a few steps closer, but first I glanced at Beth again to make sure she was sleeping and not just resting. If she overheard me talking to Mateo about their relationship problems, she would probably get cagey and snipe at me despite my good intentions.

"Did you guys have a fight?" I whispered to Mateo as I put the borrowed purse down on the bed.

His dark eyes looked haunted. One corner of his mouth tugged up. "I suppose you could say that."

Utterly paranoid she would wake up, I looked her way again. It occurred to me maybe I should try to lure Mateo out of the bedroom and into their living area across the hall. I'd feel more comfortable talking to him with more privacy.

That time when I looked at her, though, something felt off. From a distance I hadn't noticed the way her arm hung stiffly to the side. I tilted my head, moving forward unconsciously. The closer I got, the harder my heart began to beat. She wasn't moving, not at all. Her chest wasn't moving the way chests move when a person breathes.

All the signs were there, but I couldn't connect the dots, not until I reached out and touched her arm. She didn't move, and she was cool to the touch. Not cold, but definitely cooler than she should be. And pale. She was cold and pale.

My stomach dropped, but it couldn't be. It was impossible. Beth was too young to die. I had to know, and even though logically I knew I could just voice my fears aloud and Mateo would tell me, I reached my hand to her neck to check her pulse.

She didn't have one.

Gasping in horror, I jumped and started backing away from the body. Oh, my God. Beth couldn't be... dead. I was tempted to feel for a pulse again, but I knew it would be pointless. I already checked and there wasn't one. It wouldn't come back. Somehow... somehow Beth was dead. Everything was coming together at a horrifying pace. My brain understood that she was dead, and that's why Mateo looked the way he did, but how? Why?

Her recent unhappiness and disinterest in Mateo and the life they had together sprung to mind. I knew she was unhappy, but God, she couldn't have been that desperate, could she?

Would she really kill herself to get away from him? To hurt him? I could imagine those spiteful thoughts going through her pretty head when she was being dramatic, but I couldn't envision her actually acting on them. Who would give up their life just to spite someone they used to love? Mateo couldn't have known she was that desperate. Surely if she had gone to him, if she had told him it was that bad…

I was struggling to process it all myself, but one loud, clear instinct emerged from the befuddlement. Mateo. I needed to go to Mateo. Oh, my God, did he just find her? He must be completely traumatized.

Swallowing, I looked over at him still sitting against the wall. He knew I was over there, but he wasn't looking. Maybe he couldn't look at her again. Maybe he just couldn't deal with my grief on top of his own.

Conscious of that, I tried to put a lid on my own feelings. I was still reeling, but I wasn't the one who had just lost my partner. I could deal with my own feelings later. Beth was my friend, but she was the mother of his *baby.*

My stomach plummeted, a new horror gripping me. "Oh, my God. Where is Isabella?"

"Isabella is fine."

Mateo's voice was rough, raw in a way I'd never heard it before. My heart split for him. Without wasting another second, I went over and slid down the wall beside him, curling my legs behind me so my body was facing him. I had no idea what to say. What could I say in that moment that would even matter?

I didn't know, so I touched his thigh, wanting to offer comfort but without even a clue as to how. He turned his head and met my gaze. I knew my eyes were full of sympathy. His were full of loneliness that wasn't entirely new, and it broke my heart.

"I'm so sorry, Mateo. I didn't think… I didn't think things were this bad. I didn't think she would… I'm so sorry."

Then he looked me straight in the eye and asked, "Why did she hate me so much?"

Words stuck in my throat. Even if I knew the answer to that question, I wouldn't give it to him. Not in the wake of such a tragedy. Instead, I offered, "She didn't hate you."

"She fucking hated me," he stated, not as generous with the line between truth and lie as I was being. "She's the one who chased me. She's the one who…" He trails off, shaking his head. "I know I'm not the easiest person to get along with, but I gave her everything. I gave her fucking everything. Why wasn't it enough?"

Instead of offering useless words, I closed the distance between us and hugged him. After a moment, I finally managed, "This was not your fault, Mateo."

He laughed shortly, the sound devoid of humor. "Yes, it was."

"No," I insisted, shaking my head. I felt him finally give in to the hug, felt his strong arms slide around my waist to return it. My stomach dropped immediately.

Grieving or not, I probably should have known better than to hug him. Mateo's touch can't feel platonic. Even in the throes of deep grief, his arms locking around me that way felt shamefully intimate, reminiscent of a time when the embrace had *been intimate. The way he drew me against his hard body and pulled me close… his masculine scent, his singeing heat.*

Comfort wasn't the need I felt from him in that moment, and I wasn't sure he was thinking clearly enough to register that I couldn't be less available to offer him that *kind of comfort. Mateo would never make a move on me on an ordinary day, but it was no ordinary day. I knew we were different people, and I was aware his grief may come out differently than mine would.*

I swallowed, pulling back to signal I was ready to break the hug, but his arm remained locked around me, holding me firmly in place. With his other hand, he brushed a stray lock of dark hair off my face, a surprisingly tender gesture, coming from him.

Feeling the need to shift his focus back to Beth, I told him, "She loved you, Mateo."

When my words registered, his tone went cold. "She fucked someone else."

My eyes widened in disbelief. "What? No. No way. That's… there's no way."

He nodded, a humorless smile crossing his lips. "She did it just to hurt me. It wasn't love or lust, it was… She wanted to hurt me more than she already was with her fucking distance. She wanted to rip my fucking heart out. I guess at least she got what she wanted."

That time the sting behind my eyes caused real tears to well up. They didn't fall, but I definitely felt moisture flooding my eyes. That actually did sound like something Beth would do at her worst. She had it in her to be selfish and vindictive.

The idea of his already damaged heart being ripped out made me want to cry, and I forgot why it was a bad idea to hug him. What else was I supposed to do when one of the strongest men I knew was hurting so much?

I didn't know what to say, so I just rested my head on his shoulder and held onto him, hoping it would help in ways my words couldn't. "You didn't deserve this," I told him softly. "I know you loved her, but you deserve better than someone who would do this to you."

It was a brave thing to say at all, let alone with her death so fresh. He could have snapped at me, protective of her memory. It was fine for him to air those issues, but maybe it wasn't okay for me to comment on them.

I know some people feel it's wrong to speak ill of the dead, but I'm more concerned with the living. With the people left behind to deal with the loss, to try to make sense of it all. I figured I would rather comfort a grieving man who was still alive than lie about the virtues of the dead girl who broke his heart.

He didn't get mad or defend her memory. He said nothing for a long time, then, still holding me, he declared with a solemn finality that broke my heart, "Maybe that's too tall an order. Maybe I'm unlovable."

"You are not," I said fiercely, pulling back to meet his gaze. "You're sad right now so I'll forgive that stupid thing you just said, but you are not unlovable. Beth was unhappy with herself. No matter how much stuff you lavished on her, you couldn't change that. You couldn't make Beth like Beth. How could she ever really love you if she couldn't even love herself? You weren't the problem, Mateo. You loved her hard. You tried your best to make her happy. Please don't internalize this and take all that damage for her. Beth thought only of herself when she did this. She abandoned you, she abandoned Isabella." I shook my head, my gaze dropping. "I'm sorry, but I think it's awful."

"You wouldn't do that, hm?" he murmured.

I stiffened, feeling his breath on my neck, knowing the hug was too tight and I needed to pull out of it. "No, of course I wouldn't do that to Dante," I responded, a subtle reminder that I belonged to his brother.

"What about me?" he asked rather casually, given the question. "Think you could have survived me?"

I liked to think I could have, but it didn't matter. I cared about Mateo, but my draw to him was completely different from my draw to Dante. More surface-level, more casual, definitely not made to last. It had been a raw, sexual, magnetic pull—but it wasn't love. Mateo didn't love me either, he just had an aching void from Beth's death and he was looking for something—anything—to fill it until his heart mended. I didn't know if he would ever actually *try to take me from Dante just to ease a temporary ache, but I did know it wouldn't end well for anyone if he did.*

Trying once more to ease back, I told him, "I think we shouldn't do this right now. Or, you know, ever." Pointedly looking down at his strong arm locked around me, I added, "I also think you might wanna ease up a little."

"Remember when you worked at the club? When I used to come visit you," he mused, his gaze drifting down the curve of my shoulder, exposed in my strapless dress. His finger followed the path and my heart fluttered at the sensation of him touching me again. Inappropriate memories began to trickle back into my mind, and I searched more fervently for the escape hatch out of that moment.

"I need to go back downstairs. Come with me. Dante is downstairs with Adrian. It's not good for you to stay in here with…" I glanced back at the bed, but I couldn't look at her for more than a split second. "Come on. I'll get you a drink. Adrian will get all this cleaned up." I tried once more to pull back, but his hold remained steely. Like his brother, there's no getting out of his hold if he doesn't want you to. Finally, I pushed against his chest more adamantly. "Come on, Mateo. Please."

"All right," he finally said, letting his hand drift down my side and come to rest on my hip.

Dante's clipped tone from the doorway nearly stopped my heart. "What the fuck are you doing?"

I gasped and sprung away from Mateo. Gracelessly, I stumbled to my feet while trying to keep my short dress covering my ass. "I was just—"

His eyes flashing with hot anger, he didn't wait for my answer. He stormed across the bedroom and grabbed my arm, yanking me in his direction. "Get the fuck away from him."

"Dante," I objected, instinctively trying to pull my arm from his too-firm grasp.

"You were practically in his fucking lap," Dante snapped, glaring at me.

"I was—" Jabbing a finger toward the bed, I blurted, "Beth… He found her… I was just trying to comfort him. It was just a—an innocent hug."

Dante's lips curved up cynically and he looked from his brother to me. "Is that what he told you? That he fucking found her like this?" Looking back at Mateo, his tone harder, he said, "I guess she probably wouldn't have pressed her tits against you if you told the truth, huh?"

Flushing, I muttered, "I was not pressing my—"

"He didn't find her like this," Dante interrupted, his eyes snapping back to me. "He killed her. Strangled the fucking life right out of her. Still want to give him a hug?"

Horror threatened to balloon up inside of me, but it couldn't rise past the disbelief. "What? No…" I glanced back at Mateo for his denial, because Dante had to be wrong. Mateo might be bad, that's inarguable, but he wouldn't kill Beth, the woman he loved.

Mateo's dark gaze met mine, but he offered nothing. While I stood there looking back at him, waiting for a denial that wasn't coming, Dante's hand tightened around my wrist. I didn't bother resisting as he dragged me out of his brother's bedroom without another word.

I expected he'd let me go once we were in the corridor outside, but he didn't. He hauled me downstairs and right back out the front door.

"What are—? We're leaving already?" I asked.

"You are," he clipped, releasing my wrist and opening the car door. "Get in."

I didn't know what to say. There were a million thoughts flying through my head, but at the top of the list, I couldn't believe he was so angry at me for giving his grieving brother a hug*. I couldn't believe Beth was dead at all, and I certainly couldn't believe Mateo would have killed her, even if she did cheat on him.*

I didn't say any of that, though. Dante's jaw was locked, alerting me that it wasn't a good time to poke the bear. His jaw ticked when I took too long to obey. When his glare landed on me, I put my head down and slid into the passenger seat.

Once I got my legs inside, he slammed the car door and stormed around to the driver's side. He said nothing when he got in, said nothing until we were off the long driveway and on the road away from the house.

"That was a stupid fucking thing you did back there," he finally said.

Crossing my arms defensively over my chest, I looked out the window instead of at him. "Yes, I'm so sorry I thought to comfort your grieving brother upon finding his girlfriend dead. What a thoughtless, insane thing to do."

"He could have hurt you," he snapped. "He's not in his right mind. He just fucking killed a woman, Colette."

"Well, I didn't know that, did I?" I snapped right back. My heart dropped, acknowledging that, accepting it as the truth. "Are you even sure he killed her?"

Dante's gaze took on a crazier gleam, more guarded and angry. "What did he tell you happened?"

"He didn't tell me anything. I just found her like that and… I guess I assumed, and he didn't correct me." A moment passed and Dante didn't say anything else. Finally, I got tired of waiting and offered a morsel of information to see if it was news to him. "He said she cheated on him."

"Yep," Dante clipped, his gaze not leaving the road.

"Is that why he killed her?" I asked, quietly.

He looked over at me, a glint of danger in his eye. "Does he need a reason beyond that?"

My stomach plummeted, and I turned my attention to my lap rather than look at him. I would never cheat on Dante or anyone else, but given the conclusions he had just jumped to finding me innocently offering Mateo comfort… "Is he sure she cheated?" I ask. "I mean, did she admit to it, or…?"

Dante didn't immediately answer. I couldn't tell if he was considering what to tell me or just torturing me, but I felt tortured.

"Don't worry about it," he finally said. "You shouldn't even know this happened, but he got emotional and it made him fucking sloppy. We'll get it cleaned up. You put it and her out of your mind." Then,

looking over at me still with that crazy, dangerous glint in his dark eyes, he added, "And don't ever let me find you alone with him again."

After Dante dropped me off at home, he went back to his brother's house to help Adrian clean up "the mess," whatever that entailed. He gave me no further details and I knew better than to push, but I couldn't believe he was denying me information after I already saw so much. It wasn't business, it was very much a family affair. If they executed my friend for the crime of alleged infidelity, I'd like to know they were positive it actually happened. I wanted to know I *wouldn't be denied a trial and murdered because I hugged someone and my boyfriend took it the wrong way.*

Dante had always been territorial, but it had never scared me before.

That night, I had to admit; I was a little scared.

The rest of the evening went by at an agonizingly slow pace. I didn't hear from Dante at all, but I assumed he was busy. When he still wasn't home after midnight, I gave up waiting for him. I took a shower to wash the yuckiness of the day off myself, then I put on pajamas and climbed into bed. My anticipation for bedtime earlier that night crossed my mind, but it felt like a lifetime ago. I guess my dress will stay intact tonight, after all, *I thought.*

Normally when Dante came home late, I didn't wake up until he climbed into bed with me, if then. That night he was noisy when he came in, undressed, and went into the bathroom to take a shower.

Since he was home, I didn't even try to fall back asleep. I'd been trying to turn off my brain all night, but it hadn't worked. The way I was feeling in the aftermath of our aborted family dinner that evening, I needed Dante to set my mind at ease. I needed him to quiet the reasonable doubts that had been echoing around in my head since he dropped me off at the house.

My heart kicked up when I heard the shower turn off. A few minutes later the bathroom door opened, and before Dante shut the light off, I caught a glimpse of him.

Dante is a beautiful man and his exterior more or less matches his insides—dark and hard, but exhilarating when he gets close enough. He didn't bother to put clothes on after he got out of the shower, so my gaze traveled all over his muscular physique, then settled on the hard cock standing at attention.

My insides melted a little at the sight of it. Dante caught my eye, seeing I was awake, but we only held eye contact for a split second before he turned off the light in the bathroom and crossed to the bed.

My heart hammered as he approached—my side, not his. Without a word, he grabbed a fistful of my hair and hauled me off the bed. I inhaled sharply, dropping to my knees in front of him and looking up, a bit uncertain.

"It's not going to suck itself, is it?" he asked carefully.

My eyes narrowed and I huffed at his insolence, but nonetheless took his angry cock in my hand and began stroking him. I eased forward, taking him inch by inch into my mouth. I worked him for a few minutes just the way he liked, but despite getting exactly *what he wanted even though he was being a bit of an asshole, Dante got bored. Restless. I could feel it in him and I didn't think it had a thing to do with sex; that was just how it was manifesting. Morelli men are good at a lot of things, but communication is rarely one of them.*

Fucking is *on the list of proficiencies, so next thing I knew, Dante was lifting me up and throwing me down on the bed. I twisted, trying to get out of my pajama bottoms while he climbed on top of me and cursed at me.*

"Why are you wearing these fucking things?" he demanded, dragging them off and tossing them behind him.

"I didn't know when or if you were coming home tonight. I thought I'd just be sleeping."

He wasted no more words once my pussy was unobstructed. He fucked me hard, like he was exorcising demons of his own or punishing me for wrongdoing. After the evening we'd had, it could've been either. It could have been both.

Usually I had no problem taking it when he gave it to me like that, but it was harder that night. I had images of Beth's rumpled bed and dead body in my mind, memories of Dante's face when he essentially told me his brother was right to murder a girlfriend they assumed *was unfaithful. I needed reassurance that nothing like that could ever happen to me, that Dante loved me more than that, but I didn't get it. Instead, I got sex that felt like a punishment, lacking in warmth and fueled by anger. Cleaning up a murder was probably nothing Dante hadn't done before, but walking in on me with Mateo was, and I had a strong feeling that was to blame for his extra roughness.*

When he finished with me, I was weak and boneless, sprawled on my stomach with my limbs tossed every which way. While I tried to catch my breath, Dante pulled out of my body and shifted onto the bed beside me, but he didn't even reach out to pull me into his arms. I turned my head to face him, watching as he stared up at the ceiling, lost in his own thoughts.

"Are we okay?" I asked, tentatively.

He turned his head and his virulent gaze met mine. "Should we not be?"

"You're not still upset about me hugging Mateo, are you?" I asked, more specifically. "I was only being nice."

His lips curved up faintly and he returned to staring at the ceiling. "Nice is overrated."

That was not reassuring. "Will you at least tell me more about Beth's death?"

"You don't need to know about that," he informed me. "She's gone, that's all you need to know."

I knew that was the usual way of business matters, but surely there was some exception for something so personal? "She was my friend, Dante."

His gaze still on the ceiling, his tone verging on bored despite the callousness of his words, he told me, "She was a self-absorbed, trifling whore with no loyalty to anyone but herself. You don't need friends like that."

"She was the mother of his child. He couldn't have just… killed her. They were family. Doesn't that mean anything?"

His angry gaze snapped to mine and I knew I had said the wrong thing. "Family?" He spat the word, like I was his enemy for even daring say such a thing. "You don't get to be family if you're not loyal to your own, Colette. That's what family is. Beth was a gold-digging whore who didn't give a single fuck about my family. That makes her not *family, whether she squeezed out his kid or not. Lot of fucking regard she had for the poor kid, too. Trying to sink all of us," he muttered, shaking his head, but I didn't know what he was talking about. "Fuck Beth. She knew what she signed up for. She couldn't fucking handle it, and that's no one's problem but hers. Beth is in the past now and she earned her spot there, so don't worry about it."*

That was easy for him to say. Him, the man with all the power. Dante had no idea what it felt like to have to trust anyone with his life, let alone a dangerous, volatile man like him.

Letting me know he was done talking about it, Dante shifted and pulled up the covers so he could drag them halfway across his naked body. "It's late. We've both had a long day. Let's get some sleep."

I tried, but I wasn't like Dante, I couldn't shut my feelings off like I had them hooked up to a switch. I couldn't turn off my brain or quiet my own doubts. While he drifted off to sleep, I drifted away down a long, lonely highway of paralyzing fear. It was impossible not to put myself in Beth's place, not to envision a future where I crossed Dante, and it was my cold, lifeless body lying on the bed, waiting to be "cleaned up" and swept under the rug.

I might have been lying mere inches away from him on our king-sized bed, but I'd never felt farther away from him. After what I had experienced at Morelli mansion that night, I wasn't sure I'd ever find my way back. I wasn't sure I even wanted to anymore.

3

COLETTE

"COLETTE, honey, why don't you get up on the bed? Some sleep will do you good right now."

I pull my thoughts from the past at the sound of my aunt's voice. I look up at her from my spot on the floor and try to focus, but the present feels foggy. As terrible as those days after Beth's death were, some part of me would rather be there than here. If I could go back, I could change everything. I could make a different choice and stop all this from happening.

I will never forget the day I realized that the man I loved was dangerous, the torturous evening when all my doubts about our future were born. I'll never forget the sleepless nights that followed, or the punishing distance I felt from him—punishment for a crime I didn't even commit.

After what happened to Beth, I was so afraid for myself that all I wanted was to get out while I still could, but I should have stayed. I'm the one who chose to get involved with Dante. I knew exactly who he was. I knew what I was doing. On some level, I knew what I was signing up for.

Declan didn't. All he saw was a quiet, lonely florist who kept to herself and had weird, paranoid quirks because of a toxic past relationship that didn't end well.

Declan is a lawyer, so it took a while before I opened up about that ex, before I finally told him it was Dante Morelli—yes, from *that* Morelli family. The dangerous, powerful mob family that runs so much of Chicago, you can never even be sure who is connected to them and who isn't.

Was a lawyer, I mentally correct myself. Declan *was* a lawyer.

Fresh tears spring to my eyes, the horrifying reality of my present wrapping its claws around my throat until I can't breathe. Panic sets in and I struggle to draw air into my desperate lungs.

This isn't the first time this has happened today, so my aunt isn't entirely unprepared this time. She kneels on the ground beside me, pushing aside the big, tulle puff that is my wedding dress. She tugs on me urgently, attempting to pull me upright.

"Come on, Colette, sit up and breathe, sweeting."

I dissolve into tears, collapsing against her shoulder. "This is all my fault, Aunt Aggie."

"No," she assures me. "Don't think like that, Colette. You're not responsible for anyone's actions but your own. I know this hurts, I know it's a horrifying loss you're suffering, and so early in life, but you listen to me," she says firmly. "You didn't know he was in danger, and you couldn't have done anything to stop this."

She holds me and rubs my back, murmuring empty reassurances that everything will be okay, but I don't believe her. I'm pretty sure nothing will ever be okay again, and I *know* I'm the one who put Declan in harm's way, whether I meant to or not.

"Maybe I could have. I should've… I shouldn't have said yes when he asked me to marry him. I shouldn't have tried to—" My voice breaks on a sob and my aunt continues to rub my back.

"Nonsense. That's nonsense, Colette. You were living your life; you weren't doing a thing wrong. There's no evidence they even did this," she adds, refusing to utter their family name, like that might summon them. "It was a tragic accident, that's all it was. It's no one's fault."

"It wasn't an accident," I whisper, shaking my head and pulling back from her shoulder to swipe a hand under each eye.

"Now, now, Colette. Don't let your imagination get carried away with you."

After all this, how can they *still* think this is all in my head? I'm too tired to argue. My aunt tells me how okay everything will be a few more times like she can will it to be true, then she props me up so I'm leaning back against the bed.

"I'll get something to settle you down."

Resentment rears its head through the grief as I watch her leave my bedroom. I don't want pills or empty reassurances. Why doesn't anybody understand? This monster isn't in my head, it's in my past, and now he's burst into my present and ruined my life. Punishment for daring to have one without him in it. Punishment for leaving, even though he let me go.

Nobody understands. Nobody believes this was him, and I'm so tired of people doubting me. I'm so tired of people acting like I'm crazy for feeling afraid of his very real danger. Dante isn't some monster I've made up; he's real, and he just struck, and these fucking people all want to believe it was an accident.

When my aunt returns, she has a small white pill and a glass of water. Anxiety meds. I don't have anxiety; I have a fucking hellhound right on my heels, but nobody believes me.

I let her dump the pill into my hand, but I don't take it right away. I don't want to take it at all. I fucking hate taking these pills. They don't really fix anything. Sure, they calm me down so I can breathe easier, they slow my mind down and bring me some measure of peace, but I don't deserve peace. I led the devil right to Declan's doorstep, and it's my fault that instead of a wedding, his mother will be attending his funeral.

The pain comes back and the pill starts to tempt me. I know I don't need it, I know I'm not crazy, I'm just haunted. I know that, but the temptation of relief... just for a little while....

Before I can think better of it, I pop the pill in my mouth and swallow. I grab the glass of water from my aunt and drink it all, even though it's lukewarm tap water with a funny taste.

"There you go," my aunt says, her tone comforting as she rubs my back. "I know it hurts, sweeting, but just let yourself get some rest and you'll feel better soon."

I SAT *on the edge of the black leather couch, my clammy hands clenched tightly into fists, my shoulders so tense that I knew I would be sore later. My nerves had been fried since before I told him we needed to talk, and having him bring me into his study—which was usually reserved for* business—*didn't make my heart race any less. I looked down at the hardwood floor so I didn't have to look up into Dante's face while I broke both our hearts.*

He sat a glass down with purpose, the clink as intimidating as he intended it to be. I jumped, glancing up just enough to see his shiny loafers slowly moving across the floor in my direction.

"What do you mean, you don't want to be with me anymore?" he ground out.

I tried to swallow, but bile rose in my throat. Despite the distance between us in the days leading to that point, I knew he hadn't anticipated I'd try to leave him.

I also knew he didn't take rejection well, so my insides were quaking. Memories of Beth came flooding back, and I wondered if he might hurt me for trying to leave—was that as great a sin as cheating, like Beth allegedly had?

"Do I not take care of you?" he asked lowly, reaching out and placing his hand under my chin, tilting my head up so I had to look at him.

"You do—of course you do," I said a little too obsequiously. I didn't want to piss him off, but none of the sleepless hours I spent rehearsing my logical speech mattered at all, considering my mirror was not nearly as intimidating as the man standing before me.

"Then what? Is there someone else? Is it him? His fucking girlfriend's dead now, so you see an open spot—"

"No!" I blurted, eyes widening. "No. God, no, Dante! Don't be ridiculous, it's nothing like that—"

"Then what?" he asked, eyes narrowing on my face.

I looked away, side to side, anywhere but at him. It was foolish, but I felt like I might burst into tears at any moment. Knowing I couldn't do that—he would pounce on the show of weakness and talk me right out of my good sense—I pulled myself up, squared my shoulders, and said quietly, "A woman died the other day, Dante. A woman I was close to, even if we didn't always see eye to eye. She would be alive right now if she hadn't gotten involved with your family. I know I'm already involved, but I don't want to be anymore. I don't want to get in any deeper than this. I don't want this life."

He was quiet for a moment, then he said, "I know this lifestyle isn't ideal for you, but it comes with me, Colette. It's a package deal. There's nothing I can do about that."

"I know," I offered, quietly. "That's why I want out."

He sighed loudly, irritated that he wasn't getting his way. He shot me a menacing look that would make much tougher people squirm, at least inwardly. It did rattle me, but I didn't let him see that. I knew I couldn't. If he believed I had doubts about my decision, he would never let me go.

"You don't love me anymore?" he asked simply.

Feeling my heart contract painfully in my chest—was that possible? It felt possible—I had to stifle a raw groan, just at the thought of telling that lie.

No, I wouldn't do it. I couldn't.

"Of course I still love you," I told him, quietly. "I don't know if you know this about yourself, but you're not an easy man to stop loving."

The left side of his mouth turned up just slightly, but he didn't smile. "You've tried, huh?"

Nodding hopelessly, I said, "It isn't that. I miss being normal. I miss not being afraid. I don't want to do this anymore. I don't want all this drama and danger. I mean, when we first got together it was stupidly sexy and exciting, but I've aged a lot in these two years, Dante. I can't imagine how much I'd age—if I survived them—in another two."

"You talk like you're an old lady," he remarked blandly.

"I feel like one sometimes. Do you have any idea how much I worry about you? For Christ's sake, if you don't answer your phone for a half hour, I think you must be dead."

"That's stupid," he informed me. "Nothing is going to happen to me, Colette. Things are getting better *for us now that Mateo is running things, not worse. I have more power than I ever had when Dad was in control, and it's only going to grow from here. You stick with me and you'll see. You are not fucking Beth. I won't let anything happen to you."*

Feeling more despondent since his reaction wasn't as violent and angry as I had prepared myself for, I shook my head sadly. "I don't want to. I mean, okay, a part of me wants to, but... no part of me wants *to want to, and... even if I did, I'd have to overrule that desire. It's time for me to grow up and make this change for myself. It's time for me to be sensible, not follow my fool heart."*

"What if I say no?" he asked, turning and picking up his glass, swirling it for a second and then tipping it back and draining the rest of the amber liquid.

"That's not how this works," I said, for lack of a better answer. "I'm not one of your lackeys, Dante."

"You don't think I can make you stay?" he asked, disbelief evident on his handsome face.

"Of course you could make me stay," I said, not stupid enough to think otherwise. "But you can't make me want to be here. It would only make me resent you, and resentment poisons love. Before long, what would be left of the girl you love?"

"So it's like that," he said evenly.

I watched him cautiously; I couldn't tell what he was thinking, and the uncertainty was more than a little unnerving.

"I'm not trying to hurt you, just... telling you how I feel," I told him.

Dante was silent, staring off at nothing, his lips pursed in mild irritation. Until that point, I felt the conversation was actually going as well as could be expected, but I couldn't tell what his next move would be.

Finally, he uttered one word: "Fine."

My eyes widened a little. It seemed suspicious that he was letting it go just like that. "Fine? So... you're letting me go?"

He turned a rather cynical smile on me and made a little noise, like a tenth of a laugh, because that was all that comment deserved. "No," he replied, almost sympathetically. "You can leave, I won't stop you, but I'll never let you go."

Unsure of exactly what that meant, I nonetheless took his permission to leave at face value. I picked up my little leather clutch, smoothed down the skirt of my too-snug dress, and glanced at him uncertainly. Should I give him a goodbye hug? That might be stupid, since all of my possessions were in his house, so it wasn't like I'd never see him again.

When I hadn't been sure how things would go down, I packed an emergency bag with a little money and enough clothes for a week, but I had a walk-in closet full of clothes in our bedroom. It would take much more than one trip to clear everything out.

"Thank you, Dante," I said, before I could think better of it. "I wasn't sure… how this would go."

He didn't respond, merely picked up his empty glass, turning his back to me, and went over to the decanter to pour himself another drink.

After standing there awkwardly for a moment, waiting for him to turn around or say something, I finally accepted that he wasn't going to. I had been dismissed. It stung, but it was better than a fight, so I turned around, swallowed the lump in my throat, and walked out the door.

4

COLETTE

THE WHOLE WORLD is blessedly fuzzy. I feel freer in my own head, disconnected from my body and my aching heart. The drugs make me feel so dissociated and that's normally what I hate about them—though my aunt gave me double my prescribed dosage, and I don't think she did it by accident—but today I'm happy to be high. High above Colette Fontaine and her horrifying reality.

It could be minutes or hours passing by; I'm in such a fog, I can't tell the difference.

Given how dazed I am, I am too disconnected from my own pain to react as I should when the bedroom door swings open so forcefully, it bangs against the wall. A tall, broad-shouldered man barges into the bedroom, a thunderous scowl on his devilishly handsome face. He's wearing a jet black suit that hugs his muscular physique perfectly, a snowy white dress shirt underneath—a stark contrast to the black heart that beats beneath the attractive surface.

My heart leaps at the sight of him, sweeping in like a dark, avenging angel, a harbinger of death and misery with his sights set on me. He looks braced for a fight, but I don't know if I want to give him one. I know Dante. I know how he treats his opponents, and despite the fact that he's here to steal me away like some dark prince in a twisted fairy tale, I know enough about this man and his family to know whatever affection for me he once had—or might even still have—isn't enough to protect me, just like it wasn't enough to protect Beth from Mateo once she had made the fatal mistake of crossing him.

A man like Dante can't lose, because he refuses to. Whatever he has to do to win, he'll do it. If there's a line drawn to show how far is too far, Dante will step over it like a meaningless crack in the pavement. He won't bat an eye at doing things far worse than I could ever even imagine.

I can't afford to lose any more than I already have. I can't afford to cost *anyone else* more than I have. I've seen now how dirty he'll play, how unimaginably low this monster will sink, and I know I don't have the arsenal to win right now.

I wait silently on my bed, in my wedding gown, suspended in my diazepam bubble. I know my concerned aunt is in the next room, and if I fight Dante the way I'd love to, ripping into him, clawing at his handsome mask to reveal the monster hidden beneath, maybe she'll try to save me.

Maybe he'll kill her for getting in his way.

Wouldn't be the first time he killed to possess me. Wouldn't even be the first time *today*.

He came prepared for a war, and I'm not foolish enough to believe he has a moral qualm about stacking up casualties. On the other hand, he knows I do.

"You," I mutter lowly, watching him as he approaches my bedside.

"Me," he says evenly, holding my gaze. He pauses at my bedside, his eyes raking over my big, puffy white dress. Then he looks over my once-familiar face, only today my features are stained with heartache and smudged mascara. He put it there—every bit of hurt, every sad smudge belongs to him, and he doesn't even look remotely ashamed in the face of it.

My tone low, I demand, "Why are you here?"

"You know exactly why I'm here," he states, no nonsense, as fucking usual.

A crack of sadness penetrates my bubble. Tears well up in my eyes, but I hardly feel them. "To take more from me than you already have? To cause more destruction, to hurt more people, to ruin more lives?"

"If I have to," he says, his dark gaze locked on mine. "If that's what it takes to bring you home."

He's so selfish, I could scream. Even knowing how useless it is, I can't help lashing out at him in some small way.

"My home will never be with you, not now. You went too far. I hate you, Dante. You were the worst mistake of my life and I wish I'd never met you. Get out of my house. Get out of my *life*."

"No," he says, simply. "We already tried that, remember? It didn't work."

"It *did* work," I shoot back, glaring at him. "It worked for me. I was finally *happy* again, and you destroyed it."

He rolls his eyes at me like I'm overreacting. Like he accidentally scuffed the toe of a favorite shoe instead of murdering my goddamned fiancé.

"Go away," I say, more loudly than I intend, but his

dismissal enrages me. "You've already taken everything from me, isn't that enough punishment? Just leave me alone."

"No," he says again.

Jabbing an accusatory finger in his direction, I open my mouth and release stupid, reckless words. "I know you did this. I know you did. And I won't let you get away with it, either."

"No?" he questions, as if faintly amused by my histrionics. "What do you think you're gonna do about it, beautiful?"

His old endearment slices right through me, but the stab of pain only makes me want to lash out more. In a less drugged up state, I might call on enough common sense to think of Beth and hold my tongue, but in this moment, the only victim of the Morelli family I can think about is Declan. At the moment, I don't give a fuck if Dante kills me, as long as he knows how much I despise him first.

"I'll go to the police," I threaten.

His brown eyes go dead, no longer amused. Pointing at me, he says, "Don't say a stupid fucking thing like that again, Colette."

"I mean it," I swear.

"No, you don't."

"Yes, I do. Declan wasn't a part of your world. He wasn't fair game. You murdered an innocent man, and you're going to pay for it."

Dante looks over his shoulder, checking to make sure none of the goons he must have brought with him are within hearing range. They must not be, because rather than deal with an urgent mess I've made by running my mouth, he looks back at me and shakes his head irritably. "Say another fucking word, Collette, I dare you. I'll send Luca back here tonight to pay your auntie a visit."

The venom drains out of me, along with the color in my face. "You—" I start to say he wouldn't, a practiced belief, but then my new reality asserts itself, forcing me to shut my mouth.

If he has decided he wants me back for whatever reason, of course he would. He'll do anything to get me back in line, hurt anyone to control me.

He's a monster. The beautiful man I loved turned into a monster.

Or maybe he always was a monster, I just didn't see it before.

I'm so fucked.

He cocks an eyebrow, seeming to know what I almost said. "Wanna test me? Want to find out if I mean it? Say another stupid fucking thing like that and I promise you, you'll find out just how serious I am."

"This isn't fair," I whisper, shaking my head. "He didn't deserve to die. You don't deserve to win."

I don't realize I'm crying until Dante takes a step forward and brings his thumb to my cheek, dashing the wet drop away. "Life's not fair, beautiful. Now, shut that pretty mouth before it gets you into trouble. You're coming with me, whether you want to or not."

Without another word, he positions one arm around my back and one under my legs, then lifts me. Perhaps to be cruel, he holds me bridal style as he carries me out of my bedroom—me in my crumpled white wedding dress, him in his sharp black suit. He's stepping right into Declan's shoes without anyone's permission, and it makes me want to spit in his face. He doesn't deserve to wear Declan's shoes. Declan was gallant and sweet, Dante is selfish and cruel.

I think he enjoys this, so while he holds me and looks right in my face, I tell him coldly, "You don't hold a candle to the man I wanted to marry, Dante. You never will."

A hateful, intimidating look shoots through his dark eyes and his jaw clenches. I know my jab landed, and it makes my broken heart *so* fucking happy.

"We'll see about that," he says, simply.

5

COLETTE

I WATCH OUT THE WINDOW, leaning my head against the hard surface as the driver navigates us toward Dante's house. From a few nostalgic, wine-fueled research sessions I'd never admit to in an unaltered state, I know he still lives in the same place he bought when we were together—the house I helped him pick out, back when we both envisioned our future together.

Growing up, we never owned our own home. My family moved around a lot, and while we made each rental our own while we were there, it was always disheartening when we inevitably had to leave. I didn't like never having a back yard to play in as a child, or a place I knew we'd never have to leave as I got older. I told myself that when I grew up, I'd buy a great house to raise my own kids in. As soon as I got my first job at 17, I started saving money out of every single paycheck to make it happen.

When I outgrew my first job, I made a more risqué choice

for my second—I applied for a position as a cocktail waitress at a swanky strip club. I wouldn't have to take off my clothes, but I could work fewer hours and make more money. Since I was thinking about going back to school and trying to find something I was passionate enough about to pursue, that sounded like a win-win.

I got the job, but Dante's family owned that strip club, so I also got much more than I bargained for. I was only there for the better pay, the ability to save more money toward my future, but I got caught up with the distractions.

I had dated before, but I had never been pursued by anyone very impressive. When I started at the club, I drew the eye of not just Mateo Morelli, but his brother Dante, too. Dante seemed more reluctant to strike. He would eye me from a distance but he never even talked to me. I had no idea he liked me—at first, I actually thought he hated me. His brother was a different story. Mateo isn't the least bit shy, and it wasn't long before he was cornering me in darkened hallways, running his hands along my body in ways no man ever had.

Mateo's attention finally forced Dante out of the shadows. He didn't like his brother pursuing me, didn't like that I *liked* being pursued, and even though he had no right and no claim to me whatsoever, he had no problem telling me so.

He was an absolute brute with an awful lot of audacity to be telling me who I was allowed to hook up with when we'd never even communicated beyond wordless stares from across the room. But it turned out, I liked that. Turned out, I liked him.

I started dating Dante and everything changed. My once-small world began to expand.

For a while, I kept sight of my goals and still saved house money from every paycheck, even after he told me I didn't need to. The problem was, Dante loved to travel, so he was less interested in being tied to a house than I was. Back then, he lived at his family's home—more compound than home, really. Living there with his brothers meant as long as he could get the time off work, he could easily surprise me with a spontaneous trip to Barbados, or a week holed up in a beautiful seaside Mediterranean villa.

As he and I grew closer, as we went on adventure after adventure together in place after place, my idea of 'home' began to shift. It became less about a specific building to raise my future children in and more about a person to have those kids with. As fondly as I'd always dreamed about a home of my own, my adventures with Dante became more important. Wherever I slept, as long as Dante was there sleeping beside me, I was at home.

Then on my 22nd birthday, Dante told me he was going to buy us an actual house.

I was ecstatic. Home shopping together was an amazing experience, too. In addition to being crazy in love with the man himself, I was in love with the house we picked out, in love with the life I thought we'd build together inside those walls. I'd walked dreamily through the bedrooms I believed would belong to our children someday. The bedroom where we would read our daughter stories each night was yellow, but her bathroom was princess pink. Our son's bedroom was blue, and there was a basketball hoop in the driveway where he and Dante would play ball in the summer. The child in me who had never had even a small one was thrilled with the spacious back yard ours would have to play in. Dante would set up a swing set with a treehouse and a slide for them to play on. We would still have adventures, they would just be different ones. We would be a perfect little family, and I knew nothing could make us happier.

Back when I didn't think his danger mattered, or at the very least, I refused to believe it was a dealbreaker.

What a fool I was back then. Young and in love, recklessly devoted to a dream I had of who he was instead of the reality. Now his reality has bankrupted me and countless others, and I don't know how I'll ever escape that guilt.

The car veers left sharply and I look up, my heart dropping in expectation of seeing something alarming. I don't think my aunt would have been crazy enough to call the police after Dante took me, but if I've learned anything in the past few years, it's that you never really know what people will do.

The driver doesn't appear to be alarmed though. He's taking a sharp turn, but his face is relaxed. A glance out the back window shows no blue and red flashing lights, nothing to get excited about.

As if reading my thoughts, Dante replies casually, "He's just an aggressive driver."

The spike of alertness pierces my Valium-fog and brings me over the threshold into awareness. Awareness is terrible and heavy and it expands like anxiety in my chest. I regret not thinking now, not at least telling Dante before he hauled me out of the house to please bring my medication. Then again, I'm sure Dante Morelli will have no trouble procuring drugs for his captive ex-girlfriend—he just has to know I need them.

Swallowing and sinking back into the seat, I turn my face to look out the window again. "If you're planning to keep me for a while, I need Valium."

Apparently thinking I'm joking about the hardship of being

in his company, a short, scoff-like laugh escapes him. "Sure you do."

"I'm not kidding," I snap. "I don't take it all the time, but I have anxiety attacks and when I do, they help calm me down."

Since he dismissed my initial request, I look at him to make sure he's taking me seriously. My chest tightens up just thinking about being in that situation, trapped inside my own fears with no escape, nothing to ease the intensity.

Dante's face is set in a ferocious scowl. "What are you talking about? You never had anxiety when we were together."

"I'm aware. I do now."

"Why?" he demands, like if I just tell him, he can scare off whatever demons sneak inside me and fix it for me.

I can't help but shake my head at his obliviousness. He really has no idea the effect he had on my life, does he? It's normal to him that I found my friend dead, that I comforted her murderer with whom I once had a romantic entanglement. He doesn't understand how terrifying it was to leave him after all that, and he *clearly* doesn't understand that even after I left him, he was never really gone. Instead of a warm, physical presence in my bed each night, he became a terrifying ghost, haunting me, living inside my mind as an ever-present threat that no amount of hours spent in therapy or a considerate boyfriend-turned-fiancé doing his best to understand what I'd lived through could fix. Nothing the normal world had to offer could heal the wounds Dante and his family left on me. I may have gotten out alive, but I never truly escaped them.

Now I know I probably never will.

In a sick, twisted way, it's almost reassuring. I didn't want to be, but boy, was I right. I wanted *Declan* to be right. I wanted my therapist to be right. I wanted it to be true that my fears were a mere result of an unhealthy experience, scary scars from a dormant trauma, but the threat wasn't real. It was all in my head.

Now the threat is sitting beside me, so what the fuck did any of them know?

Still oblivious to all this, Dante demands, "Did that lawyer get you hooked on fucking drugs?"

"Please don't," I say quietly, shaking my head as much as I can with it leaning heavily against the back of the seat. "Don't talk about him. Declan didn't get me hooked on anything. I have a prescription from my psychiatrist, but I don't imagine you'll let me see her anymore, and my bottle is back at my aunt's house."

Dante is completely lost by all this new information about my reality. Maybe it should reassure me that he wasn't full-on stalking me, but it doesn't really matter now. "You see a psychiatrist?"

"Don't worry, I was careful not to talk about anything that could implicate anyone in your family in any of the criminal bullshit I know about. There's doctor-patient confidentiality to begin with, but… I covered your asses, anyway."

"That wasn't…" He trails off, still frowning, and shakes his head. "That's not why I was asking."

I know he doesn't get it. I'm furious at him about a lot of things, but not about that. I'm aware that it's not his fault and he doesn't know any better. I know Dante's family isn't normal; I know his way of *thinking* isn't normal. I lived that life with him for a while, and when I left, I remember the jolting culture shock of ordinary reality afterward, but Dante has never been removed from his way of life.

Morellis do not see therapists. They *need* to more than most of us, but they don't. Any therapist worth their salt would try to help them unravel the layers of their dysfunction, and their way of life depends too much on preserving it. Normal has no place in their world, and if you live there with them for long enough, it becomes worthless in yours, too.

I can't let that happen again. I can't let him pull me back in. Not now. Not after what he has done.

Somehow, some way, I need to keep my heart closed this time—no matter how forcefully he tries to get back in.

6

DANTE

I EXPECT to have to deal with Colette's temper when we get home, in fact I'm almost looking forward to it, but now that she's mentioned needing Valium, I look at her calm sadness a little differently.

I don't like Colette drugged up and foggy. I've seen the men in my employ use that method of controlling the girls we sell, but the idea that I let Colette go back to the outside world where she was supposed to be safe from those risks and it happened anyway when I wasn't there to protect her? Un-fucking-acceptable. I'm even more satisfied I killed that useless lawyer fuck now. Clearly he was not a man and couldn't take care of her, regardless of what Colette convinced herself.

I look over at her again, listlessly staring out the window. This is not the Colette I left behind. My Colette knew her place, certainly, but that's not what this is. This isn't natural. This isn't respect or submission or even going along with something she actually fucking likes, this is just… I don't know, but I don't fucking like it.

I tell myself she just needs to sleep off the drugs her aunt gave her, sleep off the shock of today. Even though I hate like hell to admit it, what she's been through today is probably enough to traumatize anyone. It won't last forever though, and once it runs its course, I'll have my Colette back.

By the time we make it back to my house, Colette is asleep. I pick her up and she stirs, but rather than react like I'm her enemy, she curls her arm around my neck like she used to and murmurs, "I smell violets."

She sure as shit does not. A little thread of affection winds its way around my heart. "You want me to get you some violets?"

"Mm. I like violets," she murmurs before her head drops heavily onto my shoulder.

I know she's only being pleasant because she's high and half-asleep, but hearing the tone of her voice sound the way it used to when she talks to me makes me feel so fucking good. Even though this might get off to a rough start, I know it will all be worth it in the end when Collette is mine again—heart, body, and soul.

God, I can't wait. I wish we could fast forward to that part, to her softness, her sweetness, the loving way she had about her. I spent so many nights missing her tender touch, and now she's finally back in my bed, even if she doesn't want to be here.

I put her down on her side of the bed and she tucks her hands under her face. Her eyes are closed and she's still in that godforsaken wedding dress, but I want to hold her while she's not in a position to fight me. Sometimes I like a little fight, but not right now.

I ease down on my side of the bed, kicking off my shoes and sliding closer to Colette. I wrap my arm around her, ignoring the scratch of the rough fabric that makes up her dress, and yank her back against me.

A soft little moan escapes her and she rests her hand over mine. A hot surge of lust goes straight to my cock at the sound of it, at the feel of her receptive to my touch. On impulse, to free her from the tight confines of the gown, I start undoing the pearl buttons that go down the back.

My intention is only to loosen the dress so she can sleep more comfortably, but the sight of her bare back is so irresistible, I have to lean down and place a tender kiss against her skin.

Colette sighs and moves restlessly. I should stop bugging her and let her sleep despite the swatch of white lace I can see now, despite my desire to further undress her, to peel off that lacy bra and take her beautiful tits in my mouth. God, it's been too long. I almost let her go and ease back off the bed, but then she turns her face toward me and sighs softly as my hand brushes her back.

Fuck me. My cock strains against the crotch of my dress pants. I roll her over just to see what will happen, climb on top of her like I used to. I'm close enough that she barely has to move her arms to reach me and when she grabs a fistful of my black jacket and a fistful of my dress shirt, I assume the jig is up and she's about to lay into me.

Her eyes drift open, but I can see she's still not right. Half-asleep, dazed, not really with me. There's a dreamy look on her face like she's happy to see me, and that sure as hell wouldn't be there if she were fully awake. I wait to see what she'll do, then get a shock when she yanks me closer to her body and nuzzles her face into my neck.

"Beautiful wedding," she murmurs, almost incoherently. "Oranges on top of..." I wait for her to finish, but she trails off and slings an arm around my neck. I don't do the decent thing and wake her up—I let her pull me in for a kiss I don't deserve. I've been craving the taste of her for so damn long, I can't even remember a time I wasn't waiting to feel the soft brush of her lips again.

She's not as passionate as she usually is, given her state. It's like I'm rousing her with my lips, kissing her awake. I've done it before, back when she welcomed such a thing, but I know I'm probably pushing my luck right now.

I just don't care. Colette's lips soften beneath the brutal, crushing stamp of my mouth on hers. I'm not here to be tender, I'm here to mark what's mine, and that's my mistake.

The roughness of my kiss rouses her. I catch her gasp against my mouth, then she lets go of my clothing, unhooks her arm from around my neck, and starts shoving at the solid mass of my chest.

"What are you—Get *off* me, Dante!"

Rather than get off her, I grab her wrists and trap them against the mattress on either side of her. "What if I don't want to get off you?"

Her blue eyes flash angrily, and that spark of real emotion pleases me, even if the emotion is negative. "I don't care what you want," she tosses back. "Just like you don't care what I want. This isn't a relationship anymore, it's captivity, and I'll be damned if I let you forget it."

"Well, if you're my captive, I might as well treat you like one, right?" Just to get a rise out of her, I grind my cock against her, a coldly dispassionate enough look on my face that *her* expression shifts through several emotions—shock, panic, then a glimmer of real fear. She opens her mouth, an inaudible denial on her lips, then closes her mouth again, just like she did back at the house when I threatened her aunt.

"No, I suppose you would," she says, just as dispassionately. "Well, go on, then. If you've brought me here to use me like a whore, go ahead and do it—just don't expect me to care for you this time, because I won't."

There's my little stick in the mud. I could smile, but I don't; that would alert her that the threat isn't real, and I feel like playing with her. Reaching down like I'm going to unbutton my pants, I tell her, "Well, as long as I have your blessing…"

Alarm jumps in her eyes again and my facial expression nearly cracks. "That was not my blessing," she says, hurriedly. "I'm not—I'm on birth control, but I don't have it with me. If I can't keep taking it, it won't be effective."

That drains the faint trace of humor right out of me. My blood boils thinking of Colette going to get birth control so she can fuck somebody else. I'm glad she was careful and didn't want to have his babies at least, but he shouldn't have had his hands—or any other body part—on her to begin with.

I struggle to rein it in because there's no point making things worse, but I don't want to. I want to make her hurt the way that hurts me. I want to paint her a picture using excruciating detail. I want to tear off this godforsaken wedding dress and tell her that Declan's death wasn't quick and painless, that the impact from the crash didn't get the job done, and the way his car rolled didn't kill him, it only crushed vital organs so that when Luca climbed down to check on him, he could see the pained way her fiancé struggled to draw breath. I could tell her about the relief on Declan's stupid fucking face when he saw Luca, thinking someone was there to help him get back to her, and I could tell her instead, I had my guy finish the fucking job. It was practically a mercy killing at that point. Not what I wanted, personally, but Luca talked me out of killing him myself. He knew I'd be too angry, and anger makes people sloppy. Plus, in case anyone asked questions about Declan's death once I took Colette back, I needed to have a solid alibi.

As long as Declan ended up dead before he married Colette, it didn't matter how it got done. Still, I kinda wish I'd done it myself. Kinda wish I could hold up the hands that ripped him apart and make Colette kiss each fucking knuckle, showing me her repentance for daring let another man touch her.

Of course, I wouldn't get that right now, either.

Covering her body with mine, holding her captive beneath my weight, I lean down and drag my lips across her jawline. "What's wrong, Colette? Don't want to have my babies anymore?"

She turns her head trying to escape me, but she can't. "Stop it, Dante."

"What if I treat you the way you say I'm treating you?" I ask, kissing her cheek even as she struggles against me. "What if I take you anyway? What if I take you every night until I *do* put a baby in you?"

Gasping as she shoves uselessly at me again, she says, "I'm not playing these games with you."

"It's not a game. This is your life now," I tell her, calmly, my grip on her wrists tightening as she struggles harder. "Will you hate my baby like you hate me?"

Tears glisten in her eyes as she looks up at me like I'm being unspeakably cruel. "Stop it. Stop perverting my old dreams."

I shrug my shoulders like her words don't matter to me. "You know it's in my blood, Colette. I don't need your consent to take you, to keep you, to make you mine. You know I don't."

"You're not as cruel as your—" She stops again, her expression unfocused for a minute, then she looks me dead in the eye. "Actually, maybe you are."

Colette knows enough about my family history to know I'm the son of a monster, but she also knows that unlike my brother, no fiery hatred for the old man burns in my gut. I'll admit the old man did some horrible things, but he had his reasons so I'm not gonna judge him. While the comparison to my father is a clear insult, it doesn't burn me the way it would if she said it to someone else.

My brother, for instance. Mateo despises our old man, but he has more personal reasons than I do. There were things Dad did to hurt Mateo and his loved ones that he never did to me. Mateo has never been easy to love. He was a weird kid who grew up to be a dangerous man—a king in his own right, his power more or less unchecked. When we were just kids, though, our dad earned a permanent spot on Mateo's shit list when he cost him the friendship of the only person Mateo knew he could always count on—our maid's son, Adrian Palmetto.

He works for us now, but only by way of coercion and Mateo's clever knack for manipulation. Adrian hates Mateo, but he has his reasons and he still serves the family loyally, so I don't have a problem with the guy for his personal feelings.

My big brother, though. He claims not to hold grudges, but sometimes he makes exceptions. When he does, his vengeance is fatal if you're lucky, catastrophic if you're not.

Currently he's sitting on Dad's throne, running Dad's family, while our old man battles terminal illness. If it were possible to *give* someone a terminal illness intentionally, I would assume Mateo did. I don't complain though because I like the way Mateo runs things, the leeway and power he gives me that our father never did. Our dad clutched his control in a tight, greedy fist. Mateo delegates—mostly to me—to free up his own time for the aspects of the business he prefers, like cushioning our bottom line and growing our portfolio of legitimate businesses.

Since taking over, my brother has busied himself multiplying our already massive family fortune, making it look so damn easy I wonder why our dad didn't try harder. Sure, we always had plenty growing up, but the only thing better than a lot of money is a lot *more*. I always thought Dad was a good businessman, but Mateo is far better. Smarter, more focused, more in control of his emotions and much less impulsive. He got the best of both of our parents, I guess, and our dad got the worst of his.

When it comes to love and women, especially, our father's legacy is famously horrendous. Only woman he ever claimed to love ended up dead by his hand—a path Mateo has already followed once, and if my instincts are as good as they usually are, a path he's probably about to head down again.

Not me, though. I've never killed a woman I was romantically involved with. Colette is the only woman I've ever really loved, and I damn sure wouldn't kill her.

I'd hurt her, though. I already have. A nobler man would have let her move on and marry someone else if that's what she wanted, but I've never claimed to be a noble man.

At least the worst is over. Now that she's here with me again and I know mine are the only hands touching her, I can wait for her to stop being pissed at me.

You wouldn't know the worst is over by the hatred in her eyes as she looks up at me right now, but it's better than her numbness. Somewhere in there I know she's still the same old Colette, because even though she means it right now when she insists she hates me, even though she *wants* to wound me like I've wounded her, she won't say those hateful words. Regardless of how great her anger at me is right now, she won't proclaim hatred for our unborn babies.

Colette's deliberate thoughtfulness is one of the many things I love about her. A lot of people will say things they don't mean in anger. Colette doesn't. If by some chance she did, it would gnaw at her until she apologized and assured me she didn't mean it. It'd kill her to do it, but she wouldn't be able to help it.

One of the perks of loving someone so much my opposite.

I'll always be able to outmaneuver her pretty little ass.

The thought brings a smile to my face. Colette misinterprets it, probably figures I'm taunting her, but really I'm just happy she's here. She's seen more of my smiles than anyone else so she should know when it's a real one, but right now she's pissed off and she sees what she wants to see.

Glaring up at me, trying again to shove me away, she huffs and struggles, then finally stops and holds my gaze. "Are you done? I'm tired."

Best thing I can do is let her get some sleep. The sooner she sleeps off her grief, the sooner she can get back to accepting that she's mine. "For now," I tell her, nodding once.

"Good. Get off me."

That time, I do.

7

COLETTE

My back aches from sleeping so long and my body is too warm from being wrapped up in blankets all night. It's summertime, but Dante keeps the air in the house cool, especially at night because we always enjoyed snuggling under the covers. There was no snuggling last night, though judging from the sight of the wrinkled bedsheets on his side, he did sleep in here with me all night.

I sit up and look over at his empty spot, waiting to feel it, but nothing comes. No shameful trace of pleasure, no bitter pang of a once-sweet memory, not even sadness. I guess I'm still fogged from the Valium I took yesterday. That's probably a blessing, so I won't complain.

Fabric rustles as I push my legs over the edge of the bed and I look down to see I'm still wearing my wedding dress. It's loose, halfway off my upper body. The sight of it makes me sick now, so I abruptly stand and wrestle my way out of the once-beautiful gown. It's ruined from sleeping in it all night, anyway.

That's okay. I never want to see this dress again. Once I get out of it, I bend down and ball it up, then I carry it into the bathroom and shove as much of it as can fit into the small waste bin.

As soon as I make my way back into the bedroom, it occurs to me I have nothing to wear now. I go to my old walk-in closet, wondering if perhaps Dante had the foresight to buy me a couple of outfits. Actually, lack of foresight isn't likely the reason if he didn't. Of course he would have thought of it, but he might have decided not to get me clothes anyway as another form of punishment, or even just practicality—I'm less likely to try to escape if I'm naked.

I hate having these nuggets of knowledge. I hate some of the darker things I know Dante's family is responsible for because I can't think about it now without chiding the younger version of myself, demanding to know why it didn't bother me as much then, why I didn't get out then, when maybe I could have.

I keenly remember one of the first times it hit me. We were curled up on the couch, eating popcorn from a shared bowl and watching some dramatic thriller about a ring of human traffickers. Naturally, they were the bad guys in the movie, but it hit me they were the ones he sided with when I caught us shaking our heads at the screen at the same time, but for very different reasons. Me, I felt bad for the girl cowering and afraid. Him, he was impatient with the head bad guy in the scene for being too soft. We were still pretty newly dating, so I didn't know exactly which dark deeds his family had a hand in. As we kept watching the movie, I realized my boyfriend sympathized with the villains, not the protagonists. On a hunch, I started asking him questions between handfuls of popcorn and sips of red wine—why the bad guys did certain things, or why they *didn't* do certain things. He had all the answers. It was like watching the movie with a pro. Even though his knowledge led me to the impression the rumors about his criminal ties might be legitimate, it didn't scare me.

It should have. It should have occurred to me as I sat on that couch with him, drinking that wine he poured, that perhaps I was a mark myself. That even if I wasn't, that he could ruin lives so casually and then go home at night to watch movies with his date like he hadn't a care in the world meant he was someone I should stay far, far away from.

Instead, the verification of his danger turned me on. When he took my wine glass from me and put it down, when he pushed me back on the couch and climbed on top of me, my heart certainly pounded, but not from any kind of fear. I was seduced by him in every way, no matter what atrocities he was personally responsible for.

I was a dumbass.

A humorless smile tugs at the corners of my lips as I replay that memory of old Colette, foolishly falling for Dante instead of using her head and running for the hills. *You dumb bitch,* I tell her, now that it's too late to save either of us.

I finally pull open the door of my walk-in closet, reaching inside to turn on the light. I remember the last time I opened this door, too—to clear out all my shit when I thought he was letting me leave. I'd been so uncertain that day, already missing him, wondering if I was making the right decision. My heart ached merely moving my things out of his house, so how much more intense would the ache get?

The closet isn't empty, but it doesn't have as many items as it used to, either. Dante always spoiled me when it came to material possessions, and I think he has more money now than he did back then. A few nice dresses hang from the racks, a few pairs of shoes line the bottom—black, shiny, patent leather pumps, some Manolos that tell me he remembers my favorite brand of shoe. I spot a cute pair of Manolo sandals with a shiny black strap around the ankle and across the toe that I instantly love. Dante could never pick out a shoe to save his life, though, so the sight of these perfect ones only pleases me for a moment before settling in my stomach like a ball of unease.

Did someone else pick them out for him? It may seem unfathomable that a normal man might make his girlfriend pick out shoes for the woman he was ditching her for, but Dante is such an asshole sometimes, I honestly wouldn't put it past him. He wouldn't even lie about it, he would just straight up tell her she had to pick out some pretty shoes for me, and I had better like them.

I draw the Manolos out and try them on. It's a low heel so it's more comfortable than some of the ultra high ones he has bought for me in the past. Leaving those on, I check out the other shoes and also fall in love with a warm, cinnamon-red pair of pumps that make me think of Christmas. Stepping inside, I move each hanger to see what I might be able to wear. Other than the dresses that look suitable for family dinner at Mateo's house, there's just a green silk skirt with a white blouse and blue blazer.

I actually would have probably worn a pencil skirt around the house when I was dating Dante, but now that I'm stuck here I don't care about impressing him. I want to be comfortable, so I step out of the shoes, push all the heels back where I found them, and shut the closet door.

I go through all his dresser drawers next, thinking maybe he cleared one out for me, but there are no comfortable clothes belonging to me here. On top of the dresser is a recognizable pink striped bag from Victoria's Secret. I can't imagine him going there by himself either, but I peek in the bag and see it's full of bras and panties in my size. He must have bought these to tide me over until he retrieves my things. At least, I *assume* he will at some point retrieve my things. Seems a waste to leave all my perfectly good clothes at my aunt's, where I was staying until the wedding since my apartment lease was up a month prior.

I wonder now if doing things differently would have changed how it all turned out. I had lived with Dante outside of marriage, but even engaged to Declan, I wouldn't move in until we were married. If I'd been in bed beside him on the morning of our wedding, if I'd been in the car with him on the way to the church, would he still be alive? I don't think Dante's goons would have run the car off the road with me inside, but perhaps Dante would have just acted sooner.

Or maybe the fact that I refused to live with my fiancé helped him justify his actions, helped him sell himself on the lie that I didn't love Declan, that he could squeeze him out of the picture and win me back if he really wanted to.

Leaving the bag and shaking off thoughts of Declan, I rummage through drawers trying to find something to put on. Dante mostly wears suits and button-down shirts, so there's not much in the drawers. Gym clothes, a few sweaters, a pair of high-quality charcoal gray vacation shorts, a pair of jeans I don't recall ever seeing him wear. Sleep pants and a few T-shirts. I suppose I could wear one of those.

Sighing, I grab a black T-shirt that smells like him and pull it on. Figuring I'm here by myself, I don't bother with pants. My stomach clenches around nothing, reminding me that after being in bed for so long, I'm also starving.

As I make my way out of the bedroom, I can't help wondering if Sonja still works for him. I imagine she does, but I obviously don't know her schedule anymore.

Sonja had never been particularly fond of me *before* I left Dante, and the loyal servant won't like me any more after all that went down. A sane person might think that Sonja would hate him as much as I do, but that sane person would be wrong.

Knowing what I know about his family's business, I doubt she's so much a paid housekeeper as an unpaid domestic worker. I don't know for sure, Dante never confirmed, but I know Mateo's housekeeper is unpaid, and that woman is as devoted to him as Sonja is to Dante. I don't know if the women are crazy, they've developed Stockholm syndrome, or the lives they led before were really so bad that being owned by the Morellis is a step up in life for them. Whatever the case, they're indoctrinated, so I expect my exit will have left a bad taste in Sonja's mouth that will be quite evident when I see her again.

Much to my chagrin, it doesn't take long for the reunion to happen. When I get to the kitchen, I see the older woman standing at the sink, hand-washing dishes despite the top-of-the-line dishwasher installed beneath the counter. I approach warily in case she hasn't noticed me yet, but my movement catches her attention. Sonja flicks a glance in my direction only long enough to acknowledge and dismiss my presence, then she returns her attention to the plate she's scrubbing clean.

"Is he here?" I ask, my voice sounding rough even to my own ears.

Sonja's tone is brusque with a hint of annoyance. "No. He'll be home for lunch. You slept through breakfast."

In the old days, regardless of her feelings toward me, Sonja would've offered to whip up something if I wanted it.

"I'm not hungry anyway," I lie, seeking out coffee instead. Dante always had some with breakfast, strong and black, so bitter it made my toes curl, but there is none left in the pot for me this morning. Maybe there was, but Sonja dumped it out just to be spiteful when she realized I was awake.

I could be just as petty and ask her to make me a fresh pot, but I'm too tired to battle with Sonja today. Going to the fridge, I grab a bottle of cold water instead.

Since real breakfast isn't an option, I grab an orange out of the fruit bowl. I consider taking it over to the table, but I don't want to stay in here with Sonja.

"I'm going outside for a few minutes."

"Don't go far," Sonja warns, leveling a look of censure over her shoulder.

"I'm not even wearing shoes, Sonja."

I hear her muttering at me, but I don't wait to hear what she says. Dante's house is huge—not as big as his brother's, but it's not meant to house as many people so Dante doesn't need an entire compound. Still, it's significantly larger than anything a single family really needs. Sonja lives in a small gardener's cottage on the property so she's never far in case Dante needs something.

There are several living rooms, but I head to the one at the back of the house. Sunshine spills into the room from the many windows. Dante's house is situated right on the lake, and from here, I have a perfect view. When we first bought this place, the lakefront back of the house was a real selling point.

The "back yard" is fenced in to protect the babies we expected to have someday from wandering down here, but the yard is so large it's sectioned off. The fenced in, kid-friendly area is more of a side yard, and the actual back yard is back here on the lake, an adult haven. When I open the towering back door, it leads out to a massive stone patio off the back of the house. It overlooks the lake and our private beach, accessible via the stairs off the back patio. Two loungers are still set up where they used to be with a little table between them. Dante and I would sit out here in the evenings, talking about our days and watching the water. Sometimes we would go on evening rides on his boat, and it was so convenient—we barely had to leave the house to go.

Curling up on the chair that used to be mine, I alternate between studiously breaking off a piece of my orange and gazing out at the smooth, blue water.

It feels so wrong to be sitting here in my favorite peaceful place. I don't deserve to have peace. Dante sure as hell doesn't. A wave of exhaustion rolls over me just thinking about it though. I know Dante murdered my fiancé, I know I am morally obligated to be miserable and make *him* miserable in tribute to Declan, but I'm glad he's not home because I just don't have the energy right now.

I should have brought wine. Instead, I sip my water and finish my orange. I stay outside until Sonja comes looking for me. I figure she is just checking to make sure I didn't waste my time and hurt my feet trying to escape, but then she calls out and tells me Dante is on the phone for me.

"I don't want to talk to him," I tell her.

"I don't care," she snips.

I roll my eyes but nonetheless climb off my chair and head back inside the house. Dante still has a landline. Sonja lifts the phone to tell him she found me—like I was missing—then hands it over. I feel a bit like a sullen teenager in the presence of a stifling authority figure when I take it from her and put it to my ear.

"What?" I demand.

Sonja shakes her head at me and mutters something in a language I don't know. I'm sure it was insulting.

Dante's voice is warm on the other end. "Good morning to you, too."

"I woke up in your bed, so it's not a good morning," I inform him.

"You could've woken up in a ditch, then it'd be worse, wouldn't it?"

"Jury's still out," I mutter. "If you're going to make me stay here, I would at least like my own room. I know you have the space."

"I do, but we're not going to sleep in separate bedrooms, Colette. That's not how this is going to go."

"How do you think it's going to go, Dante?" I ask him, leaning against the counter. "I'm not your girlfriend. I'm your slave. Just one more defenseless woman whose life you've stolen like it was your right."

"Poor you," he says, dryly. "Make sure Sonja gets out the mop to wipe up all the tears you must be crying all over the marble floor."

"Money isn't everything. You should know that by now. I'm as much a prisoner in this big, expensive house as the girls you *sell.*"

The line falls silent, but I can practically hear his annoyance at me for referring to his criminal activities over the phone. Even though I hate him, the sharpness of his voice makes me flinch when he snaps, "I won't be home for lunch.

Tell Sonja when you're hungry and she'll make you something."

I don't care that he won't be here, not really, but since Sonja just finished telling me he *would* be home for lunch, I argue. "Sonja said you would."

"Sonja was mistaken," he states.

"Will you be home for dinner?"

His tone is entirely noncommittal, forcing me to earn company I don't even want. "Perhaps."

Gritting my teeth, I do my best to ignore impulses that have lain dormant for so long, I thought they were gone. Dante generally chose to be nice to me, but he can play me like a fiddle when he wants to. An unpleasant symptom of part of his *job* being to train women to want to please him, he knows how to dangle his approval in front of you like food in front of a starving dog, to make you crave it and him, even when by all rights you should want to rip his head from his shoulders. The Morelli men of my acquaintance are all very manipulative and adept at bending the wills of weaker minds to align with theirs.

My mind isn't weak anymore, though. I swear it to myself, shaking off the old instinct. Refusing the temptation to worry that I've displeased him, the errant thoughts already skating across my mind that I could fix it if only I said or did some certain thing.

No. I am not his pet, not this time. I'm not here to do his bidding or make him happy. I don't need or want his approval. I'd rather he got sick of me and realized this has all been a mistake. He may have wasted Declan's life, but at least I could save the rest of mine.

Not that it feels like that's worth much anymore. The guilt holds me under, makes me feel terrible for even drawing breath when I'm the reason Declan is gone. He was a lawyer, a protector of innocents, and now he's gone so this vicious criminal can have *me*.

If one of us had to die for my stupid involvement with Dante Morelli, it should have been me. I'm the one who made these choices, and no one else should have paid for them.

There's relief in my cocoon of sadness because at least there I don't have to think. I curl up with it as I successfully resist Dante's attempt to control me, as I offer back an apathetic, "All right."

He's better at this than I am. Seeing my rebelliousness for what it is, he ups the ante by disconnecting the call without so much as another syllable. Displeasure sinks in my gut when I realize he hung up on me. I swallow it down, along with the vague sense of embarrassment. Sonja is standing right here watching, so she knows I didn't say goodbye, but I replace the phone on the hook anyway.

A smug smile pulls faintly at the wrinkled corners of her mouth, like she's satisfied that he hung up on me. Straightening my shoulders like it doesn't bother me, I grab my water. I could go back outside, but all I want to do is curl up in bed by myself, so that's what I do.

8

DANTE

ALL MORNING I looked forward to going home to Colette for lunch. First time in years I got to do such a simple fucking thing, and she had to ruin it.

Colette used to love when I made trips home to see her. I always worked a lot, even more back then than I do now. Now Luca handles a lot of the workload, but back then, that stolen hour made all the difference. When she knew I was coming, she usually dolled herself up and made our lunch herself instead of letting Sonja handle it.

Now she acts like a fucking brat and forces me to avoid her.

I have to eat somewhere, though, so I shoot Luca a text and let him know I'm stopping over and I'm hungry. By the time I get there, he has one of his girls preparing us lunch.

"I thought you were eating at home with your woman today," my friend and associate, Luca Delmonico, remarks from his seat at the table.

"That was the plan," I admit. "Unfortunately, my woman is

being a pain in the ass today and I didn't feel like dealing with it."

Luca shakes his head in disapproval. "Sounds to me like you're being too nice to her."

He doesn't know the finer details of my relationship with Colette, but he was behind the wheel of the car that drove her fiancé off the road, so he knows the gist of our situation. Leave it to Luca to suggest that murdering Colette's fiancé and kidnapping her was me being *too fucking nice*.

"I'm not being too nice to her," I mutter, dropping onto a chair at his kitchen table.

"Yes, you are," Luca disagrees. "She doesn't fear you. Doesn't respect you." I don't know if he's looking to demonstrate what he thinks my relationship should look like or it's a coincidence, but he suddenly leans forward and grabs a fistful of brunette hair, yanking the girl kneeling on the floor by his legs up closer to his face. "Did I say you could look at me, whore? Did I give you permission to do that?"

Shaking her head desperately, fear in her eyes, she says, "No! No. I'm sorry."

He yanks her hair harder, lifting her several inches off the ground. As she whimpers, his voice drops low and he demands, "You're sorry, *what?* How do you address me?"

"Master," she says breathlessly, tears welling in her eyes. "No, Master, you didn't say I could look at you. I'm so sorry."

He slaps her across the face and releases her hair abruptly so she hits the ground hard. I glance at the girl, note her labored breathing as she hunches over and rubs her scalp, but she knows better than to abandon her position, so she quickly pushes herself back into the kneeling pose Luca likes.

Flicking a glance in my direction as he leans back in his

chair, Luca says, "This one can't listen for shit. Good thing she's pretty, because she's a fucking moron." Looking down at the girl, he says, "Look at me. You're a moron, aren't you?"

Her cheeks heat with embarrassment, but she nods her head. "Yes, Master."

I shrug and tell him, "She's still pretty new."

"She's stupid." Looking back at the slave girl at his feet, he tells her, "I don't want to look at you anymore. Go wait for me in my bed, naked. I'll be in shortly." She starts to stand, but he puts a hand on her shoulder to stop her and gives his head a firm shake. "Crawl."

I watch the girl clad only in underwear crawl across the floor and down the hall, then I glance back at Luca. "That is not what I want my relationship with Colette to look like."

"Doesn't have to be so cold. You're warmer than I am. You have feelings for her, that's fine. But she should know what you're capable of. She should know how lucky she is that you love her, 'cause it sounds like she forgot." His lips curve up faintly and he suggests, "Send her to me for a week, I'll make sure she's grateful to have you when I return her."

I know he's not serious, because he knows what I did to the last guy who touched Colette. Luca doesn't have feelings though, doesn't understand possessiveness. To him, if it would mean training Colette to act right, it would be worth letting another man work on her for a week and saving myself the hassle. He is 100% not relationship material—a fact my younger sister learned the hard way.

"I'll pass, but thanks for the offer," I tell him dryly.

He's not invested either way, so Luca merely shrugs. "The longer you let her act out, the less she'll respect you. You've gotta let her know the way things are going to be, let her know she has no choice so she better get on board."

"You're the last man I'd ever ask for relationship advice, Luca."

"Good," Luca says. "Relationship advice sounds like something women talk about, not men."

"Speaking of women, how are things going with the brunette with the big teeth?"

Shifting to business mode, Luca sits forward. "I was about to give up on her, mark her for prostitution since she's not good for much else."

"But you're not now?"

Sighing, he says, "She's pregnant. Hopefully the kid gets my teeth or it'll be born looking like a beaver. I don't know what they were thinking when they acquired that one. Low quality shit like that is for scrappers, not us. Don't know what we'll do with her after she pops the kid out, but just keeping her alive that long is gonna be a job. She's mouthy, got a real bad attitude. Real pain in the ass all the way around. Might have to send her to Ivan's house for a few months; if she stays here, I'm liable to kill her before she delivers."

For all his internal flaws, Luca is a very well-made man on the outside. Strong features, a good physique, good teeth, very healthy. In all the time I've known the man, I don't think he's ever been sick. Women tend to find him attractive, especially the ones who mistake how uncomfortable he makes them for attraction instead of what it really is—when you encounter a dangerous psychopath and every instinct you have screams at you to get the hell away from them.

"The pretty, stupid one will be good though," he tells me,

looking more optimistic. "She cries a lot, can't say I enjoy fucking her, but she may toughen up over time. Like you said, she's still new."

"Well, try not to get that one pregnant," I offer, a bit dryly. "She's got the right look and she seems trainable. We can get a good price off her."

Luca nods his head. "That's the plan. I use condoms with her, don't want to risk it." He glances up as the underwear-clad girl who was cooking comes over, keeping her eyes down as she puts two plates of food down in front of us. Luca grabs her chin and forces her gaze to him, uttering some three syllable s-word in a language I don't know. The girl promptly drops to her knees to take the place of the one he sent away.

Casually as can be, Luca grabs his fork and starts eating. "You should bring your girl over for dinner one night. Maybe once she sees what her life could look like, she'll be a little more grateful."

I'd never let Colette's life look like this, and she knows it. She might be pissed at me for ordering the hit on the lawyer, but I don't think I could ever be mad enough at her to make her live in the kind of hell Luca's girls live in. These aren't relationships, they're trainees, and despite Colette's ignorant claim that she's as much my slave as these girls are Delmonico's, she's dead fucking wrong. Delmonico's girls would never dream of saying the shit Colette says to me. They know if they did, he'd throw them across the fucking room.

Colette just doesn't know how good she has it, that's all. Luca's right. Maybe I *should* bring her over here one night, let her get a look at how much worse it can be since she seems to think she has it as bad as anyone. Curled up in fucking luxury in my giant-ass house while Delmonico's charges sleep two to a mattress used by loads of girls who came before them.

I treat her like a fucking queen, and maybe she needs to take notice.

9

COLETTE

DANTE DOESN'T RETURN HOME until late that night, and when he comes in, I pretend to be asleep so I don't have to talk to him. I'm so lost in my misery, it doesn't even occur to me what day it must be until Dante comes in the following afternoon, throws open my walk-in closet door, and steps inside. He emerges with a black dress in one hand and a pair of heels in the other hand.

Meeting my gaze, he dangles the outfit and says, "Time for you to shower and get dressed."

"Why?" I ask, not moving from my corner of the bed.

He sighs, looking no more excited than I am for whatever this is. Then my stomach drops when he finally answers, "Family dinner night."

Family dinner night. My blood runs cold as memories of the last one I attended wash over me, finding my friend dead and Mateo traumatized—or, so I imagined.

"At your brother's house?" I ask, even though the answer is

clear. I push myself up and move my legs over the side of the bed. "I have to go to that? Can't you go by yourself? I don't want to see him."

"Neither do I," he answers dryly.

ONCE UPON A TIME, I felt pleasure when we pulled through the gates to Mateo's house. I enjoyed the sense of family, even if this particular family is stuck in time with their somewhat archaic practices. Sunday means I'll spend the whole evening cooking and serving my man while the men drink and talk shop —or whatever it is they talk about—in massive wing chairs in Mateo's study.

When Beth first started seeing Mateo, she found it all charming and kind of fun. A chance to play dress-up—she always embraced it and went all out, red lipstick and pearls—and serve her man. Then, as she didn't really want him to be her man anymore, the charm wore off and it became a chore.

Tonight, I get it. I'd rather stab Dante than serve him dinner, but I don't know what will happen if I refuse. Given his sensitivity to Mateo when I'm around, I imagine rejecting Dante in front of Mateo would lead to a fit of rage the likes of which I probably haven't seen before. It probably wouldn't be worth it… but maybe.

Dante lightly grips my wrist and tugs me into his side as we walk in the door. Keeping his voice low, he murmurs, "This should go without saying, but behave yourself tonight."

"I'm not a child," I chide, trying—and failing—to yank my wrist from his grasp.

Grip tightening, he says, "Then don't act like one. This is

the only warning you get, Colette. Try to make me look like an asshole, and you'll damn sure get one. I won't put up with any shit tonight. Not here. Not in front of him."

"Then you should have brought a willing date," I state, narrowing my eyes and finally looking at him.

Lifting a dark eyebrow in warning, he tells me, "Piss me off and you'll pay for it later."

His words shouldn't send a trail of heat through my core, but they do. I shake it off and do my best to install a wall of ice around myself. I don't want to be here and I won't pretend otherwise. I don't give a damn about pleasing Dante. I don't care if I piss him off. He's pissed *me* off. What about *my* wrath? That doesn't count?

Besides, if I embarrass him in front of Mateo, it's his own damn fault. He should have known better than to drag me here tonight.

When we used to come to these, we would meet Mateo and Beth in his study or here in the foyer, but tonight Dante sends me to the kitchen without so much as a glimpse of Mateo.

In the kitchen, I hope to find Dante's younger sister, Francesca. I had hoped she would be here so I would have *someone* to talk to, but instead I find a chummy pair of blue-eyed blondes, both young and alert to the new girl sliding into their fold. Dante told me in the car on the way here I don't need to make friends with either of them, so I don't try to. If we have to do this every week, it would be easier if we all got along, but I don't want to attach to another soon-to-be dead girl.

Instead, I keep to myself and pound glass after glass of wine like a deflated housewife at the end of a hard day.

10

DANTE

"So, how is it going with Colette?"

I look up from my drink, turning my attention to my older brother, perched on the edge of his mahogany desk, holding his own drink and watching me. We've been talking about our problem with the Castellanos family up until now, but business apparently exhausted, I'm the next most eventful item up for discussion.

"She's fine," I clip, looking back down at my glass before taking a long drink.

"You didn't bring her in to say hello," Mateo points out.

"Nope," I agree, offering nothing more.

Mateo gives me a moment to share, but when I don't, he presses me. "Is she adjusting well? Has she tried to run?"

I shake my head shortly. "'Course not. She knows better."

"Well, does any part of her seem happy to be back, or is she just angry?"

"Why do you care?" I demand. "Adrian's not here anymore so you have to butt into *my* business? Stay out of it."

Cocking an eyebrow in surprise, he shrugs. "Fine, don't share if you don't want to. I thought I might be able to offer advice if that would be helpful, but if you prefer to muddle your way through it alone, be my guest."

"I don't need your fucking advice," I mutter, taking another drink. "You don't even know how to handle your own shit, what makes you think you can handle mine?"

His lips curl up faintly, but his temper isn't engaged. "Tell yourself what you need to, Dante. I handle my shit just fine."

"Yeah?" I challenge, lifting an eyebrow.

Meeting my gaze with narrowed eyes, he says, "Yes."

I shake my head, but don't bother locking horns with him over something I care so little about. His lady problems are his own. Unlike him, I only feel compelled to impart advice when his love life starts getting in the way of our business. "Whatever you say, big brother. You handle your personal business and I'll handle mine separately. Colette falls under *my* territory, not yours. Her involvement with your circus will be limited to the very occasional Sunday night dinner. Don't expect us to come to these things and socialize like we used to. We're here because we needed to talk about Castellanos and I didn't want to leave her alone. It won't be like it was between us before. Vince may not have a choice letting you mingle with his woman, but I do, and it's not gonna happen."

Not bothering to hide his amusement, Mateo shakes his head. "You can't honestly believe I'm still interested in Colette, Dante. I'm not. She's yours. My only motive in asking about her is wanting to help you see something you might be too close to see yourself. That's it."

"Doesn't matter," I state. "I don't want her getting close to you or your fucking women—nothing. That's not how it's gonna be this time."

"Woman," Vince says, sharply. "He has *one*."

I glance back at our younger cousin, Mia's boyfriend. There's a challenge in his dark eyes like he dares either of us to disagree with him. I'm not here to fight with him, either. I couldn't give a fuck less about whatever is going on between him, his girlfriend, and Mateo—all I care about is keeping Colette out of it. I made the mistake of letting her get close to Beth and then when Mateo's drama blew up, it fucked *my* world up right along with his. That's not going to happen a second time.

Ignoring Vince, Mateo keeps his gaze trained on me. "Well, if you change your mind or it gets too hard, I have my own insights into what makes Colette tick. I'm happy to share. No strings attached."

Yeah fucking right. There are always strings with him.

I know that, so I stay away, but the more I drink the more I brood about it. The more I wonder what kind of insight he has into *my* woman. It eats away at me thinking there are things he might know about her that I don't, thinking if things were different and Mateo was the one after her, maybe he would do a better job of catching her. My brother is much smoother in certain ways than I am, certainly more adept at manipulating women to get what he wants from them. My approach is more direct, more forceful, but my approach isn't getting quick results. When Mia was staying at the mansion with Vince and she first met Mateo, he had the wool pulled so far over her eyes, she'd get in fights with her own boyfriend defending the devious bastard.

Maybe he has a point. Maybe his approach is better than

mine. Maybe gentler manipulation is better than brute force. After all, despite all he did to damage that girl, she's in his kitchen right now fixing all of us dinner. Colette looks at me like I'm the worst person in the world, and Mia still looks at Mateo like he's just fucking misunderstood.

Of course, it could just be because she's a lot younger than Colette. I guess Colette *used* to look at me like that. I don't know what it would take to get her to look at me with softness again.

Maybe Mateo does.

As much as it kills me, after a little time has passed and Alec gets off on a tangent talking to Vince, I take advantage of their preoccupation and make my way over to stand beside Mateo in front of Dad's old desk. He flicks a glance at me, but doesn't say anything.

"Suppose I did want your insights about Colette," I begin.

"All right," he drawls, watching me.

All my words feel stuck in my throat because I don't want to ask him for advice, but Luca is fucking pointless to talk to about shit like this, so I really don't have anyone else. "Colette is pissed about the lawyer. I don't even think she loved the bastard, not really, not like she did me, but she's clinging to this idea that he was the good guy and I'm the bad one. You know how she can be sometimes about all this shit."

Nodding as he takes a sip of his drink, he murmurs, "If there's a right side, Colette will always take it."

"Yeah. And right now that means opposing me. I'm sure I can break her down over time, but if there's a quicker way… it'd be nice to get there faster."

"Well, you can't always take the quickest path. Not if you want the best long-term result. In your case, though, it's simple. Right now Colette's on the lawyer's side, and he's dead, so he can't do anything to fuck it up. That puts you at a severe disadvantage. You're bound to do plenty to fuck up any good will she might have for you, and she's going to fight it even if she does feel a passing wave of affection for you because she feels it's her duty. She's putting him before you, and because she's Colette and that's who she is, she's always going to, even once she starts to waver. Until you give her someone more important to prioritize."

"What do you mean? I already threatened her aunt. I mean, I could do it again, but one more threat and if she disobeys, I have to follow through. I don't think killing her aunt is going to earn me any favor, just make her hate me more."

Mateo shakes his head. "Not her aunt. Your child."

"I don't have—" I stop dead when I take his meaning.

Mateo nods. "Get her pregnant. Give her a stronger tie to you than the lawyer. Colette's easy to trap, Dante. She wants the perfect little family she never had. She won't hold onto her stubbornness at the expense of it. She'll always try to put the needs of others ahead of her own, so push out the lawyer and give her a baby to devote herself to. That day's a bit fuzzy for me so I don't remember exactly why, but I do remember the day everything happened with Beth making a mental note that if I ever wanted—if *someone* ever wanted to trap Colette, knocking her up would be the quickest path toward her unwavering allegiance. Once someone makes her a mother, they don't have to worry about her going anywhere."

Heat creeps up under the collar of my dress shirt and I tug at my tie, glaring at my brother. "You thought about how to trap *my* girlfriend?"

Shrugging it off, he tells me, "You know how I am, Dante. I

can't help inventorying everybody's weaknesses and filing away the methods I could use to control them. Doesn't mean anything."

"Doesn't mean anything, my ass. I walked in on you two *embracing* and now you tell me you were thinking about impregnating her?"

"I didn't say—" My brother's not one to waste time repeating or over-explaining himself, so rather than continue down that path, he meets my gaze and says meaningfully, "It doesn't mean anything *now*. Whatever confused, lonely thoughts I may have had that day are no longer relevant. I'm not that man anymore. I've moved on, but you haven't. If you're still set on Colette after all these years, there's got to be a reason. Commit to a course and lock her down."

I consider his words for a moment, then nod slowly as the idea wraps itself around me. "Getting her pregnant crossed my mind, too. How fucked are we?" I shake my head, mildly amused. "She still hates me though. I need something quicker to push past that, to make her like me again so we can *get* to that part."

Mateo considers my situation, weighing his own thoughts, then he rocks his head from side to side. "You could probably speed things up. Wouldn't be painless."

I don't give a fuck about painless, I only care that it's effective. "Like how?"

"It would help if you could make yourself wounded. Colette can't resist taking care of the wounded."

"You mean physically?"

Mateo shrugs. "Emotionally, physically, either way. Physically would probably be easier for you to pull off. Brawl with

Luca or stop by my gym one morning, I'd be happy to beat the shit out of you."

I roll my eyes at him. "Yeah, I bet you would."

"Hey, like you said, I don't have Adrian anymore. I need someone to spar with."

"I don't think a black eye will get the job done. She'd like to give me one of those herself."

"Perhaps a non-fatal gunshot wound, then," he suggests. "Pretend you got nicked in a shootout with someone from Antonio's crew. Give her a scare, make her consider what it would feel like if she lost you. Then once you've tapped into her softness, milk it, let her take care of you. If you can wrap all that up with a pregnancy, you're set. She'll fall right back in love with you, even if she doesn't want to."

Lifting my eyebrows in surprise, I ask, "You think I should take a fucking bullet?"

"I probably would," he says, like it's nothing. "I told Mia once about Luciana and her throwing stars. Mia's a nurturer, much like Colette. Much less sanctimonious than Colette, but she has a big heart and cares about the pain of others, even if they don't entirely deserve her concern. Even while I was actively hurting her, when she saw my scars, that evidence of my pain, her tender heart swelled. She kissed them." A glimmer of affection glistens in his eyes and his lips tug up in a faint, faraway smile. "You can't manufacture moments like those, but if you're lucky enough to get one, it's worth taking a bullet for." More focused, he returns his gaze to me. "Besides, it's within your control. You decide where the bullet goes. It's little more than a scrape. It's not like you'd be in any real danger."

Shaking my head, I tell him, "You're a methodical bastard, you know that?"

Smiling faintly, he tips his glass up to take a sip, then looks over at me. "I do."

DINNER DOES NOT GO WELL. Apparently, neither lady in the kitchen interfered with Colette's wine intake and by the time we all sit down to eat, she's drunk.

Wine has always made Colette maudlin, and since right now she feels more anger and sadness than any pleasant emotion, rather than getting a pleasantly affectionate, handsy drunk, I get an annoying, difficult one. Even after I warned her to be on her best behavior in front of my family, she's fucking mouthy and rude at the dinner table.

We make it through half the meal uneventfully, but then Mateo's current girlfriend sees fit to try to pull Colette out of her pouting and into the conversation.

"So, Colette, you've been here before?" Meg inquires.

Without looking up from her plate, Colette nods her head. "Long time ago."

"Not *that* long ago," I clarify.

"A lifetime," Colette says, finally looking up to glare over at me. I ignore her gaze and take a sip of wine.

My brother attempts to keep things pleasant, addressing Colette before she can get sidetracked hating on me. "Things seem to be going well. Now here you are, Dante's… companion again."

"Prisoner," Colette mutters at him. "The word you're looking for is prisoner."

I refuse to reward Colette's sulking with my attention, so I ignore her some more and reach across the table for a dinner roll. As I do, I notice Mia and Meg exchanging understanding nods. Both of them have spent some time as prisoners of my family, so they know the score.

"This is fun," Vince remarks from his spot beside Mia. "You guys should come more often."

I think he was being sarcastic, but nonetheless Colette responds with a curt, "Hard pass."

Eyebrows rising, Meg murmurs, "Damn," and grabs a drink to avoid the awkwardness.

My fists clench of their own accord, rage pulsing through my veins. It feels like everyone's fucking staring at me, but it's worse—everyone is trying to look away. Mia stares at her plate, Vince shakes his head and reaches for a salt shaker. Meg gulps down her water like she's chasing a plate of hot wings, meanwhile Alec and Cherie focus on shoveling food into their mouths. Only Mateo is unperturbed, but he knows more than the rest of them about how Colette is being right now since we talked privately over drinks.

I can't let her bullshit stand, so without another word I shove back my chair, grab her arm, and haul her out of the dining room.

"Hey," she complains, stumbling to keep up. Drunk and in heels—what a fucking mess. "Let go of me."

"Shut your fucking mouth," I snap.

She gasps. I don't look back at her, but I can feel her glaring at me. I don't say a word as I drag her down the hall and into my brother's study. I pull the door shut and push her against the wall right beside it, moving in on her.

Fear leaps in her pretty blue eyes—not a violent fear, just a practiced wariness because she knows better than to act the way she's acting. Giving her one last chance to repent, I point a finger in her face—ignoring the way she flinches, like I'd ever fucking lay a hand on her—and tell her, "This ends now."

Colette swallows, but steadily glares up at me. "You're not my boss."

"Yes, I fucking am. You may not have picked me this time, but I'm your boss all the same. I warned you not to make me look like an asshole in front of my brother, Colette. Did I not warn you? Was I not clear?"

Swatting my hand away, she tells me, "You were perfectly clear. I just didn't listen."

I straighten, sucking in a breath to try to push out some of the rage coursing through me. I'm used to grown men following my orders. I'm not used to pushback from 100 pounds of self-righteous anger in a tight black dress.

"This is done," I say again, looking back down at her. "You're done fighting me. You're done disobeying and being a pain in my ass. I am done with this attitude. I don't fucking like it."

Having the nerve to inch forward until her tits are pressed against my chest, she looks me dead in the eye and says, "Good. I don't *want* you to like it."

"Keep it up, Colette." I push back, forcing her back against the wall. I block her in with one arm on the wall beside her head and anchor the other one on her hip. "I'll do something *you* won't like."

"You already have," she informs me, daring to look at me like I'm the one who betrayed her. "You lied to me. You told me I could leave, then chased me down and ruined my life for having the bad judgment to believe you. You destroyed a good man—"

Cutting her off, I lean in and grab her chin, lifting it to force her gaze on mine. "I don't want to hear another word about that prick, you understand me? He touched what belonged to me, and he got what he got. Don't fucking defend him anymore. It pisses me off—and yes, before you mouth off some more, I know you want to piss me off, but I don't have the patience for it. Mouth off one more time tonight, Colette, I dare you. I won't warn you again, I'll just impose the fucking consequences."

She tries to hold her ground, continuing to glare up at me, but the wariness in her eyes gives her away. "What consequences?"

My lips curve up faintly and I reach out, pushing a chunk of dark hair behind her ear. Then I trail my finger lightly across her jawline and tell her, "Test me and find out."

She holds my gaze, doesn't flinch when I run my thumb over her bottom lip. Finally, she says quietly, "I'm mad at you. Why is that not allowed?"

"You can be mad at me," I tell her. "There are more appropriate places and more enjoyable ways to express that anger. Don't do it here."

11

COLETTE

I SUPPORT the weight of my aching head in my hands, spreading my fingers to glare at the radio which Dante has turned up like we're at a rager. "Can you turn that down?"

"Why?" he asks innocently, not touching the dial.

"Because my head is pounding, I want to stab something, and you're the nearest fleshy thing available," I mutter back.

"Maybe next time don't drink a whole bottle of wine while you're cooking dinner," he suggests.

Reaching forward and cranking down the volume myself, I offer back, "Maybe next time don't drag me over there in the first place and then I won't have to dilute my alcohol with blood."

Dante smirks, and I replay what I just said.

"Shit. My blood with alcohol. Whatever, you knew what I meant."

Dante shakes his head, a roguish smile playing around his lips. "You're drunk."

Shoving him in the arm, I tell him, "I need to be to deal with you."

"I'm not so bad," he lies.

"You *are* so bad. You're the worst. You're bossy and mean and I want to punch you in the face."

"You can try," he assures me. "Can't be mad when I retaliate though."

"And punch me in the face?" I mock.

"More like smack that pretty little ass until you're squirming."

My stupid body soaks up his word and turns them into heat, pooling low in my belly. I scowl at my reaction and turn my head to look out the window while I unscrew the cap of the bottle of water Cherie handed me before we left the mansion.

"Are you and Cherie close?"

I glance over at Dante and see him frown in mild confusion for a moment, like he's not sure who I mean. "The maid's daughter?"

"She's Vince's sister, too, isn't she? So she's your cousin."

Dante shakes his head. "We're not close. She's closest to Vince. Why do you ask?"

I shrug, screwing the cap back on my water. "She was much younger last time I saw her. It was strange seeing her almost an adult. It was strange seeing everyone," I admit, glancing down at my water.

Dante's voice is hard in the way it always is when he's guarded. "You mean it was strange seeing Mateo."

It was a little strange seeing Mateo, but I'm hesitant to respond to what feels like a trap. I am mildly curious about the changes in his life since last time I saw him. I'd like to see his daughter, too, but Isabella wouldn't even know who I am anymore. She wouldn't remember all the times I held her, daydreaming about a time when Dante and I would have an adorable baby girl just like her.

"Adrian doesn't come to family dinner anymore?" I ask, rather than touch the subject of Mateo.

"No. He doesn't work for us anymore. For now, anyway. If I know my brother, he'll find a way to suck him back in."

My lips tug up faintly. "Probably. He's too attached to Adrian to let him go."

"Mm hmm," he murmurs. "The men in my family aren't too good at letting go of the things they've grown attached to."

Smoothing down the fabric hugging my thigh, I tell Dante, "The women in *my* family don't like being referred to as things."

"Who said I was talking about you?"

I roll my eyes. "Oh, how presumptuous of me. Did you kidnap a toaster you were especially fond of, too?"

"It made my toast just right. Never burned it. No one could blame me."

Despite how awful he really is, I can't help cracking a small smile. It's shamefully nice to fall back into a comfortable pattern like this with him.

I always felt special that Dante gave me access to his lighter side, because there is nothing light about this man. He's a beast in every sense of the word—physically intimidating, massively built, and his insides burn dark to match the exterior. He was brought up around dysfunction and twisted up even more by the path of crime he followed. Even his friends are droll and business-oriented. Dante feels like a dark fortress to me, adept at keeping everyone out. I'm the princess he keeps locked away in his tower, and as the sole resident of his dark heart, I get to see the sides of him no one else does.

It surprises me that in all our time apart, Dante never replaced me. He couldn't have, though. If he had, I wouldn't be here right now.

"Tell me something," I request, glancing in his direction. "Why didn't you fall in love with anyone else?"

Dante's gaze never strays from the road. "Not everyone gives their heart away as easily as you do."

I nod my head as he intentionally insults me. "So, my love is less special because I chose to share it with someone else when I thought our relationship was over?"

"That's right."

He's such a dick. "If my love is so cheap, why do you want it? Why didn't you find someone else—someone better—to meet your needs instead of fixating on me?"

His dark eyes cut in my direction. "Oh, I had plenty of someone elses meet my needs, Colette."

Ew. I scowl at him and a pit of jealousy opens up inside me. I try to ignore it and shut it down, but I feel everything more intensely when I'm drunk. It's like the polar opposite of being on my meds. "And *I'm* the faithless whore for being in a single committed relationship with someone else. Got it."

"You can be as insulted as you'd like. You're the one who left my bed empty. That wasn't my choice, it was yours."

"And you're the one who left my *heart* empty," I launch back, shooting him a dirty look. "You're the one who comes from the fucked up family where murdering first and asking questions later is apparently an acceptable way to deal with an errant girlfriend. I'm sorry if I wasn't willing to risk my life to be in a relationship with you, Dante. I'm sorry that I wanted something normal and safe where I didn't have to feel afraid all the damn time."

"Yeah?" he asks, almost amused. "How'd that work out for you, Colette? Did you find that safety you craved?"

"No," I snap, memories of all the times I was afraid slamming into me. "I never got to feel safe. I never got to feel like I was free. I never stopped looking over my shoulder." Shaking my head, I tell him, "Apparently there *is* no life after you. Not unless you're dead. I suppose you wouldn't be able to hurt me then."

"Is that what you want, baby? You want to put a bullet in my chest?"

"Sometimes," I fling back, only halfway meaning it. "At least then I'd finally be free."

"Would you?" he asks, rather casually. "'Cause you thought you'd be free of me if you left me, and that wasn't true. Maybe you're wrong about this, too. Maybe you think you'd be free, but really you'd be damned to a life of missing me and never being able to have me again."

The damndest thing is, the arrogant bastard is probably right. When I originally got involved with him, I had no idea he would be so much like an infection with no cure. I didn't know that the longer I spent with his sickness, the lower my chances of ever experiencing health again. He should have come with a warning label, something to advertise that being with him meant passing a point of no return. Once you let him in, he'll ruin you—not just for anyone else, but for yourself. You'll never be able to leave and feel well again. You'll become dependent on him in ways that don't even make sense.

Dante isn't a sickness you can shake and recover from; he's a disease, and once he infects you, he's with you until you die.

The really terrible thing is how much I *missed* his darkness when we were apart. I missed that sick feeling of needing him.

When I met Declan, I liked so much about him, but there was something he lacked. No matter how much I enjoyed his company, I never needed it. His love never wrapped me up like a warm blanket; I never craved him so much I missed him when he went to work. It wasn't unhealthy, so it didn't feel like love.

He wasn't the only one, either. I'd gone on lots of first dates after leaving Dante, trying to find someone else I connected with, trying to capture some other fish in the sea. No matter how many guys I met, none of them had his unapologetic roughness. No one was as confident or aggressive as Dante. They asked me too much and told me too little. Everything was too polite and nothing—*nothing*—was raw.

Dante was raw. He may be brutal and mean, he may do things I hate, but nothing matched the animalistic need we felt for each other when we were together. I don't like the tickle of it I feel right now, thinking of him with other women. I'm not a violent person by any means, but if he armed me and pointed his finger at some random woman who occupied my side of his bed while I was gone, I'd shoot her dead.

Mine.

No, Colette.

I worked too hard to pull myself out of this toxicity the first time, I won't let him pull me back in.

Attempting to shake it off, I do my best to remember the healthier life I got used to living without him. I don't know how I'll hold onto it when he's forcing me to live with him, but I have to find a way.

Normal may have been far less exhilarating, but it was also less dangerous and heartbreaking. I need to stay tethered to the world where murdering people for pissing you off is not okay.

The real world is vanilla, not death by chocolate.

Mm, now I want cupcakes.

"Can we go to Francesca's bakery?" I inquire.

Dante glances over at me, one dark brow rising in surprise. "It's Sunday. The bakery is closed."

"I want cupcakes," I inform him.

"We can stop at the store and get stuff for you to make your own cupcakes," he offers.

"That's fine. I probably need to be supervised so I don't burn myself on the oven though. I had a lot of wine."

"I think I'm qualified to keep an eye on you," he assures me.

12

COLETTE

MAKING cupcakes gives me something to do to pass the time once we get home, but having Dante stand against the counter with his arms folded over his massive chest sets my nerves on edge. Despite his claim that I had too much wine while preparing and eating dinner, he opened another bottle as soon as we got home.

I grab my glass and take a long swig as my gaze is tempted toward him again. I see him shift out of the corner of my eye and I want to investigate, but I do my best to pretend he's not here. Replacing my wine glass on the counter, I resume scooping cupcake batter into the paper-lined cups.

Dante moves too obviously in my direction and I can no longer ignore him. I look up at him as he tips the wine bottle and refills my glass. My gaze drifts to his strong arms—a real weakness of mine. Now that we're home, he's taken his dinner jacket off. He has the white sleeves of his dress shirt casually rolled up to just below his elbow, his strong, lean arms on display. I can see the pronounced veins in his forearms and I want to reach out and trace one with my finger.

I sigh, my heart and mind teaming up to torment me with memories of those strong arms wrapped around me, making me feel more secure than I ever had before.

And God, how I missed him when I first left. It was the hardest thing I'd ever done. I loved him so much, I craved the life I saw us having, and I knew I could only have it with him. Dante isn't like other men. He's not replaceable.

I surprise myself and him by asking quietly, "When you came to the flower shop that day, why didn't you warn me?"

He sets the wine bottle back on the counter and plugs the cork into the mouth of it. "I did," he says, simply.

My eyebrows rise and I drop the spoon in the bowl, turning to look at him. "Excuse me? No, you did not."

"Yes, I did," he answers calmly. "Not explicitly, but all the information was there, you only had to put it together. I swore to you I'd never set foot in the flower shop again after you left, so my presence there alone should have been enough to make you alert. The fact that I knew you were engaged should have told you I'd been keeping tabs on you, and the fact that I *asked* you not to fucking go through with it and to come back to me should have painted the rest of the picture. I wanted you back, and you knew it, but you told me to go away. You made your bed, Colette. I'm sorry if it's uncomfortable."

"That's not—I don't mean telling me you want me back. Any normal ex could say that and it wouldn't mean, 'if you don't come back, I will murder your fiancé.' That's where you needed to be much more explicit."

"More explicit?" he demands, his dark eyebrows rising. "You knew what you signed up for, Colette. For Christ's sake, we were going to get married! Apparently that's something you'll sign up for with more than one person, but not me. It meant something to me. For better or fucking worse, that's the promise, right? But you didn't hold up your end of the bargain."

"We weren't *married,* Dante. We weren't even formally engaged!"

"You knew my intentions," he states, not accepting that defense. "We talked about getting married, we talked about the family we were going to have together, we bought this fucking house," he says, looking around at it resentfully, almost like it became his prison once I left it. "We had a life. We had a plan. We had a commitment, and you walked away from it."

"You let me," I remind him, quietly.

"You were young," he states, flatly. "I thought it was a mistake you needed to make. I thought you'd *realize* it was a mistake and come back home. I thought you'd make it right and we could get back to how things were." Shaking his head, he says the meanest, most upsetting thing he has ever said to me. "You disappointed me."

I grab onto the counter's edge to keep myself steady, but my heart freefalls out of its cavity, hits every rib along my rib cage, and splats somewhere on the floor of my stomach. "You really put *all* the blame on me, don't you? It doesn't matter that I was afraid, or that I had a legitimate reason to be—"

"Legitimate reason, my ass. You should have trusted me. I know I handled the situation like an asshole, but I thought you knew me well enough to know I'd never lay a hand on you in violence, let alone kill you. We weren't Mateo and Beth, we were Dante and Colette. Entirely fucking different people. Entirely different relationships. You left me over something Mateo did. How fucking fair is that?"

"Fair?" I demand, wide-eyed. "You all but accused me of being inappropriate with Mateo *on the day* Mateo killed his girlfriend for cheating. You acted like you caught us in the act when all I was trying to do was comfort a grieving friend! Where the fuck was my mind supposed to go, Dante?"

"It wasn't just cheating, there was more to it with Beth. Shit you didn't know because you didn't bother hanging around long enough for the dust to settle. Once shit got real, you couldn't get out of here fast enough."

"Yes, because I wanted to live!" I stare at him, wide-eyed, not understanding how he still isn't getting it.

"Because you didn't fucking trust me," he says.

"With my life? No, I guess after that, I didn't," I admit, shaking my head. "I don't know what you want me to say. Beth trusted Mateo—"

Not letting me finish, he seethes, "Beth trusted Mateo? *Mateo* trusted *Beth* and she turned out to be a fucking *rat*."

That knocks the wind right out of my sails. "What?"

Dante shakes his head, looking off irritably at the kitchen cabinets, then back at me. His dark eyes flash with fury and he says, "She didn't just sleep with someone else, Colette. She slept with a cop. She tried to take Mateo down. Tried to turn fucking witness and get him put away. What was he supposed to do, huh? She knew what he would have to do if he found out. That bitch gave him no choice but to kill her."

My heart beats faster than it should when I'm standing still. I search my memory for some sign that she was trying to turn on Mateo, something she might have said that struck me as odd, but nothing surfaces. "I don't..." Looking back at Dante, I ask, "Why didn't you tell me that?"

"Because my whole fucking world was in chaos, Colette. My

brother was heartbroken, we had a mess with the cops on our payroll since we had to deal with one of them—everything went to hell because of what she did. I had a lot on my plate, and I didn't know I had a time limit on how fast I needed to report back to you with all the information to keep you from abandoning ship."

"But I asked—you said, 'does he need another reason?' when I asked, like it was just the cheating."

"Even if it was just the cheating bullshit, it would have been enough," he says, not at all apologetic. "Selfish fucking assholes who are more than happy to reap all the benefits during the good times but cheat when shit gets hard deserve to die. I make no apologies for that stance. But you weren't going to cheat, so it wasn't your fucking problem—or so I thought."

"I did not cheat on you," I state, carefully. "That's the problem, right there. You say I didn't trust you, but you're the one who didn't trust me. I didn't want to die over a misunderstanding. I would have never cheated on you, but I don't know how sure you had to be that I was doing wrong. If you walked in on me, naked in bed with another man pumping inside me, then sure, fucking shoot me, because it would never happen. But if hugging your brother when he's mourning a loss—as far as I know, at least—is over the line for you… then we have a difference of opinion, and given the penalty is death, it was an irreconcilable difference."

"I don't know why you think we're so fucking sloppy we kill people if we aren't sure they're guilty," he states. "It wasn't a *guess* that Beth fucked someone else, it was a documented fact. We don't carry out executions on a hunch, Colette. We're a little more fucking diligent than that."

"Well, you wouldn't tell me anything, Dante."

"It was business. It was none of your concern."

I shake my head, turning back to the bowl of batter and carefully picking up my spoon. "It *was* my concern," I inform him. "I didn't mind playing along with your chauvinistic bullshit as long as I knew, at the end of the day, you really respected me and viewed me as a partner, an equal. And I thought I knew that—until Beth happened, and all of a sudden, I didn't rate high enough to get any answers. None of my loyalty mattered, my actions with Mateo were suspect even though I had a completely normal reaction. That was bullshit, Dante. Lay all the blame on me if that's what you need to do, but it's bullshit. You could have handled things a lot better. You could have been more communicative, more open. You could have treated me like your partner that you were so damn committed to rather than treating me like someone untrustworthy, someone who had better be careful not to step the wrong way and piss you off. I was *afraid* of you, Dante. I wasn't afraid of you before."

Folding his arms over his chest again, he falls silent, glaring across the kitchen while I fill the rest of the cupcake holders. Once I've finished, I take them over and pop them in the oven. After setting the timer, I return to my wine glass, grab it, and chug the whole thing.

Now I kind of wish I hadn't decided to make cupcakes, because I am drained. All I want to do is go climb into bed and wake up tomorrow to find it's my wedding day and all of this was a dream. I won't even get married. I'll call Declan and tell him I can't go through with it, then I'll find Dante and tell him not to kill Declan because we're over. Once everyone is safe, I'll change into casual clothes and go to the flower shop. During the slow times, I'll find a new apartment to live in all by myself since I let my last lease lapse when I planned to move in with

Declan, and I'll start saving up money to travel alone to the places I went with Dante. I'll see what the world looks like alone, and hell, maybe I'll never come back to Chicago, because the more geographical distance there is between myself and Dante Morelli, the less the chances of him retrieving me.

Trying to marry someone else was my mistake. Maybe he would have left me alone forever if I hadn't tried doing that.

I knew he was the "if I can't have you, nobody else can either" type when I started dating him, so really, this is my fault. I should have taken him more seriously. I shouldn't have tried to move on because I knew he was crazy.

I am basically the one who killed Declan, and for that, I deserve to pay.

And pay I will, in the grossest way possible. I'm a prisoner in the home of the man I never stopped missing, but I can't love him anymore.

Forced to be here, but unable to be with him.

Torture. This is going to be torture.

Perhaps it's what I deserve.

Putting the now-empty wine glass down on the counter, I look up at Dante's handsome face, still stony with aggravation. My cheeks feel warm from all the alcohol and I need a shower to wash this day off me. "Will you take the cupcakes out if they're done before I come back down? I need to take a shower and change out of this dress."

Dante nods, and I head upstairs without another word.

13

COLETTE

AFTER MY SHOWER, I tell myself I'll only lie on the big, soft bed for a moment, but due to my excessive wine consumption, I pass out.

I'm so drunk I would probably stay asleep, even draped across the bottom half of the bed this way, but I'm startled awake by the brush of a hand along the back of my calf. I notice the bed sag with the weight of a second person, then I feel Dante's hand skim the inside of my right thigh. My body fully betrays my mind, excitement gathering in my tummy, sensation swirling between my legs as his finger traces the lips of my pussy.

I gasp and lift my upper body off the bed just in time for the strong arm I'd been lusting after earlier to move around my neck. Heat hits me everywhere as I look down at Dante's forearm locked across my throat, as he rolls me back against his muscular chest. He's still wearing clothes, but I have on only a towel because I didn't know what to wear to bed. I had planned to find something once I'd rested my eyes for a moment.

His finger slips inside me, gathering the wetness pooled there and then going straight for my clit. It's easily excitable right now and his touch ignites fireworks, but it's too much sensation too fast, so I squirm to try to get away from him. I need to tell him to stop, but fuck, his touch feels so good.

"Let me go," I say, pulling at his forearm in a vain attempt to get him off me.

"No," he murmurs low in my ear as he continues to touch me. "This is mine to play with, Colette. Mine to fuck, mine to taste. Mine to do with as I please."

"I don't remember agreeing to all that," I tell him, my heart skipping.

"I don't remember asking." He releases me all of a sudden, but only to yank away my towel and toss it on the floor beside his bed.

I struggle against him but he holds me easily, hooking his leg around mine to control my lower body and spread my legs open. His hand doesn't move to my spread legs, though, it runs over the mound of my breast instead. My head falls back helplessly as he runs his rough thumb over my tight nipple, pulling a cord of tension tight in my core.

"I missed these," he murmurs low in my ear, massaging the soft globe in his warm palm. This would be tender, if not for the threatening arm he has locked around my throat.

Even still, it's hot. It has been far too long since I've been handled so aggressively during sex, held immobile and used by a man self-assured enough to know I want what he's doing to me, and just bad enough to not care too much if I don't.

My pussy throbs and I wish I had a bucket of ice to dump on

the damn thing. It's almost comforting knowing how much stronger he is though. Knowing no matter how hard I fight him, I won't win. There's some relief to be found in the certainty that if he wants me, he'll take me no matter what—but what a sick reassurance. This is exactly the twisted, soul-consuming shit I need to keep myself out of.

"Dante, stop," I say, twisting and trying to elbow him.

His low chuckle sends prickles of arousal down my spine. "That was a pitiful attempt to get free, baby. If you want me to believe you mean it, you'll have to do better than that."

He doesn't wait for me to try. He flexes his arm and bends my head to the side so he can reach my neck, then he leans in and leaves a trail of soft, warm kisses along that sensitive column. Finally, he releases his chokehold. I break free and scoot away, but my victory is short-lived—he grabs me and pulls me under his body, then he sits on my hips to keep me pinned down.

My heart does a somersault as he jerks the snowy white dress shirt from his slacks, then rips it open. Despite my best intentions, my gaze shifts to the glimpse of well-defined muscles just beneath. His shirt hangs open for a moment, his dark eyes on my face, watching me look him over wordlessly. It's been so long since I've seen him, but the picture of him naked is emblazoned in my mind. It's a treasured memory I've revisited many times over the years.

Once he has given me my glimpse, he peels the shirt off and tosses it. A sigh slips out of me at the sight of him straddling my hips, his muscular chest bare. There's just a dusting of black hair on his flat stomach, disappearing down into the waistband of his black slacks. I want to run my tongue down it and have a taste of the treasure I know is waiting at the end.

He leads my gaze to his hips next as he reaches to unbuckle his belt. I look up at his broad shoulders, my gaze drifting over the defined cut of his muscles. God, he's so beautiful. Someone so awful shouldn't be so beautiful.

Black ink peeks over his shoulders like a twisted king's mantle and I have a passing curiosity. I know he had tattoos on his back before, but I wonder if he got any new ones.

Now is not the time to ask. He'll read into my curiosity, and right now I don't want him to think I want any part of this.

It would probably be more convincing if I could stop ogling him, but I'm not made of stone. Bastard should have slapped a blindfold on me to help me with my self-control.

Like he has the right, like my body belongs to him, he tosses his expensive leather belt and reaches his hands out to cup my breasts. My nipples strain against his palms. To reward them for their interest, he brushes his thumbs over the tight little buds and sends two new bolts of electricity through my core. I close my eyes, hoping to hide the arousal I feel when he does that, but there's no point. Dante has explored every single inch of my body. He knows exactly which buttons to push to drive me wild.

As if to illustrate that point, he plays with my sensitive nipples some more, then bends his head and takes one into his mouth. I gasp and reach for his head to pull it away, but my fingers get lost in the soft dark locks of his hair. Rather than pulling him away, I wind up just cradling his head while he sucks on my nipple, but I regain control after only a minute and yank.

Dante's hand shoots up and grabs my wrist, yanking it away from his hair and moving it beside me on the bed. He holds my wrist, his mouth never releasing the peak of my breast. My other hand flies to the back of his head and he repeats the same motions. When he releases my breast and looks down at me, his body is angled over mine, forcing both of my wrists to the bed, rendering me completely immobile.

"You can pull my hair all you like, beautiful. I won't complain as long as you know when I fuck you, I'm going to return the favor."

"You are *not* going to fuck me," I tell him.

Cocking an eyebrow, he glances down at my naked body and wordlessly disagrees. Rather than humor me with a pointless argument though, he bends his head to lavish the same attention on my other breast. I try to struggle, but I don't waste my energy trying too hard since he has me so thoroughly helpless at the moment. Instead, I close my eyes and try to think of other things. I bring Declan to mind, reminding myself why I have to fight Dante, why he doesn't deserve to win.

It proves too painful, though. Imagining Declan while Dante's mouth is closed around my breast. I fight to free my wrists with renewed vigor he's not prepared for and I get one free, so I take advantage and shove his shoulder. I try to twist my body away from him, but it's impossible with my hips pinned down.

My face warming with anger and helplessness, I glare up at him. "Get off me, you big brute."

"Brute." Amusement flickers through his eyes, but he doesn't smile. He simply recaptures my flying hands, pushes them together over my head, and secures them with one wrist. "I guess you're not in the mood for foreplay tonight, huh?"

"I'm not in the mood for *you,*" I spit, only mildly sensible.

"Your body disagrees with you, beautiful."

"I was thinking of Declan."

His dark eyes shoot to mine, so alarmed and offended, you'd

think I fired a bullet into his abdomen. I swallow, but refuse to break his gaze despite the feeling of an ice wall rising up between us.

"Is that so?" he asks, coldly, quietly.

Dread moves through my gut, but I keep my gaze trained on him. "That's right."

Nodding slowly, he says, "So that's how it's going to be. You fling insults and lies and push me away every chance you get."

His words trigger the oddest sense of guilt, but I hold my ground. "What did you expect, Dante? I don't want to be here. I don't want to be with you. I was where I wanted to be and you snatched me away. You didn't change my mind, only my circumstances. Only my location."

He continues to nod, but my unease rises a notch higher with every bob of his head. "If I were you, I'd think twice about playing that game, Colette. I can hurt you much more effectively than you can hurt me."

"It's not a game, Dante. I never wanted to hurt you, I just wanted to get away from you."

"But you never will," he tells me, like he did that day he came to my flower shop. The first day I saw him since I'd left, the day I'd ached hearing him mention my engagement. "Might as well give up now and we can go back to how things used to be. The harder you fight, the more severely I have to punish you."

"You don't have to punish me at all," I inform him. "You can prove you love me as much as you seem to think you do. You can let me go."

At that, his lips curve up in a faint smile of cynical amusement. "See, *now* I believe you must be thinking of your Declan.

The man you describe who would do that? It's not me. Never will be."

"People can change," I offer, even though I know it's pointless.

Shrugging noncommittally, he agrees, "Sometimes. But they have to want to."

"And you don't," I say, flatly. "You're happy being a monster who murders and maims innocent people to have your own way."

Though just as sarcastic as the smile before it, he smiles again more warmly. He holds my jaw so I can't turn away and leans in, kissing the corner of my mouth. "That's right. *Now* it's me you're thinking of."

He tries to kiss me again and I turn my head, but his fingers tighten on my jaw and he forces my gaze right back to him.

"You act like I changed, Colette, but I haven't. This is who I was when you loved me before. This is who I've always been."

"Then maybe it's me who's changed," I offer quietly.

"Change back," he demands.

14

DANTE

SINCE COLETTE RUINED the mood with her mouth, rather than fuck her I settle with stripping off the rest of my clothes and climbing into bed with her. Prickly as she is, I still yank her back against me. She starts to pull away at first, but after a brief, silent battle with herself, she must decide letting me hold her is an acceptable compromise.

We don't speak again. I don't have anything to say to her right now. I'm agitated with her continued resistance, frustrated because the rules of battle are so much trickier when you're fighting someone you don't want to irreparably harm. Normally I get my way quickly and easily, but normally I don't give a shit how many causalities there are in that pursuit, either. I don't care how dirty I have to fight, or if I only win the fight because I've broken the other person's back.

I don't want to break Colette. I know how easily I could. Luca was right, if I didn't care about preserving her spirit and well-being, I could break her in a matter of days, but that's not what I want. I don't want a pet or a slave girl, I want Colette as she is, I just want her to stop being so fucking irritating. It's only her hang-up on this Declan asshole I need to strip away from her.

In her sleep, the little minx wiggles her ass against my dick until my cock is throbbing painfully with arousal. She used to do that sometimes on purpose—oh, she'd pretend it was innocent, pretend she didn't know what she was doing, but I knew by the unsubtle mischief in her eyes when I'd roll her over and take her afterward, it was her way of initiating. In just about every instance, I am the aggressor in bed, but her ass wiggle was Colette's way of chiming in with her own desires.

Currently, my cock is responding like that's still true.

I know she's asleep, so I try to keep it at bay. Try to ignore the dull throb of pain, but then her ass shifts and she butts against it again.

Fuck.

I should have known better than to sleep naked with her. We used to do it all the time, but she used to be mine in every sense of the word. If our warm bodies pressed against each other too many times and one or both of us got hot and bothered, we'd just fuck again—problem solved.

I push my hips forward, pressing my hard cock against her smooth ass cheeks. My blood pumps through my veins, my heartbeat kicking up a speed. She's still asleep, but my hand curves around her breast and I give it a little squeeze. The delicate curve of her neck is just right there in front of me, so I bend my head and place a few soft, slow kisses against her skin.

Her breathing remains even like she's sleeping, but I hear her swallow. Releasing her breast, I let my hand drift down her rib cage. I splay my hand as it travels over her abdomen, then make my touch feather light again as it makes its way across her pubic bone.

"Dante," she finally whispers. An attempt at a warning, but I ignore it. She doesn't get to warn me.

I run just the tip of my index finger along her pussy lips. She fucking loves that. Even now, even silent and rebellious, I hear her sharp inhale. I can't see her eyes from back here, but I remember the way they flutter closed as she enjoys that brief moment before I sink my finger inside her. When I do, she gasps, and I wish she wasn't turned away from me so I could've caught it in my mouth.

As I gently stroke her pussy, I snake my other hand down between our bodies to grab her bare ass. Another little sharp breath when I squeeze her ass. I push my dick between her cheeks and she grabs her pillow, probably holding on in case I take her ass.

I'm not going to do that, though. I haven't prepared her and I don't want to hurt her. Plus, the only place I want to spill my cum tonight is deep inside her pussy.

Since she's already halfway there clutching onto the pillow, I withdraw my finger from her pussy and push her the rest of the way onto her stomach.

"Dante," she says again, her voice higher, more panicked.

"Shh," I say, running a hand down the curve of her back as I climb onto my knees behind her. Since I don't trust her to keep her troublesome mouth shut, I push her face into the pillows. She struggles to push her head back up, tries to swat my hand away, but I only push her down harder until she stops fighting. Once she submits, I let her go, giving her head a tender rub before releasing her so I can use my hands for more useful tasks. Lifting her hips and positioning her, I tell her, "On your knees and forearms."

"Fuck you," she spits back.

I lift an eyebrow and smack her ass for her insolence. I don't need her compliance, it will just be more work without it. I'm not afraid of a little work. Since she's being difficult, I hold her where I want her, grasping my cock with my other hand and guiding it between her legs.

For all her bullshit resistance, she's drenched. Just the first inch inside her wet heat is incredible, but when I drive deep into her tight little pussy, the pleasure is so fucking intense, everything else disappears. Almost everything. I hear her gasp as I slide deep inside her, feel her body respond when I pull back and thrust into her again. A moan slips out of her as I pick up the pace, as I shove a little harder, as I remind her what she's been missing since she left.

What I've been missing, too. I may have had encounters with various women in her absence, but none of them felt like her. Being inside her again is a relief, like finally falling into your own bed after a long stretch of traveling and spending every empty night alone in a hotel with a shitty mattress. Now I'm home, and nothing else matters.

She's supporting her own weight on her knees now, so I run a hand up her back and grab a fistful of her hair. I give it a tug as I thrust my hips forward and pound into her. Her breathing is heavier now and she clutches onto the pillow and the bedsheet for dear life.

When I imagined the first time I fucked her again, I pictured a marathon. I pictured position changes, her body slick with sweat, begging me to come by the end of it. I pictured denying her even while I plunged into her body, refusing her pleasure until she couldn't take anymore.

In reality, I just want to fucking mark her. I want to come all over that pussy so she knows if she ever so much as thinks about giving it to someone else again, these are the consequences. I'll kill every last one of them and mark her all over again. She's never getting rid of my mark. Never.

"Dante, Dante, Dante," she whimpers helplessly, bringing me back to the moment.

She must be close. Armed with that information and ready to come myself, I tilt her hips while I thrust, stopping when I can tell by the strangled sounds she makes I have her in the right place. Then I pound into her hard and fast, so hard she can barely hang on, until she's whimpering and whining so much, you can't tell if she's being fucked or beaten. Fuck, that's my favorite part.

"Come for me, beautiful. I'm waiting for you to finish me off."

Her mind might be stuck on rebellion, but her body knows who its master is. With a sharp, strangled cry, Colette comes hard, her pussy squeezing me once, twice, three times. I groan as her body continues to convulse around my dick, as I thrust furiously into that tight, throbbing haven, then I lose control and come apart, growling and yanking her hair tight in my fist as I drive forward and explode deep inside her pussy. She cries out again but I'm too lost in my own pleasure to pay attention. It takes a minute before I can think straight again, then I realize how hard I'm fisting her hair. I release her immediately and she rubs the back of her head.

I pull out of her body and sigh, sinking against the bed beside her. "Sorry, I got a little carried away there."

She's still breathing hard as she comes back down from her orgasm, but after a few seconds, my brow furrows in confusion. It sounds like she's getting *more* worked up, not calmer. The pace of her breathing should be coming back down to normal, but instead, she's breathing so heavily it's the only sound in the room.

"Colette?" I question, grabbing her shoulder and rolling her onto her side so I can see her.

What I thought was her continued heavy breathing is in fact her struggling to breathe. I shoot up, trying to make sense of the panic on her face. My blood runs cold and I turn her all the way over onto her back, climbing on my knees and looking down at her. "Colette, what's wrong?"

It takes her a minute, but she finally manages to get out between heaving breaths, "Can't breathe."

Can't breathe? Why can't she fucking breathe? I don't know what to do, but as I hold onto her shoulders and watch her struggling to do something so simple, I note she's trembling like she's cold or terrified. I know she's not either—there's a light sheen of sweat on her forehead from fucking, and I may have been a little rougher at the end than I meant to be, but that was nothing she couldn't handle. Certainly nothing that would terrify her.

I don't know what to do, so I sit back and pull her into my arms. She struggles at first, but it's not me she's fighting, it's the panic.

Keeping my tone calm and authoritative, I tighten my hold on her, imprisoning her in the safety of my arms. "You're fine, Colette. I've got you. Breathe. Focus and breathe."

It doesn't work right away and I have no fucking idea what to do, but I never let that show. I keep calm, keep my voice commanding, keep offering direction and reminding her body to do the things it should do naturally while I rub her back and try to calm her.

Finally, I think she's calming down. She's not gasping for air like she's drowning. She's still off-kilter, but it seems to be tapering off until she suddenly breaks away from me and makes a break for the bathroom.

I spring off the bed to follow her, but hesitate when I hear her emptying the contents of her stomach into the toilet.

A feeling I'm not at all used to burrows into my gut—fear. I don't know what exactly is happening to her, but I know it's bad. Easing the door open, I step inside. Colette is hunched over the toilet, sobbing. I walk past her and grab a towel. Returning to her side, I touch her shoulder to get her attention. She looks up to take it, murmuring a low, rough, "Thank you," but all I can focus on is her face. Red with the strain of wrenching up whatever feelings just overtook her, her face splotchy from tears.

I don't know what else to do, so I kneel down and sit on the ground beside her while she uses the towel to clean up her face. Her whole body still trembles, whether from the force of throwing up everything in her system, or from whatever the fuck had her trembling in the bed, I'm not sure. Whatever the reason, she's shaking, and I fucking hate it.

"Are you cold?" I ask her.

"I don't know," she murmurs.

I don't know what kind of answer that is, but I stand up and go to get her robe, just in case. She's still on the floor when I come back, so I bend down and drape the bathrobe around her shoulders like a cloak to keep her warm.

"Come on, get off the floor. The floor's cold," I tell her, offering my hand.

She takes another swipe at her mouth with the towel, then looks at my hand but shakes her head. "I'm gross right now, don't touch me."

"You could never be gross," I tell her, grabbing her hand and helping her off the floor.

Since she feels gross, though, I haul her over to the shower. I keep hold of her hand with one of mine and lean in to turn on the shower. I know she likes scalding hot showers, but I start it just a little hotter than warm so it doesn't shock her system when she steps inside. I look back at her, expecting her to get in the shower, but she looks lost and drained. I don't even know if she's capable of showering by herself, so I peel the robe back off her shoulders, drape it across the nearby chair, then put my hand at the small of her back and usher her into the shower.

Colette is like an articulated statue as I go through the motions of cleaning her up and washing her hair. She doesn't even put up a fake resistance when I pull her back against me in the shower and caress her breasts as I soap them up. I drag the soapy washcloth down her abdomen, then between her legs, running it and my hand over her pussy. She sighs and leans her tired head against my shoulder, but again, doesn't resist.

Last time I made her come she flipped the fuck out, so I don't do it again. I play with her a little, but only to relax her, not to build up the tension. I knead her shoulders and try to rub some of the tension out of her lower back, then once she's clean and relaxed, I turn off the water and we get out.

She's finally capable of caring for herself enough to dry off once we get out, but she's still not speaking and I'm not either.

We don't need to talk. Some of our best communicating is done in silence, but I don't like what I'm hearing tonight.

Once we're tucked back under the blankets, Colette in her bathrobe snuggled up close to me, I can't help asking the one question I can't get out of my mind.

"Colette, was that my fault?"

Her big blue eyes have the power to fell me with one accusing glare right now, her sharp tongue could wound me with a single syllable. I didn't understand when she told me she needed the Valium because I've never seen anything like this happen to her before, but if it never happened to her before and now it is, maybe it wasn't the lawyer or the world that did this to her.

Maybe it was me.

All she has to do is confirm it and she'll win this round, she'll deliver guilt I haven't accepted until now, but she doesn't. There's no accusation in her gaze, only exhaustion and a touch of sadness. I'm vulnerable to a verbal lashing, but she doesn't say a word to wound me. Instead, she wraps her arms around me and buries her face in my chest, letting me know she doesn't want to fight, she doesn't want to talk, she just needs to be held.

I hold her so tight none of her demons would dare escape, but I can't outrun the knowledge that Colette never had demons—not until I gave them to her.

15

DANTE

IT'S a long night and I don't sleep well. Every time Colette so much as shifts in my arms, I wake up to check on her. At least she seems to sleep soundly, despite all the movement. Come morning, I ease out of bed, careful not to wake her, and get started on my day. I had a few things planned today work-wise, but every time I think about leaving Colette here by herself, I consider delegating those tasks to someone else and just staying home.

Well, she won't be entirely by herself, but Sonja's not the best company. I'll warn her to be nice to Colette before I leave, to make sure she makes her some breakfast and doesn't hassle her, but I still don't feel right about leaving. I never left Colette alone when she was sick, I kept her company and took care of her. Not that she's actually sick, I guess, but whatever the fuck she is, it's my job to fix it.

Much as I hate to leave, there's a meeting I can't miss this morning regarding our conflict with the Castellanos family.

Even Adrian is going to be there to fill us in on some stuff, and he doesn't work for us anymore.

So, I have to go to my brother's house.

Ordinarily these meetings don't take much longer than they absolutely have to, but today when I sit down with a cup of coffee at the dining room table, it's not just the usual men gathered around it. Vince brought his fucking girlfriend over, and inexplicably she's sitting at the table like she belongs there. I saw her in the kitchen a few minutes ago, but I assumed she was here to visit Meg, not sitting in on our meeting.

"What is this?" I ask, nodding at the cute blonde seated beside my younger cousin. "We get a new recruit no one told me about?"

Vince slides me an unamused look. "Yeah, right. Mia needs to go grocery shopping. Figured I might as well bring her here for breakfast since Maria always makes too much and the fridge is empty at home."

How fucking annoying. Normally I wouldn't be such an asshole about it. Personally, I don't know what it's like to have to budget to buy groceries, but I do know since Vince and Mia moved out of Mateo's house—and out from under his thumb—he cut them off financially, except for the paychecks Vince earns doing work for us like any other associate who needs to work his way up. It's not much, and I'm sure Mia doesn't make much helping out at our family bakery either, so they probably don't *have* grocery money. That's the part Vince isn't saying, since obviously it would embarrass him to admit in front of Mateo that he's failing to provide for his woman.

Today I don't give a fuck about their financial woes though, I only care about getting back home as quick as I can to check on

Colette. Hell, I'll slide Mia a fifty myself and tell her to go shopping if she'll just leave so we can get down to business.

Now that Vince is finished critiquing Mia's shopping skills, she turns back to Mateo to resume their conversation rather than eat her fucking food.

Mateo is seated at the head of the table like always, his dark eyes trained on the babbling blonde seated to his left. Now that I know we're just waiting for her to finish eating, every moment she spends talking to him instead of shoveling food into her mouth annoys me as much as it seems to annoy Vince.

And boy, does he look annoyed. Of course he's annoyed. The little fucking genius brought Mia around Mateo on purpose. He should've left her at home to starve because now even once she leaves us here to do business, the kid's gonna have a chip on his shoulder. Mateo will probably bait him, and even if Mateo doesn't, someone else will rib him about it and he'll get all pissy. This whole thing is going to devolve into a pissing contest before we ever even *start* talking about Castellanos.

Fucking fantastic.

Shit like this is exactly why I didn't want to meet at the mansion when Mateo summoned me here, but he didn't feel like going out. So, here we all sit, assembled around the dining room table, but with a plus one no one told me about who completely fucking blocks any business we might have wanted to discuss.

Basically, this is an enormous waste of my time.

It's a waste of his time, too, but Mateo idly stirs his coffee, nodding his head at Vince's girlfriend, not seeming to mind at all. There are a few reasons this is ridiculous. One: Mateo doesn't need to stir coffee because he takes it black. But Vince's idiot girlfriend wanted to help Maria out in the kitchen since there are so many of us this morning, and she put cream in it. He should've made her dump the coffee and get him a new cup—he certainly would've if Maria had fucked up his coffee—but he just stirs it like he's actually going to drink it. Two: this girl is actually trying to convince him—*a fucking crime king*—to donate money to some do-gooder organization whose interests align firmly against our own. Three: Mateo is not customarily amused by morons. I would say maybe he's less bothered by them when they have nice tits and a low-cut top, but that has not historically been the case.

"So anyway, I figured you probably already donate money to charitable organizations for your legitimate business interests, right? For the tax breaks or whatever?" she's saying now.

His lips curve up just slightly and he gives a faint nod—almost encouraging, if I didn't know any better.

Mia shrugs, taking a sip of her orange juice. "That's what I figured. And, yeah, I understand you guys aren't Boy Scouts, but there are worse criminals out there—there are people who do stuff like *this*. I mean… that's truly horrible. Anyone who could do something like this to human beings just to make money…" She trails off, glancing at the table like it's just too dark for her to wrap her head around.

This is fucking hilarious. I cannot believe she is asking the monster himself to help protect the victims. I nearly smile at how fucking stupid she is. I expect Mateo to be privately amused, too—he doesn't give a fraction of a fuck what people think about him, but I figure it will amuse him that this little nobody is unwittingly telling him right to his face that he's the worst kind of monster her innocent little mind can conjure.

But there's no glimmer of amusement in his eyes. The hint

of smile is gone. I don't expect him to whip out his poker face to mask amusement—that's not really his style.

Discomfort moves through me, but the idea behind it is too ridiculous to consider. There's no way he *cares* what this girl thinks about him. That's too absurd to even consider.

Brightening slightly, Mia concludes, "So, yeah, that's my pitch. If you're looking for a good cause, you should definitely give your blood money to this one. You should check out that book, too—I'm not even a big reader and I couldn't stop turning the pages."

"I will certainly look it up," he assures her.

She nods and smiles pleasantly, finishing off her orange juice. "Well, I'm going to go see if Meg's awake yet."

Mateo's brows furrow and he nods at her plate. "You haven't finished your breakfast."

"I wasn't that hungry," she insists, pushing back her chair and rising. I doubt that's true, but I get the feeling she knows she's intruding now. Rather than continue to hold us up, she just won't eat anymore.

Too fucking considerate, but I'm glad. Now we can get on with the business portion of this fucking business meeting.

Mia leans over to give Vince a kiss. "I will leave you gentlemen to your... whatever. Have a good day." She offers a smile and wave to the assembled men, smiling lastly at Mateo before heading back into the kitchen with her dishes.

Once she's gone, Mateo looks into his cup of coffee. Finally, he lifts it to take a drink. Predictably, he grimaces and sets it back down.

I glance around at the other men, expecting them to be similarly annoyed. They're not. Many of them live here, though, so they're more accustomed to her presence.

I glance at Vince across the table. "Where the hell did you find her?"

"Heaven," Adrian answers, without hesitation. "She was clearly sent by God Himself to punish every last one of us."

"Did he send her without a brain on purpose, or was that an oversight?" I ask.

Vince glares from me to Adrian. "Hey, don't be assholes."

"She just earnestly asked a human trafficker to donate money to an anti-fucking-trafficking organization," I state, dumbfounded.

"She doesn't know we're into that shit," Vince defends. "How the hell would she know the details of what we do?"

My eyebrows shoot up helplessly and I gesture to Maria, approaching the table now to get Mateo some drinkable coffee. "How does she think Maria came to be here? Why does she think Adrian had to work for us to have Elise? Seriously, how fucking dense can a person be?"

"She doesn't ask questions," Vince states, glaring at me.

"You know who doesn't ask questions?" I offer back. "Fucking morons."

"That's enough," Mateo says, leveling a significantly less pleasant look at me. "We're not here to discuss Mia."

I nod my agreement, checking my watch. "You're right, we're not. We're all here to talk business, but you let her come to the table so we've all wasted our morning listening to Elle Woods launch her anti-trafficking campaign. I don't have all day, you know. Some of us actually have important shit to do."

"Then go do it," he challenges, holding my gaze.

I give him a mild glare, but I cross my arms over my chest and settle back in my seat. I'm pissed I had to leave my house in the first place, but I'm more pissed that he's okay with wasting my time. Maybe if he would've been the one who told Mia to get out of here so we could work it'd be okay, but I don't like that he sat back and let her get in the way. Gives me a bad feeling.

With the girl gone, we can finally get down to the meeting. I'm impatient the whole time, waiting for it to be over from the moment it starts, but despite the current crisis, the meeting is brief. I'm fucking glad. We all push back from the table, leaving our respective coffee cups for the maid to clean up, and everyone heads off in their own direction. Alec slips out first. Adrian hangs back to talk to Mateo. I turn my sights on Vince, who is about to leave without so much as a goodbye.

"Hey, I need you to do something for me."

Vince halts and looks over his shoulder uncertainly, like he thinks I got the wrong guy. "Me?"

I nod, reaching into my back pocket and drawing out my wallet. Vince scowls at it, but looks back at me wordlessly to see what I want.

"I need some Valium," I tell him, pulling two crisp fifties out of my wallet.

"How much do you need?" Vince asks, looking at the cash.

"Just a standard bottle, like someone would get if they had a prescription. Colette had one at her aunt's house but I didn't bring it when I took her. You can go to her aunt's house and retrieve that bottle, if you feel like it. Then you can keep all the cash for yourself. I don't especially care how you get the job done, I just need the pills today."

"Is her aunt home?" he inquires, since he's pretty good at picking locks.

"No idea."

Pulling out his cell phone, he opens it up and hands it to

me. "I'll find out. Give me her address. I can let myself in and grab Colette's medicine. Need anything else while I'm there?"

"For an additional fee?" I ask knowingly.

Vince smirks. "Hey, guy's gotta eat."

I shake my head. "She doesn't need any of her old shit. Just get me her pills." I start to put my wallet away, then I stop, remembering the horrible thought that crossed my mind somewhere around 4am. Opening my wallet back up, I draw out another fifty. "Actually, on second thought, I do need one more thing. Not from Colette's house, but you can pick it up at a drugstore on your way to drop off the pills."

Vince takes the cash and looks up at me. "What's that?"

"A pregnancy test."

16

DANTE

BY THE TIME I get back home, Colette is awake. I find her on the back patio, sitting in her old chair with a cup of tea in hand, staring out at the calm lake. Her long, dark hair is a mess, pulled back and twisted up, secured with a clip I didn't buy her. Colette is still in her bathrobe, but I guess I didn't really buy her any relaxing clothes to wear around the house. I figured once she got comfortable we would go out and she could do some shopping, but I probably should have had more waiting for her when she got here.

I'm not trying to be stealthy, so I walk heavily enough that she hears me approach from the slap of my loafers against the ground. She looks up at me as I come to a stop beside her chair and offers a tremulous smile. "What are you doing home already?"

Home. She already refers to it as home again. I like that. Taking the seat beside her, I tell her, "Not much going on today." That's a lie, but a harmless one. "I'll stay here and keep you company."

"You don't have to do that," she tells me, like she knows why. "I'm really fine. I told you, sometimes I have panic attacks."

"Well, Vince is bringing your pills this afternoon," I tell her. "If that happens again, we'll be ready."

"That's nice of him," she murmurs, looking back out at the lake. "You should give him a cupcake as a thank you. I don't know if they're any good, but I frosted them before I came outside."

I nod in acknowledgement of what she said, but I don't give a shit about cupcakes. "How are you feeling today?"

"Tired."

That's not exactly what I meant, but I guess it's all she wants to give me. That's all right. Rather than press her for more, I lean back in the chair and join her in looking out at the lake.

"Do you still have the boat?" she inquires, after a moment.

"Sure do. We can take it out this evening, if you want. Pack up some cheese and fruit, bring some wine, watch the sun set."

It's the kind of night she used to love, but asking her now seems to make her sad. I'm afraid making her sad could trigger another attack like last night, so when she doesn't answer, I don't say anything more about it.

I guess my presence must have ruined her enjoyment of the lake view because after just a few minutes, she gets up and heads back toward the house.

Sitting forward in the chair and looking back at her, I ask, "What are you doing?"

"I'm going to lie down," she answers, before disappearing inside the house.

WHEN THE DOORBELL RINGS, I'm instantly irritated. Vince could have just texted me to let me know he's here, he didn't have to ring the damn doorbell and risk waking up Colette.

When I pull open the door with a scowl on my face, prepared to ream my younger cousin, I have to do a double take. It's not Vince standing on my doorstep, but a blonde girl in a white top and denim shorts seemingly designed to draw my eyes to a pair of long, shapely legs that damn sure do not belong to my cousin.

Do-Gooder Barbie herself, Mia Mitchell.

"What the hell are you doing here?" I demand.

Mia's eyebrows rise, then she holds up a plastic grocery bag expectantly. "You asked Vince to get some stuff for Colette."

"Yes, I asked *Vince.*"

"Well, Vince had work to do, so he asked me to bring it over," she explains, glancing past me into the house. "Is Colette here?"

"No, she's at the zoo."

Mia gives me a dead-eyed look. "Hilarious."

"I'll give you the schedule for my stand-up tour so you can follow it." I hold out my hand to take the bag, but rather than hand it over, she pulls it back toward her as if reluctant.

"Actually, I was hoping I could give it to her," she tells me, her tone and her big blue eyes indicating she's asking my permission. I do like that, but I don't like her ringing my damn doorbell or getting in my brother's head, so I open my mouth to tell her no. She must sense it coming, because she quickly starts talking again. "I got her some other things, girly things, things she might need. I remember when Mateo kept me…" She flounders for a nice way to say captive, but fails to find one. "… in his room, there were things I would have liked to have. I couldn't even shave my legs." Shrugging, she concludes, "Anyway, I bought some things for Colette you may not have thought of because you're a guy."

"A captive care package. How thoughtful," I remark, dryly. It is thoughtful, though. The damned girl doesn't even have enough money to buy groceries, and here she is wasting her money buying shit for Colette.

Since I haven't bitten her head off yet, she appears to gather courage. Looking up at me, she adds, "Also… if she is pregnant, she probably shouldn't be given Valium. Some medications can harm the baby. I'm not positive that's one of them, but you might want to check with a doctor first. If you're having a hard time keeping her… calm, maybe I could talk to her. I understand what she's going through, I've been there myself, so—"

"Been where?" I ask, just to make her uncomfortable.

She hesitates, but at least holds my gaze this time. Again, I see her searching for a non-confrontational way to refer to the heinous shit Morelli men are so often responsible for. "Just… there," she says with a shrug, refusing to put a name to her passive accusation.

Leaning against the doorframe, I cross my arms and cock my head, as if confused. "Where?"

Mia sighs at me, leveling me another look of minor annoyance. "Why do you need me to say it?"

"Say what?" I ask innocently.

Her blue eyes narrow, but she doesn't answer me. Seeming

to understand I'll keep giving her a hard time if she keeps letting me, she straightens and says, "I'd just like to see Colette, that's all. I want to make sure she's okay and give her the things I picked up for her."

"You don't even know Colette. Why should you care how she is?"

"I met her last night," she says.

"She was mean last night," I point out.

Mia shrugs. "Well, yes, but she's undoubtedly not having the time of her life right now, so... people handle that in different ways. In any case, it doesn't matter if she's mean or nice, I would still like to check in on her while I'm here."

"Why do you think she needs to be checked on?"

Looking me dead in the eye, she says, "Because last night she seemed like she would rather blow you up than look at you, and today I'm delivering a pregnancy test."

My lips curve up faintly at the little peek of irritation. "Am I getting on your nerves, Mia?"

"I don't care about you," she states. "I just want to make sure Colette's okay. I know she doesn't want to be here, I know what she may be going through, and as someone who has come out on the other side, I just think I have the experience and perspective Colette might need right now. I can be sympathetic without interfering in a way you wouldn't like. I'm a Morelli-safe visitor, it's not like you have to worry I'll try to rescue her. I'm not here to judge you for whatever you may or may not have done to her, I just think it'd be a real dick move to make her suffer alone when she doesn't have to."

Losing the faint trace of humor I had, I straighten to my full height and take a menacing step toward her. She must not be a complete moron, because she takes two wary steps back.

"Watch how you talk to me, Barbie. I'm not my brother, I don't find you charming."

"You don't have to find me charming," she says, carefully. "I don't know you, I don't know your deal, but I think if you care about Colette at all, you should consider what I'm saying. It's not easy dealing with all this Morelli bullshit alone, it's not easy being locked away with no one to talk to. She can talk to me. I get it. I can help you both if I can give her a way to vent. Wouldn't you rather her say mean things about you to *me* than you?"

Yes, actually, I probably would. Rather than say that, I decide to get rid of the girl once and for all. The quickest and most effective way? Scare her.

Grabbing a fistful of her white shirt, I rotate our positions and shove her up against the outside of my house. She gasps, grabbing at my hand on her chest to try to break my grip, but all she ends up doing is touching my hand, so she quickly lets go and looks up at me, her blue eyes wide with alarm. "What the hell do you think you're doing?" she demands, despite her naturally submissive physical response.

"You're right to think I'm dangerous. You're wrong to think anything you say will get you into my house—and given your assumption about my predilections, you should probably be thankful for that." I let the silent threat hang in the air just long enough for her to lose a shade of color, then I go on. "You're also wrong if you think there's a shot in hell I'll let you befriend Colette, regardless of your level of Morelli expertise."

"I only wanted to help—"

I cut her off. "I know what you're trying to do. Here's the thing, sweetheart; when Vince kills you in a jealous rage someday, I'm gonna have enough shit to deal with, I don't need to add a grieving Colette to my already full plate. So, you keep to your side of town and I'll keep to mine. Got it?"

She swallows, clearly still wanting to argue. She knows better though, so she nods tersely. "Let go of me."

Instead of releasing the balled up fabric clenched tightly in my fist, I make a show of looking her over real slow. I hear Mia swallow and imagine dread pooling in her taut little stomach, but enough of it needs to pool there to keep her the fuck off my property, so I take a little longer. Given I'm clutching the fabric right on top of her breasts, my fingers are pressed close enough against her that I can feel her heart pounding beneath my fingers. Good. Be afraid, little pest. Be very afraid.

Slowly, I bring my gaze back to her eyes. I look at her like she's property to be sold, but just far enough out of my reach that I'd have to lean to catch her, and that's too much work. Finally, I release her shirt, but I don't take a step back, so she's still caged between me and the exterior of my house. "Enjoy your oblivious illusion of safety while you still have it," I advise her.

"Vince isn't going to kill me," she states, but now she won't meet my gaze as she straightens her shirt and inches away from me.

"Yes, because he's certainly never hurt you before."

Despite her wariness of me, Mia glares. "That was—Mateo—He wouldn't *kill* me."

My tone bored, I reply, "Tell yourself what you need to." Holding my hand out for the bag, I raise an expectant eyebrow.

Mia thrusts the bag at me, clearly mad at me now. "I feel sorry for Colette."

"I feel sorry for whoever will have to dig your shallow grave and dispose of your lifeless body," I offer back.

Making a noise of disgust, she storms down the stairs and hastily makes her way back toward her little piece of shit car.

I almost let her leave, but on second thought, I take a couple steps forward and call out, "Hey, Mia."

She spins on her heel and shoots me a dirty look, but waits to see what I have to say.

"Don't mention this little encounter to my brother."

I don't like making the request, but I don't know this girl well enough to know if she's a whiner. I know she was volleyed between my brother and cousin and somehow she manages to be on good terms with both of them now so she must be some sort of peacekeeper, but I don't want to risk it. I have an uncomfortable hunch that if she tattled to Mateo about my treatment of her on my front porch today, he wouldn't be very happy about it.

"Wasn't planning on it," Mia calls back. "I'm pretty accomplished at keeping all your family's dirty secrets."

I crack a smile. "If only you weren't also so accomplished at taking all our cocks, maybe I could have let you be Colette's friend."

Her jaw drops and she gasps in outrage. "Screw you, Dante."

My smile widens and I hold up the plastic bag. "Thanks for all your help, Elle."

"That's not my name," she mutters, shaking her head as she opens her car door. Then she drops as heavily as she can into the driver's side seat and slams her door shut.

It's really too bad she can't be friends with Colette. She's right about her experience with my brother potentially helping them bond, and I couldn't give a shit less if Mia judges me, as long as she stays out of my way, regardless.

I don't know if I'd want Mia regularly hanging around my

house given my brother's interest in her, but even if I wanted to avoid him potentially sticking his nose in my business, once Colette adjusts, they could be shopping buddies and Mia could play chaperone when Colette wants to go out. The girl could have been damned useful, if only my brother hadn't noticed her —or if he'd noticed her first, I guess. In any case, my powerful brother and hot-headed cousin *both* having some kind of vested interest in her makes it far too risky.

Before Beth and Mateo fucked everything up, we had a nice system with them. Colette got to have a friend, I never had to worry about outsiders influencing our relationships with their clueless bullshit.

I don't hate ragging on Mia either, I just can't risk letting Colette get close to another potential Beth.

17

COLETTE

When my eyes open, it's because the mattress shifts and jostles me as Dante takes a seat on the bed. He's still wearing charcoal gray slacks and a white dress shirt, but he has taken off the jacket and tie he was wearing when he got home. His shirt sleeves are rolled up to his elbows, exposing his strong forearms. My gaze lingers there for a moment, but then drifts to the plastic bag on the bed next to him. My curiosity stirs. I was expecting my meds today, but the bag is too full for just a bottle of pills.

Before I can ask what's inside, Dante asks, "How are you feeling?"

Groggy, but I don't say that. "Fine."

"I was going to let you sleep as long as you needed to, but Sonja is finishing up dinner and you need to eat."

It's dinnertime? Wow, I slept the entire day away.

Not that it really matters. I'm a glorified prisoner with

nothing to do and nowhere to go. Sinking back down into the bed, I pull my blanket up over my head.

Dante tugs it right back down. "Come on, it's time to get up." He picks up the bag and opens it, peering inside.

"What's that?" I ask, since he brought my attention back to it.

"I asked Vince to pick up some things you might need, remember?" He draws out a small orange bottle with a white lid and label, and relief pours through me. "Here are your pills."

"Thank you," I say, reaching for my medication, but Dante moves the bottle before I can grab it. He places the bottle on his nightstand, out of my reach unless I crawl over to his side of the bed. "Am I not allowed to have them?" I ask.

"You're calm right now," he points out. "You have to be careful with those, Colette, they're addictive."

"I don't need to be told how to handle myself, Dante. I'm not a child."

Ignoring me, he reaches into the bag for something else. I'm not sure what I expect him to pull out, but certainly not a pink and white rectangular box with a picture of a pregnancy test on the front.

Arching an eyebrow at him, I demand, "Are you serious? I know you Morelli men think a lot of your virility, but you just fucked me less than 24 hours ago. Even if by some slim chance you did impregnate me, it won't show up on a home pregnancy test for at least a couple of weeks."

Dante doesn't look at me. He shakes his head, looking at his lap instead. "That's not what it's for. After last night it occurred to me—" He stops, perhaps considering how to word what occurred to him, then he looks me in the eye and says, "I just need to make sure every last trace of him is gone. I need you to take this to set my mind at ease."

When I catch onto his meaning, I want to punch him right in the face.

I take the box, all right. I take it from his hand and fling it across the room as hard as I can. "Fuck you, Dante."

"I have to be sure, Colette. If you're difficult and you refuse a home pregnancy test, I'll take you to the doctor."

"*Please* take me out in public. I'll scream my head off and tell everyone who will listen that I've been abducted by a madman."

"You will not," he says, not even mildly threatened.

"I am not pregnant. I don't need to take a home pregnancy test. Not that it's *any* of your business, because it isn't, but Declan and I were always very careful. I told you I was on birth control. We also used a second form of protection." His hands fist so I quickly conclude, "There is a zero percent chance I was pregnant when you took me from my aunt's house. I don't need to take a test."

"*I* need you to take it," he states, immovably.

"I don't care what you need," I inform him, point blank.

He stares at me for a long moment, so long that I start to feel a little guilty for saying it, but it's the truth. I don't know why he thought he could storm into my life, commit a murder, and we'd pick up right where we left off. I don't know why he thought the foolish younger version of me who loved him might still exist. When he came to my shop and asked me not to marry my fiancé, when he asked me to come home and I said no, that should have been his answer. But Dante doesn't know how to take no for an answer, and now here we are.

He seems to realize it the same time I do, because he stands, leaving the plastic bag on the bed with me. "Make sure you go downstairs and have some dinner."

My gaze follows him as he heads toward the door. "Are you going somewhere?"

"Yes," he states, offering nothing more.

DESPITE MY CLAIM that I wouldn't take the pregnancy test, I take it the following morning. I know it's a complete waste of a pregnancy test, but Dante didn't come home until late last night, and when he did, he stayed on his own side of the bed and didn't touch me. I caught myself thinking about it off and on while I was alone, fast forwarding a month or so ahead of time, imagining the possible repercussions if I remain stubborn about not taking the test and Dante *does* end up getting me pregnant.

The possibility that he would believe Declan might be the father instead of him opens up too many horrible doors that I can't bear to think about. I know Dante, I know what he's like, and I know there's not a shot in hell he would let me have anyone else's baby. I envision that future and find myself huddled in a corner, arms protectively covering my abdomen, begging him to believe me. Protecting our child—whom he would never hurt, if he believed it to be *our* child, but if he thought it was Declan's? I'm not so sure.

So, by morning, I acknowledge that the best thing I can do is take the damned home pregnancy test.

He's already gone and I don't have a phone to take a picture and text him the negative result, but I used to have an actual camera and I didn't take it with me when I left, so perhaps it's still here. It didn't occur to me when I took the test, but I've heard if they sit for too long, the result can change. It would be horrifying if Dante returned home late this evening and the warped stick told him Declan *did* get me pregnant.

Dante's side of the closet hasn't changed much. I notice that as I step inside and check the drawer we used for odds and ends, my old wallets that I didn't want to let go of or a pair of cuff links he had stopped wearing. Essentially, it was full of stuff we should probably throw straight away because we're done with it, but we can't quite admit that.

It seems like the place he would put a camera if he found it while I was gone. I'm surprised as I root through it to find some of my things are still in here. I pull out a sparkly rhinestone costume bracelet I used to love—at least, until it caught on one of my favorite tops in Madrid and snagged the damn thing. When we got home, the damaging bracelet went straight into the closet junk drawer.

I can't help smiling faintly as the memory replays, though. It wasn't a good memory; I was incredibly annoyed at the time, but I loved traveling with Dante. I loved when he was relaxed and romantic. Those memories are the ones I replayed most often in our time apart, not because of the locations necessarily, but just because of how he was when we weren't at home. I felt like a princess on the arm of a prince. It was no longer complicated by what he did for a living, there was no conflict—he was Prince Charming, dammit, and I was the luckiest girl in the world.

I slide the bracelet on my wrist and look at it for a moment, but now it feels like it belongs to someone else. Someone I can't be again.

That makes me sad for a lot of reasons, but most of all

because I'm not sure Dante will ever accept that, and even if he does, I don't know how long it will take or what comes after. Will he eventually tire of not coming home because he doesn't want to be around me? Will he finally give up and return me to my broken life? The thought doesn't bring me much relief, but the idea of staying here and growing more and more miserable as Dante tries to cram me into a box I don't fit into anymore sounds worse.

I shuffle through the drawer and rescue another piece of jewelry—a necklace he bought me at a shop in Athens. It had a hopeless knot in the delicate chain and I tucked it in here one day until I could take it to a jeweler and have them tug the knot out with their precise tools, since my fingers were too awkward to get the job done.

The last thing I find lodges in my gut like a grappling hook. A red Cartier ring box is pushed to the very back of the drawer. I draw it out and take the lid off the outer box. Inside is a smaller ring box, so I draw that out next.

I know what this is. Some part of me thinks I shouldn't look at it, but I can't resist. I crack the box open, and there nestled in a soft black bed is a beautiful, sparkling engagement ring. My heart breaks for all of us—the Dante who bought this, the Dante who tucked it away in the junk drawer after I left, and the Colette whose heart would have flown out of her chest if she'd ever actually received it. I don't know when he bought the ring or what he was waiting for to propose, but I suppose he thought there was no rush. That was how I felt, too. We both knew where we were headed and we weren't in any rush to formalize it.

Swallowing a sudden lump in my throat, I tuck the ring back into the box, then put the box back in the drawer. I tug off the bracelet and slide the pink jewelry box from Greece back inside, too. I can't have any rescued jewelry when Dante gets back or he'll know I got into that drawer, and if he knows I got into that drawer he'll guess that I saw the ring.

I close the drawer feeling sicker and sadder than I have all day. Since there's little else to do, I give up my search for the camera and climb back into bed.

18

DANTE

DAYS PASS and not much changes at home, so I focus more on work. It's easy to do because everything there blows the fuck up.

Some of the work Vince was too busy doing to deliver Colette's things to my door Monday was apparently squiring Mateo's chatty girlfriend around town and then out on a date with my brother. An ordinary enough night—except their date was interrupted by a guy from Antonio's crew. Meg ended up getting shot, but the bullet that hit her was meant to take out Mateo.

Consequently, my work life is a complete shitshow right now. Despite the war going on around us and our missing sister, I've mostly been doing day-to-day shit and just keeping apprised of whatever intel Adrian collected and passed on before he left.

That is no longer an option. All hands were already on deck, but now it's more than that. Now we have to strike back, and harder. Now it's not just a conflict over territories and leadership style; now it's a fucking war.

On the bright side, with Meg in the hospital and everyone feeling sorry for my brother, Adrian is already back working for us. On a temporary basis, he says, just until we get the war with Castellanos under control, but he's fooling himself. He's taken the bait, he's on Mateo's hook; my bastard brother will find a way to keep him here if he has to kill Meg himself, make it look like an accident to stir more sympathy and make it seem like he needs Adrian around to keep us all alive.

Scheming prick.

I don't care about any of that. Adrian's good at what he does, so if my brother manages to bring him back into the fold, it's a good thing for us.

Meg getting shot makes me feel a lot better about my decision not to let Colette befriend her or Mia, but it also brings to light the danger that could follow me home. I decide that until everything is settled with Castellanos, I need a trusted guard on Colette anytime she's not with me so I can make sure no one hurts her.

I'd really like to put Luca on her. He's a fucking beast, he can rip a man apart without a weapon. Luca's too much though, and if I took him off his slave house, I'd have to put someone less qualified on it. Last thing I need is some bitch making a break for it when the monster's not home, maybe getting out, getting attention.

My brother is already on edge from the failed assassination attempt. If I fucked things up that way in the name of keeping Colette safe, he'd throw it in my face like I threw it in his face when he wanted to keep Mia instead of testing her a few months ago. He cost me my girl, and I cost him his. It's not a game I want to keep playing now that I finally have Colette back.

I call in Xander instead. I tell him not to talk to Colette unless he has to because Colette would absolutely hate him. I don't like him on a personal level either, but he's a good soldier, so it doesn't matter. He's not here to be her friend, only to ensure her safety. For the most part, he should be stationed outside the house. Due to the risks of my line of work, I've made sure my home is pretty secure already, but as much as I hate to alert Colette to what's going on, she probably needs to know.

I manage to put it off until Friday. Colette only had the week off from her flower shop (she was planning to spend it in the Bahamas on her honeymoon) and I had hoped by the time that window closed, she and I would be on better terms.

We're not, but the time has come and it can't be delayed any longer.

When I return home from working Friday, I search the whole house before finding Colette sitting on the back patio looking out at the lake again. My blood runs cold at the sight. Before the shooting, I didn't mind, but right now? Sonja was supposed to keep Colette inside the house so no Castellanos goons could sneak past Xander or accost Colette via the beach. Our area of the beach is private, but there's a public beach access just up the road. If I wanted into my house and I saw a guard out front, I'd park down the road and walk up the beach. Walk right up my steps onto my back patio where Colette would be sitting, completely defenseless, with a fucking cup of tea.

Because of my concern, my voice is sharper when I demand, "What are you doing out here?"

Colette turns to look at me over her shoulder, surprised by my anger. "I—What?"

"You were told to stay inside the house," I clip, grabbing her arm and tugging her out of the chair, checking the perimeter just to be safe. I'm far from a nervous person, I barely remember the fucking feeling, but right now it's sparking all my nerves. My hand on her arm tightens when she tries to pull it away from me.

"Dante," she objects, but I don't waste time arguing with her. I haul her ass into the house and lock the back door once we're inside.

Yanking her arm away from me, she pivots and glares up at me, her blue eyes stormy and dark.

"Is this how it's going to be, then?" she demands, her voice rising. "I'm your literal prisoner, locked up inside? I'm not even allowed to go out on the back patio? What could possibly be the reason for that?"

"Mateo's girlfriend was shot."

Caught off guard by that bit of news, Colette's blue eyes widen, then she loses a shade of color. "What? Why? Is she okay?"

"She'll be fine."

"Who shot her?" Colette asks.

I sigh, glancing out the window at the lake. As soon as I moved into this house, I had all the windows replaced with bulletproof glass, so I'm not real worried about anyone getting in. Part of my wine cellar also doubles as a panic room, but I don't know if Colette remembers how to use it. I dread having to have this conversation with her, having to remind her how dangerous my life is when this was one of the excuses she used when she left.

Well, dangerous or not, there's no leaving this time.

Walking around the couch, I take a seat and pat the cushion beside me. "Come sit down. We need to talk."

Colette's brow furrows with concern, but she comes around the couch and gingerly sits on the edge. "What's going on, Dante?"

"My family and another family in Chicago have had a conflict lately. It's necessary business, I don't want to get into the details with you, but they escalated things and tried to kill Mateo Monday night. They can't get to our dad because Mateo's house is a fortress, but if they are trying to take out Dad's heirs..."

Paling even more, she eases back against the couch cushion. "You're next in line after Mateo."

I nod my head. "Again, I don't want to get into details, but Adrian is back with us while we deal with this. Part of his plan is to take out Antonio's heirs. His son's in hiding, but since we can't find him, we're going after the next guy in line. If they follow the same logic, they can't get to Dad or Mateo at the mansion, so it's not impossible they might come after me. Nothing is going to happen," I assure her, lifting her chin to make her meet my eyes so she knows I'm serious. "You're safe with me, but I need you to obey me. I can't keep you safe if you don't listen, Colette. You can't go outside when I'm not here with you. I have a guard on the house when I'm not here and if you leave the house without me, he'll be with you, but you have to be cautious. I can't have you reckless and rebellious, disregarding your own safety just to spite me."

"You have a guard on me?"

"Yes. He *has* to be with you at all times. It's the only way I can keep you safe."

"I understand," she assures me, nodding her head. Her tone is calm enough that I know she means it, so I finally relax and stop adding to the tension building in my lower back and shoulders. I have enough on my plate with work; I don't want to have to deal with Colette's fucking defiance when I come home.

"I need you to go easy on me right now," I tell her, despite her insistence earlier this week that she doesn't care what I need. "Everything is a disaster and I need there to be one place I can fucking relax and put my guard down. I can't have our shit getting in my head and following me to work. I need to be on my game right now."

Colette looks down at her lap but doesn't agree or disagree. "Are you in a significant amount of danger when you're not at home?"

Answering honestly, I shrug and tell her, "I don't know. This isn't the best time to be the only Morelli not living at the mansion, I'll tell you that."

"Maybe we should stay there until this is over," she suggests with a shrug of her own. "I know living with Mateo again is not at the top of your wishlist, but like you said, it's safer there and you would all be in one place. Alec still lives at the mansion, I assume?"

I nod my head. "All but me and Joey. Well, and Vince now, but I don't see him being a target."

"Is Joey staying at the mansion?"

"No. Mateo won't let him."

Her eyebrows rise, but she doesn't bother questioning my family politics. "Would he let us?"

"We are not staying with my brother," I tell her, immovably. "We're perfectly safe here. I don't need Mateo's help to protect you. Like I said, I have everything secure as long as you listen to me. Do you remember the protocol we had in place in case anything went wrong?"

"I don't have a go-bag anymore."

"We'll pack you one tonight. We'll pack two, actually. I'll put one in the wine cellar in case anything happens and you need to go down there. Do you remember how to secure it?"

Colette nods her head, her blue eyes wide. "I remember."

We did a dry run right after I had it put in so she would know the drill, just in case, but of course I hoped there'd never be an occasion she would have to use it.

"We also need to talk about the shop," I tell her. "I know today is your last day of vacation. I was going to let you go back tomorrow, but now I want you to get someone else to cover until we settle all this. The shop isn't secure and I can't change that, not in a couple days. I could put Xander on you while you're there, but if someone wanted to, they could shoot you right through the fucking window. I can't let you go back until I'm sure you'll be safe."

She's staring at me, but not with anger, annoyance, or outrage this time. "You're letting me go back to work?" she asks, clearly surprised.

"Well, yeah, if you want to. I told you, you're not my prisoner, Colette. There's a new car for you in the garage, I ordered a credit card for you so you don't have to worry about money. I brought you here to take care of you, not to imprison you."

She seems to be at a complete loss for words, but I don't know why. I'm the one who *bought* her the damn flower shop to begin with. I'm the one who keeps it going during slow months, buying shipments of flowers for various offices that have leases on our properties so Colette can pay the bills. I know she's unaware of the second part, but she damn well knows I'm the one who encouraged her to start her own business all those years ago.

I mean, sure, I had my own ulterior motives. Didn't want my woman working at a fucking strip club, even if she was just a waitress and not one of the girls taking her clothes off. Still entirely too many other men ogling her in her skimpy outfit and trying to touch her. It was a recipe for disaster.

Anyway, she likes being a florist much better, so it was a win-win.

19

COLETTE

FRIDAY EVENING GOES MUCH BETTER than they have been, but I feel a bit guilty for letting it be that way. Dante gives Sonja the night off and orders us turkey and brie sandwiches from the place up the road for dinner. After we eat, he opens a bottle of wine and turns on *Fight Club*.

It's strange spending this evening the way we used to spend quiet evenings together. More than once my mind drifts to the engagement ring tucked away inside the drawer in the closet, but I do my best to push it out every time. To remind myself of the engagement ring I wore up until a week ago when Dante decided to take a wrecking ball to my life.

Thinking about it gives me an attitude, but then I recall his recent request. Dante needs an evening of quiet calmness tonight, that way when he leaves tomorrow to do whatever he has to do out there, he won't be distracted thinking about me. I may still be angry at him, but I don't want to be responsible for him making a fatal mistake. Regardless of what I've said to

Dante in anger, I don't want any more blood on my hands, least of all his.

I work myself out of my snit and pour another glass of wine to sip on while we finish the movie. By the time the credits roll, I'm feeling a bit tipsy. Without my inhibitions stopping me, I can't quite stifle my curiosity.

"So, tell me more about this gang war."

"There's nothing you need to know," Dante assures me.

"I know that's often the case, but you need to understand when someone I'm close to gets killed or nearly killed, I do want some details. That makes a difference from everyday business."

"Someone you care about," he says levelly enough, but I can feel annoyance vibrating off him. "You don't even know Meg."

I've had just enough wine to tell him, "You know I meant Mateo."

"You care about Mateo, huh? Maybe you wish his girlfriend would've died and left him lonely again. Maybe then he'd look your way again, save you from me, is that it?"

"Don't be stupid."

Grabbing my jaw with one hand and my wineglass with the other, Dante leans forward, extends his long arm, and puts my drink down on the coffee table without letting go of me. "Watch how you talk to me."

I grab Dante's wrist and try to yank his hand away from my jaw, but his grip is too tight. I glare at him as he eases me back on the couch, try to kick him as he climbs on top of me.

His voice is low and husky, tinged with a menace I always found sexy when he had me in this position. "I've got bad news for you, beautiful. You're not Mateo's favorite back-up anymore."

"I was never his back-up," I tell him, trying again to get him off me. "Keep being delusional and crazy though, this is good. Keep reminding me why I left you in the first place."

Releasing my jaw and going for the buttons on my top, Dante informs me, "Doesn't matter why you left me. You're not going to do it again."

"Yeah," I say quietly, holding his gaze as he unbuttons my top. "But I'm not a prisoner, right?"

"Don't consider yourself a prisoner, just a guest I strongly encourage to stay."

I scoff, glaring up at him. "Encourage. Yeah. Your family's special dictionary has a very different definition for 'encourage' than the rest of the world. Threaten. Blackmail. Force. Those are much closer to what you do. Encourage is the wrong word."

Dante's gaze drops to the swell of cleavage now visible with my top unbuttoned. His warm gaze moves over my curves with appreciation, but a fair bit of ownership, too. Then, pulling the rest of my shirt open so he can get a better look at his property, he assures me, "I can threaten, blackmail, and force you if that's your preference, Colette."

Before he even gives me a chance to respond, he leans forward and covers my body with his, sharing his heat with me. I light up like a candle wick touched by flame. My breasts suddenly feel restrained inside the soft fabric of my bra and then he makes it worse, running his finger underneath the strap up to the curve of my shoulder. He leaves a light trail there, sending jolts of excitement coursing through my body.

"Dante," I murmur.

Rather than listen to whatever I'm about to say, he covers my lips with his to shut me up. I should push him away, but I know it would be pointless. Dante goes where he wants, especially when he's running on jealousy. I know his need to dominate takes over, but I also know it doesn't mean he loves me any less. It's pure animal instinct for him, and it's one of the things I loved about Dante in its more civilized forms. One can't pick a brutish, dominant man and then be shocked when he behaves like one.

My heart aches and pounds at the same time as he snakes his hand beneath me to unclasp my bra. I break away from his mouth and push against him. "Please don't rip my clothes. I don't have enough of them for that."

He half growls at me under his breath, but wordlessly leaves a trail of rough kisses along my jawline and down the side of my neck. After a moment, he sits back enough to pull me up and peel my shirt and bra off. He tosses them on the floor past the coffee table, then shoots me a look. "Happy?"

"Yes, thank you," I murmur, satisfied.

"I suppose you don't want me to rip your panties, either?"

"I realize how incredibly high-maintenance I am to expect such delicate treatment."

Nodding like he agrees, he says, "As long as you know." Then he climbs off the couch to stand in front of it, bending to yank my shorts off. He takes my panties off with exaggerated gentleness and I roll my eyes at him.

I don't move to help as he climbs back on the couch, but this time he stays lower. He pushes my legs up and settles between them, and despite myself and the disinterest I wish I could maintain, a swarm of butterflies unleash themselves inside my tummy as he looks up at me with those dark, dangerous eyes from between my spread thighs.

Wordlessly, he bends his head and runs his tongue teasingly along the slit of my pussy. I grab above me, reaching for the arm of the couch to hold on to. My greedy pussy already aches for his attention, much less interested in principles than my mind and heart.

"Mm," he murmurs, lifting his head to give me a devious little smile. "Dessert."

Then his mouth latches onto me and the time for words passes. As long as it's been, he hasn't forgotten his way around my body, and his tongue expertly teasing my clit serves as a sharp reminder. It has been a long time since I've experienced great oral love, being eaten with this kind of determined ferocity, like I really *am* a dessert that he can't get enough of. Just his hunger for me as his mouth devours my pussy like a decadent dish sends my arousal levels soaring through the roof, and topped off with the skillful way he makes his way around? It's almost embarrassing how fast I come, squeezing his head between my thighs, wishing he could keep eating me, but too sensitive to handle any more of his touch.

I fall back against the couch, breathing hard, clutching my breasts. He likes when I play with them. I'm not thinking about that consciously when I start, but my pussy probably is. It has probably tossed my brain and my heart out of the vehicle, desperate for some more Dante action. Damned unreliable thing.

Dante watches me, his gaze heated, as I squeeze my own breasts beneath him. He's still fully dressed, so he takes advantage of the break to undress down to his boxer briefs while he enjoys the show. Climbing back on top of me, he takes over playing with my boobs. He cups one in his hand, kneading and squeezing the full globe while he bends his head and takes the other one in his mouth. He starts off tender, kissing the smooth flesh, but ends up biting me. I jump, yelping in surprise, then he switches breasts and starts handling my nipples even more roughly. I whine, snaking my body against him, a silent plea for mercy.

"Spread your legs."

I do, cradling him right against my bare pussy and locking my legs around him in hopes following his order will get him to ease up on my nipples. He pinches harder and I cry out, my upper body arching off the couch. "Dante," I say on a gasp as he squeezes harder.

"Don't complain," he commands.

I shut my mouth, but I can't keep from trying to twist away from him. "Please."

He narrows his eyes and pinches harder.

I cry out again, but force the words from crawling out of my throat this time.

"Rub your pussy against my cock, show me how much you want it."

I lock my ankles around his body and thrust myself against the hardness cradled between my thighs. I rub furiously, like I'm trying to get myself off on it. The friction is so delicious, I might if he makes me do this for too long. Rubbing myself against his cock feels so good, I forget about the pain. Need overtakes me, a craving to be possessed that runs so deep it can never be sated, not with a million orgasms.

"Dante, please."

His voice is hard and level, like he's not even turned on, but I know from the rock-hard cock I'm dry humping that's a lie. "Please what?" he demands.

"I need you to—" I need him to everything. I need him to kiss me, fuck me, torture me. The friction feels fantastic, but I know what feels even better. “Dante, please. I need you inside me right now. I can’t wait.”

“No?” His tone is too soft now, and it sends dread shooting through me. Oh, God, don’t play with me like this.

“Please,” I ask, more desperately since I know he’s about to deny me. “I need to come.”

Dante smiles, still holding onto my achy nipples. “You’ll come when I say you’ll come, and not a moment before.”

“Don’t you want to fuck me, Dante?” I ask, rubbing my pussy against him to entice him. “Don’t you want to bury your cock inside me and show me who I belong to?”

Oh, he does. His dark eyes glow with desire, but he has too much self-control to take such basic bait. Despite how much he wants what I just offered, he tells me, “Nice try, beautiful. No cock for you. Not yet.”

I throw my head back against the couch in frustration, wanting to grab his cock and shove it inside me. He’d only pull it back out though, no matter how much it pained us both. He’s a stubborn bastard when he wants to be.

On one hand, I can’t believe he’s making me work for the fuck I didn’t even want to begin with, but on the other hand, I can absolutely believe that.

“You’re evil,” I inform him.

He releases my nipples and I gasp, bringing my hands to my breasts to cover the tender peaks protectively. It almost hurts more now that he released me. They throb, but when I look up at him, they also strain against my palms like they’re trying to escape and get back to him.

Dante pulls away from my needy pussy and nods behind me. “Turn around and lean on the arm of the couch.”

Need rushes through my body in waves but I push up to my

knees and turn around, leaning my arms on the arm of his couch like he told me to. Dante crawls up behind me, wrapping one hand around my throat and bending my head back until he can lean down and kiss me. His other hand caresses my ass while he kisses me.

It feels so nice as he steadily rubs his large palm over the curve of my ass. It's almost comforting, but then he squeezes and his fingers dig in.

"You've been a pain in my ass, haven't you?" he asks.

My pussy throbs and my head nods, since apparently it has abandoned my team.

"Yeah," he agrees, he tone warm since I agreed. "Now it's time I'm a pain in yours."

I don't know if he'll just strike me or fuck it, but I don't much care. I need him inside me, I need his permission to come, and I won't get either thing if I argue with the asshole. Instead, I crane my head as much as I'm able with his hand firmly around my throat. I manage to reach him and kiss him again. He accepts my invitation, deepening the kiss and fucking my mouth the way I want him to fuck my pussy—mercilessly.

He squeezes my ass one more time as he devours me, then without warning he brings his hand down hard. I jump and gasp into his mouth, but I don't stop kissing him. He smacks my ass again, harder this time, and I try to get closer to him. Mental images of him pushing me down over the arm of the couch and fucking me surface and I moan against his mouth. Oh, God.

The need for release grows and as it does, worse things happen. All the vines that used to tie me around Dante, the ones I worked so hard to chop down… I feel them growing again, reaching for him, needing to pull him inside me in more than the most literal way. I can't have sex with Dante and not get all twisted up. I should have remained a cold fish on the couch, I shouldn't have responded. I should have fought him even if it wouldn't have worked, just so he wouldn't try to get me into it.

It's dangerous when he makes me want him, because I can't stop. Wanting Dante isn't like wanting a normal guy, it's not a satiable need. Instead of quenching my hunger a little more with every serving, every taste makes me more ravenous.

If I start wanting him again, my desire will become an insatiable beast inside me. Not only will he win, but I'll become his prisoner in the one way he can't force. I'll never be able to leave him, not because of guards or any kind of tangible cage he puts me in, but because I'll never be able to stop wanting and needing more, more, more. His love will become my prison, he will be my warden, and escape will be absolutely impossible.

I try to rally my mind to my own defense, to tell it we need to get out of here while we can. We need to break his spell, tell him no. I don't care if he listens or not, I just need him to stop doing *this*. I need him to stop possessing me, controlling my desires. I used to love that he could do that, but now I hate it. Now I know how dangerous it is and how hard it is to come back from.

Like any struggling addict, though, I can't resist the temptation of one little hit. I tell myself this is a one-time thing, I won't let him sweep me under like this again. I won't let it go this far. I won't beg him, won't be willing to do anything—to *accept* anything—if it means I can have him. Never again, but maybe just this once…

Dante must feel me drifting. He doesn't know I'm losing the fight anyway, but he stops making my ass blush and breaks our kiss, forcing my upper body down on the arm and repositioning himself behind me. He runs his soothing palm over my stinging ass and I sigh with pleasure, then he spreads me open and pushes two fingers inside my pussy.

I moan and close my eyes, hugging the arm of the couch for support. The tender, delicious assault continues—his hand rubbing my pink ass, his fingers sliding in and out of my wet cunt. He must be so smug, feeling my desire for him on his fingers like that.

"How's that, beautiful? Does that feel good?"

I have just enough of a grip on sanity to resist responding. He slides his fingers all the way out of me, then pushes three fingers inside me, thrusting a little harder.

His tone cools. "I asked you a question, Colette."

My heart drops at the tone of his voice, but I still don't respond.

His voice hardens even more. "If you want this cock in your cunt, Colette, you better tell me how fucking good it feels."

Shit. I do want that, but I don't *want* to want that, so I keep my mouth shut.

"I swear to God, if you don't speak in the next three seconds, I'll use your pussy to get myself off and I won't let you have yours."

My heart gallops again. I open my mouth to speak, but I've held out this long. I can't give in now. I can't.

"Dante, please," I mutter, holding onto the couch as he fingers me.

"You know what I want to hear. Say it now, or it'll be too late."

Fuck. Fuck, fuck, fuck. My heart races and my pussy throbs as his fingers stroke it, as if to say, "Tell him what he wants to hear, you crazy bitch!"

But I can't. I just can't.

It's only a few seconds that I hold my silence, but they stretch on forever. My silence says a lot right now, and *none* of it is what Dante wants to hear.

"Fine," he clips, pulling his fingers out of my body.

My pussy immediately clenches around the absence, but I'm not empty for long. I nearly sob with relief when Dante finally shoves his cock inside me, but my relief is short-lived. It lasts about as long as it takes him to pump inside me four times—first just opening me up to take all of his cock, second pushing a little harder and going deep. The third pump is more brutal, but the fourth is so merciless, he nearly knocks me over the arm of the couch.

Fuck yes.

That's the speed and hardness he decides he likes, so the next several thrusts are just as hard to take. I gasp and hold on tight as his fingers dig into my hips, as he pounds his cock into me like he's *trying* to throw me on the floor. The powerful way he fucks me is incredible, but it makes me feel so off balance. My tenuous grip on the couch is nothing compared to the force he's putting behind every thrust, but I know he won't let go of me, so I know I'm not really in danger of falling.

There are no more tender words, no more teasing words, not even more taunting words. He's done speaking to me, using his voice to add to my enjoyment of the experience. He no longer wants me to enjoy it because I didn't play by his rules. It's impossible *not* to feel pleasure as he rams that thick, hard cock of his inside me, but no matter how overwhelmingly incredible every stroke feels physically, mentally I know the boundaries. Mentally I know that I'm allowed to have as much pleasure as it naturally gives me to give *his* body pleasure, but when all this is over, unless he tells me I can, I won't be able to come.

I want to cry thinking about it, but I don't think he'll be that mean. I may not have submitted to him completely, but I gave him more than I meant to.

He fucks me forever. It feels so good now, but every thrust is so brutal, so aggressive, I know I'll be sore for a couple days after he finishes with me. He fills my pussy full of his cock again and again, then finally grabs a fistful of my hair, shoves deep into my body, and unloads his cum inside me as he growls with pleasure. A shudder of pleasure ripples up my spine as he thrusts me back down on his cock a few more times, pumping every last bit of his release inside me.

I close my eyes and sigh, so full of him even as he slowly slides his cock out of me. My body is wound so tight, my need to come every bit as strong as his.

I wait for him to touch my aching pussy again, to find my clit and finger me until I'm crying out and my legs are shaking, until my body is as satisfied as his.

But he doesn't. He climbs off the couch and starts getting redressed.

Still breathing rather heavily, I look back over my shoulder at him. I haven't abandoned my perch on the couch, and I'm so tense with need, I'm ready to start rubbing myself against *that* if he doesn't get over here and give me something to get off on.

"Dante."

He looks up at me as he straightens. He knows what I want, but rather than give it to me, he slips his dress shirt on and begins buttoning it, waiting for me to tell him.

"Please. I need to come."

Dante shakes his head. "You should have thought about that when I gave you the chance."

"Please," I cry more desperately, moving my hips against nothing.

"No."

I want to rebel. I want to slide my own hand between my thighs and rub myself until I come, but I know he won't let me. He won't even have to physically stop me. When we were together before, he had me trained well enough to know having an orgasm once he had forbidden it was absolutely not acceptable. I developed a mental block. I even tried to get myself off in bed one night when he denied me. He lay there next to me in the dark, watching me desperately rubbing myself. The lack of concern on his face ramped up my anxiety. I thought he should be mad I was disobeying him, but it wasn't until I rubbed myself completely dry and still hadn't come that I learned what he already knew—if he said no, my body would listen to him, whether I wanted it to or not.

He is already dividing us, my body and my mind. My mind knows I'm trying to do the right thing, but my body has abandoned the cause to flock back to its master. It doesn't care if he's a soulless murderer, it only cares that he knows exactly how to make it purr like a kitten.

I'm fucked, and not in the fun way.

Just the thought that he's fucked me over so thoroughly makes me wetter. It shouldn't since he's not on my side, but my stupid body doesn't believe that. My stupid body believes what it believed before—that he always ultimately has my best interests at heart, and if he wants to fuck with me, he knows best and somehow it is at least in part for my enjoyment, too.

The aching need between my thighs makes me squeeze

them together, needing pressure and friction. "Dante, please," I say again. "I'll do it myself, just tell me I can come. Please."

Now fully dressed, Dante walks around the couch until he's in front of me. He tips my chin up to bring my gaze, cloudy with lust, to his—clear, firm, and satisfied since he got to come. "No," he says, immovably. "Next time you think about defying me, remember how you feel right now and *don't*."

Then he drops my clothes onto the couch behind me, but it may as well be a pail of cold water he tosses over my head. I sink down and bury my face in a decorative pillow, so deeply disappointed, and so ashamed of myself for feeling that way.

20

COLETTE

TOYING with me the way he did makes me docile for the rest of the night. We watch another movie that I hope will distract me, but it takes a while for my arousal to subside. Even when it does and I can finally focus, Dante—the evil bastard—reaches over and runs his hand up the inside of my thigh. Each time he teases me, his fingers floating so high I'm straining to hold it together by the time they nearly reach my pussy... but then he stops, draws his hand away, and leaves me a needy, disappointed mess all over again.

All I can think about is being fucked. I already was fucked, but I didn't get to finish, so I want it again. *Need* it again. All I can think about through 80% of the movie is scenario after scenario where I can get his attention, get his cock hard, get him needy enough to ignore his stupid stipulation and just *give it to me.*

Unfortunately, I know it's impossible. Dante doesn't lose his mind during sex. Maybe when he comes, but I'm not sure. I'm usually too preoccupied with my own orgasm, but even when I'm preoccupied with his, I have no idea if he maintains all his mental faculties during. I sure don't, and frankly I wouldn't want to. I love letting go and giving everything up to my partner, and *because* I love it so much, tonight is absurdly hard. I'm denying both of us what we want and it *sucks*.

The movie ends and Dante starts shutting off lights, so I guess it's bedtime. I almost get excited thinking about climbing into bed together. I'll take a shower and climb into bed naked. Then I'm going to wiggle my ass against him "by accident" until he has to fuck me again. Even if he won't let me get off, I'll get the steadier, less explosive pleasure of feeling him move inside my body while he chases his own orgasm.

Back in the day, I enjoyed pleasuring him as much as I enjoyed getting my own. I loved making him come, loved every moment leading up to him coming. I don't know if it's accurate to say *he* trained me to enjoy servicing him no matter the circumstances, or if I was predisposed to that already and maybe that's why I was so crazily attracted to him.

Mateo flits across my mind and on a stroke of masochistic genius, I consider using it. If I'm feeling really brave, I could mention the times *Mateo* got me off without making me ask nicely.

That might be too far. It's pretty mean, but Dante's pretty mean, too. Fuck him. Also, if I get him mean enough, he will definitely fuck me. He can't hit me, so when he's profoundly pissed off, he takes it out on my vagina and I love every brutal second of it.

Yep, I'm gonna do it.

I tell myself that the whole time I'm showering. I entertain myself with a scenario where I completely win this fight, where

I launch my Mateo missile and make him so irrationally angry, he does lose his mind. His manly pride wounded, he *needs* to make me come. In fact, he needs to make me come several times just to make sure any orgasms Mateo gave me years ago are completely wiped from my memory.

Shower Colette is firmly convinced she has a good idea, but when I get back to the bedroom, Dante looks irritable. I wondered why he didn't join me in the shower—mostly because I wanted him to. I had another shower fantasy of him joining me just to make sure I was behaving myself and not trying to get myself off, but then once he's in there soaping me up, his cock can't be denied and he fucks me again.

All my fantasies end the same way tonight. Not very prolific with the endings, but I can't think about anything else.

Unfortunately, shower Colette's naughty plans to get fucked crash and burn when I hear an irritable Dante barking into his cell phone. He glances up when I come into the room, then wanders out into the hallway for some privacy. He lowers his voice now that I'm around, but I can still hear the aggravated hum through the wall.

Well, shit. Aggravated Dante isn't the one I want, *mean* Dante is the one I need.

And it is a *need* at this point. He's made me feel so needy tonight, and I hate it. Not just physically. When he makes me need him physically, he makes me need him in every other way, that's the problem with him. When we were together, I thought the problem was with me, I thought my sexuality had become so entwined with my emotions, I couldn't fuck without falling in love.

Then I left Dante, and that turned out not to be true. The *opposite* was true. It was like not having Dante's permission to orgasm; I could sleep with Declan 84,000 times, but I could *not* open the chamber of my heart to him that Dante had unfettered access to. I convinced myself that was because of all I went through with Dante, convinced myself that chamber simply didn't open anymore because he had demolished it… but now here it is, cracking open a mere week after he murdered my fiancé.

It's a hard thing to accept that Dante owns exclusive rights to an important part of me, but I remember feeling emptier without him. I remember feeling like I had become a colder person, unable to truly love, unable to connect and attach and be vulnerable. I thought he had broken me, rendered me unable to feel those things, but maybe he only ruined me. Maybe he only made it impossible for me to feel those things for anyone *else*.

That's where my head is at when his phone call ends. I'm trapped somewhere between resentment and reluctant admiration. I don't know how he manages it, but he truly is an incredible man. A bad one, but incredible all the same.

I'm perched on the edge of the bed, wearing only a fluffy white bath towel, when Dante comes back into the bedroom. He spares me a glance on his way over to his side of the bed. He plugs his cell phone charger in and puts the phone down, so he must be finished with it for tonight.

"Was that a work call?"

Amusement flits across his face, but he doesn't quite smile. "Worried I'm sharing my dick with other women?"

The mere thought sours my stomach, but I don't think I have to be worried about that. Granted, I don't know where he goes all day, but I never did, and I was never worried he would be unfaithful. "I imagine if you were still fucking other women, you wouldn't be so intent on *encouraging* me to stay. If you could replace me so easily, you would have by now."

"Is that right?" he asks, starting to unbutton his dress shirt.

Rather than waste time arguing over something I get annoyed thinking about, I tug off my towel and drop it onto the floor. Bare naked, I crawl across the bed and stop on his side, spreading my legs once I'm in front of him. Just feeling his narrowed eyes on me makes me wet, so when I sink a finger inside myself, it comes out glistening with my desire.

Then I slide off the edge of the bed and stand right in front of him, pushing up on my tiptoes. I run my thumb over Dante's full lower lip, then push my wet finger into his mouth. His lips close around it greedily, taking it to the knuckle, licking and sucking every drop of arousal off my finger.

"Want some more?" I offer.

He pulls my finger out of his mouth and smiles at me, a real smile. "You don't like being hard up all night, do you?"

"No," I admit, winding one arm around his neck, dragging the other down his muscular chest. "But I do like when you eat my pussy."

"I bet you do," he says, amused. "Unfortunately, I already ate your pussy tonight."

"I'll let you have seconds," I assure him.

"Oh, how generous," he teases, bending his head to nip at my jawline, lightly dragging his teeth, then bending lower to kiss my neck while he covers one of my breasts with his palm. "You know what, though? I don't think it'd be fair for me to take seconds when you haven't even had firsts."

"You want me to suck your dick?" I ask, dragging my nails lightly down his chest. Without waiting for a response, I sink to my knees, unbuckling his belt with eager fingers. I look up at him as I work it free and toss it aside. I can feel desire leaking out of me, so I know how I must look on my knees for him, taking his pants off. He knows I'm hungry for his cock, and I've been too horny for too long now to pretend otherwise.

I sigh with pleasure as I take him out. I love Dante's cock and I've *missed* Dante's cock, so I can't help leaning in and giving it a kiss. One kiss leads to a trail of them and before I know it, I'm balanced on my knees and the tips of my toes, both hands under Dante's beautiful dick, kissing my way up and down its veined length. I love the challenge of giving him head, but he's so thick, I know my jaw will be aching in just a couple of minutes.

Still, I'm eager and wanting when I take his cock into my mouth. He groans lowly, raking a hand through my dark hair, but his touch is tender to let me know he's pleased. His gesture of approval shoots through my veins like a drug that will undoubtedly ruin my life.

Once he's in my mouth, I shift my position slightly and brace a hand on his hip. I close my eyes and get lost in the back-and-forth rhythm as I take his cock deeper and deeper until he's in my throat. I struggle a bit at first because it has been so long, but my throat remembers after only a moment. A salty drop of pre-cum gathers on the head of his cock and I draw back, grasping him in my hand and running the flat of my tongue over him to lick it off. I take him back into my mouth again, feeling more wetness gather between my thighs as I suck him hungrily. Even after my jaw begins to ache, I suck and I suck and I suck. I don't stop until Dante gathers my hair in a loose ponytail in his hand and yanks me back.

I look up at him in question. My jaw aches, but I'll happily suck him more if he wants me to.

"You've earned your treat," he says lightly, a little playfully, and my insides fill up with happiness.

"You'll let me come?" I ask, as I sit back down on the edge of the bed.

"You want my cock, don't you? It feels good inside you?"

I don't fail the test this time. "It feels incredible. I'm empty without you inside me, Dante."

"Mm, good girl," he purrs, caressing the side of my face before dropping to his knees.

I could die of happiness as he spreads my thighs and buries his face between them. I think I will as I claw at the bed, rocking my hips desperately, trying to get closer to his face as he licks and sucks and chases me toward an orgasm. Finally, my world rips apart and I get lost down the jagged center, sinking to the underworld in a free-fall of bliss.

Dante kisses me on the pussy as he stands back up. He puts my legs down gently since I'm too weak to move, but instead of moving, he remains between my spread legs and grasps the cock I made hard. He positions it at my entrance, then moves his hand to grip my hip. He wraps his other hand around my throat.

Since my pussy was just used a little bit ago and he knows I've spent most of the time wet, he doesn't bother easing in the first time. His fingers dig into my hip and he thrusts me down onto his cock at the same time he rams his hips forward. I cry out from the pleasure of the impact, reaching above me for purchase, but there's nothing to hold on to.

Well, there is something. I hold on to Dante's strong forearm, the one attached to the hand he has wrapped around my throat. I hold on for dear life, watching him, barely ever breaking his gaze as he does it again and again, doing the work for both of us and fucking me so hard the bed moves with every thrust.

"Who owns this beautiful body, Colette?" he asks as he drives into me.

I'm too afraid he'll stop if I don't tell him what he wants to hear, and I want to say it too much beside the point. On a harshly drawn breath, I tell him, "You do."

"That's right," he says, rewarding me with another brutal thrust. "I do."

My back is starting to burn from the back-and-forth friction over the bedsheets, but I don't complain. This is the most connected I've felt to Dante since before Beth died, and I don't care if it's toxic, I want to enjoy every second I'm held captive by his intensity.

Whether it's from the orgasm denial earlier, the connection I'm feeling now, or some combination of both, I come twice while he fucks me. I come so hard and for so long the second time, I think I might cry, and still it takes him several more pumps into my overly stimulated body before he explodes inside me. I watch him come, still dazed from my own orgasm, but it feels so satisfying when he empties himself inside me. The inside of my body is temporarily fulfilled, but now the rest of it needs affection.

"Hold me," I say quietly, as I wait for my breathing to return to normal.

Dante releases his tight hold on my throat and eases back, looking down at my prone body for just a moment. Once he's looked his fill, he pushes me back on the bed to make some room. I use the strength left in my body to roll, then as soon as Dante climbs on the bed, I roll back up against him. Everything feels right as I settle my arm over his torso and curl up against his side.

Dante runs a hand tenderly down the back of my head, then tugs me close until I'm completely pulled into his warmth. I'm glad for the cool temperature of the room tonight. I'm glad he chased my mind away so he could have free rein over my body. I don't know how I'll feel in the morning, but I'm so glad I got to be with him tonight.

21

DANTE

SUNLIGHT FILLS the bedroom when my eyes open, letting me know I've slept too long. Colette's warm body is curled up in my arms, so I don't care.

Contentment spreads through me as I close my eyes again and just lay here holding her. We used to sleep this way all the time. Made it that much harder when she left and every night I had to sleep alone.

Now I have to get used to having her here again, but that will be a much more enjoyable adjustment.

Since I know I've overslept but I don't yet know by how long, I ease my arm out from under Colette and climb out of bed. I grab my phone off the table and grimace, seeing it's after 10. Shit, by a lot.

I hustle through the most important parts of my morning routine, so when I come back into the bedroom to get a suit, I'm bare-ass-naked, using a towel to dry my hair. I glance at the bed to check on Colette and see her staring at me, eyes wide with surprise.

"Good morning," I say, as I head into the closet to grab clothes.

"Good morning," she answers sleepily, stretching her arms up in the air when I come back out. "Why is it so bright out?"

I look at the suit I picked out, frowning at the navy blue tie, but I don't have time to pick a different one. "It's nearly noon."

"Late start today?" she questions.

"Inadvertent. I forgot to set an alarm last night."

Her voice light, she tells me, "Aww, Mateo's gonna kick your ass."

I know she's teasing me, but I don't even like hearing his name on her lips, so I ignore her and toss the towel so I can get dressed. "I sent a text to Xander already. He's on his way. He'll be out front if you need him for anything, but his job is to keep watch, so don't distract him unless it's important."

"I won't," she murmurs.

"If you see anything that doesn't feel right or get an uncomfortable feeling for any reason, don't second guess yourself, just call me." As I button up my dress shirt, I walk around to my side of the bed and open the nightstand drawer. I draw out a rectangular box and put it down on the bed beside her. "This is your new phone. I charged it yesterday and pre-loaded it with my phone number. You may call me and you may call the flower shop, but no one else unless you ask first."

Her lips press together in a firm line of displeasure and her eyes narrow slightly, but she forces herself to nod her head in grudging acceptance of my rules.

"It's just until I know I can trust you again," I assure her. "You'll get all your privileges back once you've earned them."

Now she grits her teeth and tries to kill me with her eyes. I have to bite back a smile, looking down and straightening my tie so she doesn't see how amused I am.

Since she's annoyed at me again, I decide to give her a little push and see what she'll let me get away with. I climb on the bed and crawl over until I'm on top of her, straddling her hips. I pull down the thin blanket she has covering herself so I can see her pretty tits. I know they'll miss me as much as I miss them, so I bend my head to give them each a few kisses. Some part of me expects she'll push my head away as soon as I do, but instead I hear her sharply inhale the way she does when she's getting turned on.

I wasn't planning on a fuck, but I certainly won't turn one down. My goodbye kisses to her tits and the way she arches so prettily on the bed ends up running me even later, but when I'm pumping inside her and my bedroom is filled with the sounds of Colette's pleasure, I can't seem to find a fuck to give about the people I've kept waiting.

I only collapse on top of her for a couple minutes after we finish, just long enough to recover and steal a few kisses. When she catches her breath, Colette fingers the dress shirt I didn't bother taking off to fuck her. "This is getting all wrinkled."

"Good thing I have a maid," I remark, completely unconcerned.

"You might want to change it before you leave. Unless you *want* it to be obvious you were rolling around in bed with me even though you were already late."

I roll onto the bed beside her and tug her on top of me. Then I grab a handful of her ass and tell her, "Everyone knows this is mine. They can't hold it against me if I run late so I can enjoy it from time to time."

"That's not how jobs work," she informs me.

"It's how mine works."

"I would fire you," she states.

"You could try," I tell her, touching the tip of her nose before pushing her off me and back to her own side.

She huffs at me as I climb off the bed and I have to bite back another smile. Been a long damn time since I've had to suppress so many of these.

"I was going to come home for lunch, but since it's nearly lunch now, I'll just see you at dinner." Looking back at her over my shoulder as I fix the button that popped loose, I tell her, "Wear something sexy."

"And if I don't?" she tosses back airily. "Do I lose my *privileges?*"

"If you don't want to dress up, come to the table naked," I suggest. "Those are the only acceptable options."

"I'm gonna wear sweats," she tells me, just to be defiant. "And a ratty T-shirt."

"Good luck finding either of those things in my house." I walk around to her side of the bed to grab my suit jacket that I left there.

"I don't have any of my make-up. If you want me to doll up to sit across from you at the dinner table, you need to at least get me some essentials."

I'm able to do a lot of things, but pick out make-up is not on the list. I have no female friends and my sister is kidnapped or a runaway. Wherever Francesca is, it's not somewhere I can shoot her a text and ask her to buy Colette some make-up.

"Didn't Mia give you girly shit in that bag she brought over?"

"Mia?" she asks sharply, shooting up in the bed to look at me.

"Vince," I correct, forgetting I went with the simplest version of events and let her believe Vince brought her the bag of stuff.

Shit.

"Vince brought you—" I stop trying to recover, because now it's too late. Now she's glaring and giving me attitude. It's my own fault. It was an insignificant thing to lie about; I just didn't think it mattered or that it would come up again.

"*Vince* brought me tampons and moisturizing shave gel?" she asks, her tone ridiculing what she accepted to be true until I slipped up.

I sigh, raking a hand through my damp hair. "Vince got you the pills, he sent Mia to the pharmacy and she picked up the rest of the stuff for you."

Even though I specifically said *he* sent her to the pharmacy, Colette continues as if I am the one who sent Mia on an errand.

"Then she brought it over to you while I was asleep? How sweet."

I can tell by her tone she does not think it's sweet, and she's got a sheen of crazy in her eyes. I don't know where it's coming from, but I don't have time for it right now.

Colette goes on, "You call her Mia, too. You call Meg 'Mateo's girlfriend,' but Mia… requires something a little more familiar, I guess."

Goddammit. Paying close attention to the language someone uses to get at the truth of how they feel about someone is a trick *I* taught her, and I damn sure don't like it being used against me.

"I barely know the girl, Colette. You're being crazy," I inform her.

"You lied to me and covered up that she came over when I wasn't around," she tosses back with deceptive casualness. "Why would you do that if it's innocent?"

"I didn't *lie*. I asked Vince to run an errand for me, he sent his girlfriend instead. What do you want me to say? I didn't tell him to."

"Maybe she wanted to see you. She's pretty. Has great taste in shoes, too."

What the fuck does that have to do with anything? Before I can ask, she's hurling another thinly veiled accusation at me.

"Were you two close while I was away?"

"For fuck's sake," I mutter, patting my pockets to make sure I have my phone and my wallet. "No."

"You said you slept with other girls," she reminds me, sounding none too pleased about it for someone who was *engaged* to some other motherfucker.

"Trust me, I did not sleep with that one," I assure her. "No one you would have to keep seeing once you were back where you belonged. What do you think I am, an asshole?"

"Yes," she answers, but smiles faintly anyway.

I shake my head. "Clearly you're thinking of Mateo. I don't fuck the girlfriends of my male relatives, that's him."

Her arms are still folded over her chest with leftover attitude, but now that I've assured her I didn't bang the blonde, she's settling down. "Did he sleep with her?"

"Yes."

"Is that why you said I'm not his favorite back-up anymore? Is it her now?"

I don't know how to explain that simply, and more to the point, I don't want to. "Not exactly. Anyway, I gotta go."

"Well, if your side bitch isn't doing anything today, you could tell her to bring me some make-up."

Even though she's clearly joking about it now, I turn around and point at her. "Do not joke about that. That girl has some kind of hold on Mateo. If he thought I wanted to fuck her, he'd probably find a way to sneak cameras into my house to make sure I'm not. I don't need *that* headache on top of all the ones you give me."

Colette looks a little too proud of herself at the prospect of giving me headaches. "I'm very curious about this whole situation. Maybe she can be my lunch date since you're busy; she can catch me up on all the Morelli stuff I missed."

Something like regret stabs me when she says that. By asking to have lunch with Mia, she's indicating a willingness to integrate herself back into my family's social web. I like that she's already offering to do that voluntarily, but I damn sure don't enjoy having to tell her she can't.

I wish I hadn't brought Mia up, even if inadvertently. Now on top of everything else I told her she wasn't allowed to do today, I have to add something else.

"Look, I know this isn't how it was before, but I don't want you getting close to Mia or Meg. I don't know how long they'll be around. Mia's caught between Mateo and Vince so she's bound to get herself killed, and Meg is... aside from being annoying as fuck, I don't think Mateo really trusts her. I don't know exactly what he's doing with her, maybe just passing time? But he's damn sure not in love with her, so whatever his agenda is, I wouldn't recommend getting too attached to her either. We didn't know what to expect with Beth, none of us ever imagined it would go down the way it did, but now we know what can happen. I don't want to see you go through that a second time, so I think it's best to keep your distance from these two."

I can tell she doesn't exactly love the idea of not being able to befriend the only other people who could really comprise a social circle for her, but she accepts that if I have enough doubts to tell her to stay away from them, there's a good reason. "What about Francesca?"

"She's missing. It's a long story and I don't know how that one ends either."

"So... I'm just not allowed to have any friends now? I was close to the people in your life before. Now I can't be?"

I don't know what to tell her. She sounds so disappointed, I have to throw her a bone. "Hey, maybe I'm wrong. Maybe one of them will end up making it. If Mateo ever gets married, we can assume she's a keeper and you can befriend his wife. How about that?"

Giving me a rather sour look, she says, "If Mateo getting *married* is what I have to wait for, you might as well just get me a cat."

Yeah, that bastard's never getting married. "I could get you a kitten," I offer, liking that idea much more. "Or a puppy. Pick an animal, I'll get it for you."

Brightening, she says, "I was just being sarcastic, but I like that idea. We should go to the animal shelter next time you have a day off, see if they have any furry friends we could adopt."

"It's a date," I tell her.

22

DANTE

"We need to talk."

I look at Mateo, surprised to see him at the warehouse today. He knew I had a meeting with a Castellanos informant who hasn't shown up yet, but I didn't expect my brother to make an appearance.

"I thought we decided you should spend as much time as possible at home or safely guarded until this Castellanos business is handled," I remind him, taking in the strangeness of his posture. His hands are tucked into the pockets of his slacks so he's not standing tall like he usually does when he wants to command respect. His posture is more familiar, almost like he wants to talk to me as a brother, not an inferior. That's not something we do a whole lot, so I'm not sure what to make of it. "Something else happen?" I ask, more warily.

"A lot has happened," he says soberly, nodding his head. "It's been a busy week."

"Damn sure has," I agree, shaking my head a little. Despite

the headaches it has caused, I wasn't reluctant to go to war with Antonio Castellanos. I want their territory to be ours, personally, and war is the only way that happens. Mateo hasn't wanted to go for it, though. He's more interested in growing our legitimate income than the illegal shit.

I don't think it's a choice that has to be made and I have locked horns with him over it before, but now that significant others are getting shot, things have gone too far. It used to be people in our line of work had enough fucking respect to leave the women and children out of shit like this, but it seems Antonio's disdain for my brother taking the reins of leadership from our dad has finally tipped the scales in the wrong direction. Traditional as they are, Antonio doesn't respect Mateo or his commandeered authority in our family, so he's not treating him with the respect a boss should command. He's rejecting Mateo, and he's not being subtle about it, either. This is too far, though. If *Mateo's* woman can be shot at in public by a rival family, no one among us is safe.

"I'll be glad when this is all over," I admit.

"Yeah, so will I." He makes me even more uneasy because rather than being direct, he's stalling and wasting his time. I have the distinct impression bad news is coming.

Since he's making me drag it out of him, I ask again. "So, what is it? What's going on?"

"Do you know what Joey's been up to lately?"

Our youngest brother. There's quite an age gap from us to him, so we're not as close. He's closer to Vince in age and maturity level, so it's no surprise they're such good friends. "Nah, what'd he do now?"

Little asshole is also the only Morelli of our generation who has seen the inside of a jail cell. He didn't get our father's cleverness. His mom's dead and none of us ever met her, so I can't say what traits he might have got from her. Whatever the reason, bad genes or maybe because he's the baby of the family, Joey is the closest thing we have to a fuck-up.

Mateo clears his throat, then looks me dead in the eye. "Joey's dead."

I rear back a little, hearing his words, but not making sense of them. "What? How?"

"Adrian," he answers, nodding his head to the metal folding chair in the corner of the room we're standing in right now. The chair where Adrian executes people who need killing—but not our fucking family members.

It takes me a few seconds to hide my shock, but I don't know what the fuck he's saying. I don't know what to focus on first. That Adrian killed one of his own men, or that my youngest brother is dead. "I don't… what does this mean? Did Adrian turn on us? Did Castellanos get to him?"

"No, of course not," Mateo says quickly, firmly, shaking his head to cut me off before I can get carried away. "Adrian discovered that *Joey* was colluding with Castellanos. Apparently he's the one who told them where to find me the night Meg was shot."

My brow furrows and I shake my head. "That doesn't make any fucking sense. Did Joey even *know* where you were that night? Why would Joey try to get you killed? Joey may not be close to you, but to turn on you like that? Why? It doesn't make sense."

I hear a thread of irritation in his voice. "I know it doesn't make sense."

There's only one way it *does* make sense that Joey might get dragged into a plan to turn on Mateo. "Was Vince involved?"

I search my brother's face as I ask the question, look for bursts of reaction as the words land, but he gives me absolutely nothing. His face is carefully guarded, his expression serious but noncommunicative. "No," he finally answers.

"That makes no sense. If anyone in this family has cause to want to see you dead, it's Vince, not Joey. Did Adrian question Vince?"

Mateo holds up a hand to stop me. "I'm handling it. I'm not telling you about this because I need your input; I just thought you should know... Joey's dead. I figured you should hear it from me."

Reeling a bit from the surprise of this news, I pull back the folding chair I hung my jacket on the back of and sit down by the table. "I can't fucking believe this."

Mateo nods solemnly. "I know."

Glancing back up at him, I ask again, "You're *sure* it was Joey?"

"I'm sure he betrayed me. Adrian was sure. He wouldn't execute without solid evidence, you know that."

I do, I just don't understand. I sit there for a minute trying to process what he told me. Trying to process the death of a family member. Joey and I were never real close, but he was still my brother. I guess he didn't handle the burden of our family's legacy as well as he could have, but he was young. Mateo and I have had a lot longer to adjust, plus we *had* to. Mateo was the eldest so a lot fell on his shoulders. Then when he took over the family, a lot fell on mine.

Being so much younger, Joey never really got a heap of family responsibility dropped on him like that. Maybe we gave him too much time to fuck around, maybe we should've taken him in hand and made him get serious by now, but it doesn't make sense that it led to this. To betraying Mateo? *Why?*

"There's more," he tells me.

Pulling myself from my skeptical thoughts, I look back at him. "What do you mean, there's more?"

"Not related to Joey. I don't have all the relevant details right now, but one of my guys on the force tipped me off. Someone saw something at Rob's house. One of the girls. Someone noticed something off and reported it."

Now I shove back the chair as I stand up, scowling. "What the fuck do you mean, they noticed something? Reported what to who?"

"You know what to who, Dante," he states. "They reported suspicious activity to the fucking cops."

"What—Was it one of our guys, at least?"

"No," he answers, his face solemn. "It wasn't one of our guys."

I don't immediately know how to respond to a thing like that. After a moment of heavy, dread-soaked silence, I ask, "What the fuck does that mean?"

"It means they're going to investigate. They haven't had time to get to it yet, I know that much. That just means despite all this Castellanos shit we have going on, there's one more task on your to-do list. You've gotta shut down Rob's house, and you need to do it now before they get someone to investigate."

Raking a hand through my hair, I mutter, "Jesus Christ. Okay. I don't know where we're gonna put all those fucking girls. I guess Ivan has some room, but Luca's full. Maybe we can get Rob in a different house—"

"No," Mateo interrupts. "You're not understanding me. This isn't a temporary measure. We're not redirecting and redistributing. I want Rob's house *shut down.* I want his arm of the operation *shut down.* It won't be coming back, the other two houses won't be taking on extra girls. Get rid of whatever inventory he has now and that's it."

I stare at my brother for the longest fucking minute. "Are you serious? You want to permanently shut down an entire house because of one fucking hiccup? What are we paying all that money to our guys on the force for if they can't even handle one fucking hiccup—"

Raising his voice, Mateo says, "This isn't a hiccup, Dante, it's a fucking catastrophe. What good does it do?" he echoes, in disbelief. "All the fucking good. The reason I have a heads-up and we can get ahead of this instead of getting taken down in some fucking sting operation and going to prison? That's what we pay all the money for."

"Rob's not sloppy," I argue, as if I can somehow change the reality of this situation if I fight it hard enough. "There's no way in hell he'd let anyone in the neighborhood see anything suspicious. Rob is fucking careful, that's why he runs the house to begin with."

Not nearly as upset as I am, Mateo states, "No matter how good, no one is perfect. He fucked up and someone saw." He shrugs, but manages to make the gesture decisive. "It is what it is. All we can do now is handle it."

Of the three houses, Rob's house is the least profitable, but it still turns out a good chunk of change every year. Ivan's house brings in the second highest profit, and Luca is the master—he doubles what Ivan makes because he doesn't have a soul or a life outside of work, and he has no problem pulling double duty. Luca's effectiveness is unmatched, and though I told Mateo he couldn't take on more girls, he probably can if he has to.

"All right," I mutter, running another hand though my hair in irritation. "I guess I'll figure it out."

"There's nothing to figure out," Mateo says simply, carefully, like he doesn't quite trust me to follow orders. "It's done. Collapse the house quickly and get the girls out of there. Reassign Rob to something else."

"And what about the shipment of girls he was expecting? I have 3 coming in this week."

That news shouldn't displease him, but his irritation increases. "Goddammit. I guess you'll have to redirect those three to Ivan or Luca, wherever there's room. But the turnaround needs to be quick."

I nod my understanding. "I'll send them to Luca then."

"Do whatever you have to do. Just wrap this shit up and no more new acquisitions. None. We need to clear out what we have and see where this investigation goes. I know this is usually your wheelhouse, but if I find out so much as one new girl has been brought in after these three, someone will be sorry."

Sighing, I scratch my forehead. "This probably isn't a good time to tell you Luca knocked up one of his girls."

Dead-eyed, Mateo agrees flatly, "No, it probably isn't."

"I just figured with your insistence about no new acquisitions, I should probably explain that one. The Russian girl he knocked up is ready to pop, but this new one... she can't be more than a month along."

Squeezing the bridge of his nose and closing his eyes briefly, he says, "We'll figure it out. Just pass along the order that no new girls are to be brought in, and for Christ's sake, buy Delmonico a box of condoms."

"It'd probably be easier if you looped me into the conversation with your guy on the force so he can keep me up to date on the investigation. Like you said, this is more my area of expertise than yours. If they do turn up anything, it'd be better if he could just tell me so I could handle it more efficiently."

Mateo shakes his head. "That won't be necessary. I'll make sure any relevant information makes it back to you."

"We're wasting valuable time with a middleman, Mateo. It makes more sense to let me—"

Cutting me off, he looks me in the eye and informs me, "I am not a middleman. I'm the boss of this fucking family. I tell you what you need to know. That a problem?"

I stiffen, the muscles in my shoulders tensing as I stare back at him. Mateo doesn't usually pull rank on me like that, especially when it comes to trafficking. I don't think he gives half a fuck about this arm of operations, it's just another cog in the machine to him. It's *my* baby. Together with Luca, I have personally expanded the operation, turned it into what it is today. Mateo doesn't do shit in this arena, and now here he is shutting it down and cutting me out of the conversation.

It is his call at the end of the day, but hearing it still pisses me off.

I shake my head once, stiffly. "No problem. Just trying to minimize the damage, that's all. Shutting down Rob's house is going to cost us. If the investigation dies or one of our guys can get it shut down quick, it'd be nice to know that. It's entirely possible we could get the house back up and running—"

"No," Mateo tells me, shaking his head. "Under no circumstances will the house resume operations. I need to see exactly how much it costs us, you need to see where you can redirect the people who worked at that house, but put the idea of re-opening it right out of your head. That's not an option, regardless of what happens with the investigation."

Scowling at him, I demand, "Why?"

"Because that's the decision I've made," he states, his tone making it clear he's done discussing this. Reaching into his pocket, he draws out his keys and looks down at them. I take it to mean he's ready to leave, but since Mateo doesn't normally drive himself, I'm not familiar enough with the gesture to be sure. "There's one more thing," he tells me.

I scoff, looking down at the ground and then back up at him. "That's not enough?"

"Like I said, it's been a busy few days."

"Well, what else is there?" I ask impatiently, still aggravated that he's being so unreasonable about Rob's house.

Without so much as a trace of sadness or displeasure, Mateo looks at me. That's not what I expected. I suppose it's possible he saved some good news to follow all the bad, but I don't think that's what's coming. Despite the calm, misleading look on his face, I sense a sliver of malice in him now, and that wouldn't accompany good news. I don't know what he could tell me that would be worse than what he's already said, though, let alone something he would derive any kind of sadistic pleasure out of.

That is, until he opens his mouth.

"Dad's dead."

23

COLETTE

WHEN DANTE COMES HOME, I can tell something is wrong almost immediately. At first glance I assume he just had a long day, but when I look again, I can tell by the look in his eye he's been pushed well past his breaking point. He's done with this day, and something must have happened to make it so.

Knowing there's a mob war apparently going on that he's a part of, I'm a little afraid to find out what it is that happened. I don't even know how to ask without him shutting me down, telling me it's *business*—and therefore none of mine.

We don't talk right away, not with words anyway. Even though I know he's unlikely to open up without at least some prying, I follow him to the bedroom. I have to. I'm like a magnet, helpless to resist the possibility that he's exhibiting some sort of vulnerability. I've always been a sucker for it. Dante is a fortress, hard and cold and impermeable as hell. Before I left, I didn't even think it was possible to hurt that man. He seemed invincible to me, above mere humanity. I worshipped him when we were together, celebrated his strength; I was in awe of him.

It's really something knowing that while nothing else may be able to hurt this man, I did. I'm not proud of it, I didn't *want* to hurt him, but I truly didn't know I was capable.

Now I get the feeling something else has, and since I know he's unbreachable, I know it must be something bad.

I sit down on the edge of the bed and watch wordlessly as he rips his clothes from his body like they've pissed him off. I have no idea what to expect on the heels of whatever is radiating off him so I don't know what to brace for. He seems angry, so he'll run hot, but how? Will he rage, or will he fuck me? I'll let him if he needs it. I may not necessarily like him right now, we may even be at war, but I don't have it in me to turn him away if he really needs me.

He's not hard when he strips off the last of his clothing, but I can't keep my eyes off him. Dante has the sexiest back, so strong and broad, and covered with tattoos on top of it. I haven't paid much attention since I've been back, but now that I have an unobstructed view of his back and he's not trying to fuck me, I see that he did get a new tattoo. My lips curve up faintly at how fitting it is—a bird cage with the door open and his treasured pet escaping.

Me. He put me on his back.

With a sigh, I stand and move up behind him. I touch his shoulder and feel him stiffen beneath my fingers, then I press my open palm to the newly inked skin.

I could say something inane like, "this is new," but I don't say a word. He knows and I know, and words are irrelevant. He looks back at me over his shoulder and my heart skips a beat when his dark gaze meets mine. I swallow, slowly drawing my hand away from his back. Even though I'm the one who approached him, I'm overcome with the sensation of being cornered and I need to put space between us.

I can't break his gaze but I drop both hands and take a step back. It's the wrong move, or the right move, I'm not sure anymore. He turns on his heel and advances on me, causing my heart to speed up.

He advances faster than I back up and before I know it he's grabbing a fistful of my hair and yanking me against him. I gasp at the impact. Heat from his body scorches mine and crawls up my neck, causing my face to flush. I still feel like I should turn and run, but before I can even consider entertaining common sense, Dante strikes, crushing his lips against mine and pulling me so tightly against his hot skin, I feel like I'm on fire.

I let him ravage my mouth, knowing if I didn't he would anyway. I let him rip my clothes off with an unmatched aggression. I grimace when I hear threads tear, remembering how I used to buy two of my favorite items because he's such a brute, I could never trust he wouldn't destroy one of them in his haste to get me naked.

I guess that's Dante. He's too brutish, too impatient, too rough. He destroys delicate things before he realizes he's done it, and if I had any sense, I would've left him the first time I realized that.

Dante hauls me into the bathroom and turns on the shower. Where he wasn't hard before, he certainly is now. He catches me eyeing his dick when he turns back to me. I flush, but his face doesn't betray even a trace of amusement or pleasure at having caught me.

That's odd.

"Are you okay?" I finally ask, troubled by his lack of response.

"Yep," he says, rather coldly. "I did what he couldn't, you know?"

I tense up, thinking he must be referring to Declan even though I've asked him not to. "What are you talking about?" I ask guardedly.

"I brought you back. When Belle ran away from my dad, he couldn't get her back."

Rearing back a little, I frown. "Your *dad?*"

I now have absolutely no idea where his head is at. I've met Dante's dad, but not the version of him he once was. I've heard the horror stories about Matt Morelli and his obsession with his first wife. I know she hated him and ran away with a man she actually loved. I know he found her and massacred her and the family she dared create without him. I know he's a psycho, so my crazy, murderous apple didn't fall too far from the family tree.

I *don't* know why we're talking about him, particularly in this capacity. I realized long ago that Dante and I don't see things the same way, so I guess I shouldn't be surprised he's less horrified by his father's atrocities and more competitive about having done better. While I tend to agree with Mateo that their father is a vile, despicable monster, Dante… doesn't see things that way. It hasn't mattered, though. Since their evil father fell sick and Mateo cloistered him away from the rest of the family, the vengeful old man is more or less harmless.

"You don't hate me as much as she hated him."

I think he's insisting on that more for himself than for me, but I don't say anything. I wait to see where this is going.

Turns out, it's not going anywhere. Dante has said his

piece, I guess, given me the only glimpse I'll get right now of whatever war is brewing inside him. He grabs my arm and drags me into the shower with him. The hot spray hits me as I move around to the other side. Dante pushes me against the tile and leans into me, covering my body with his. His hand drops between my thighs, his fingers covering the sensitive flesh.

"This is mine," he states.

I swallow, but don't agree or disagree.

He doesn't need me to. Without breaking my gaze, he moves his hand to my heart. Almost defiantly, he informs me, "This, too."

My heart aches and it's harder to hold his gaze. It's starting to hurt, and not the good kind of hurt. I swallow, torn between continuing to let him get away with murder just because he might be sad, and holding him accountable. My head conquers my heart and I reach up to remove his hand, telling him simply, "It was."

Dante doesn't accept my rebuff. "It still is. Always has been, even when you were gone. You ran from me out of fear, not because you didn't love me anymore."

"You say that like it's normal," I remark, looking way from him.

Bringing his hand to my jaw and guiding my gaze back to his, he says, "In my family, it is."

"I'm not part of your family," I tell him, even though the words feel wrong in my mouth. We may never have married, but at the time I felt as much a part of Dante's family as I would have as his wife.

"Yeah, you made that clear when you left."

Given this could easily stray to unfriendly waters and it

seems like he has had a hard enough day, I ask, "Do you really want to talk about this right now, Dante?"

"You're the one who doesn't want to talk about it," he states, still with that mean look in his eyes. Unease moves through me. I want to be there for him for some ungodly reason, but I don't think he's seeking comfort now, I think he's spoiling for a fight.

I don't want to fight with him, so rather than let him misdirect whatever anger someone else has triggered in him, I reach my hand out and lightly drag my fingertips across his toned abdomen. I meet his gaze and hold it, then let my hand drop a little lower until it's wrapped around his cock.

My distraction is adequate.

There's nothing tender or loving about the way he fucks me, but I didn't expect there to be. Not this time. This is more a catharsis than lovemaking, a fucked up form of therapy for a man who doesn't like using his words to express himself when he can use his body instead.

I'd like to think of it as generosity on my part, but the pair of orgasms he gives me tell a different story. When we emerge from the steamy shower, he lets me grab a towel and start to dry off, but then he reconsiders, yanking it out of my hand, dragging me into the bedroom, and tossing me on the plushy king mattress where he proceeds to draw a third orgasm out of me.

We lie on the bed in the aftermath, my pillow growing damper by the moment, the luxurious sheets wet from the sheen of sweat that developed while he fucked me or the clean spray from the shower, I'm not sure. I try to brush off the lingering sense of guilt that I went along with all that, that I comforted the monster who murdered Declan when I should have let him suffer. I grasp for several defensive arguments to feed my conscience, but it's fed up and sickened, disinterested in my lies.

I saw him hurting, and I wanted to make it stop. The end.

I hope selfishly that there is no afterlife, that Declan's ghost isn't standing at the foot of the bed, absolutely disgusted that he lost his life over me.

Before I can sink any deeper into self-loathing, I turn my head to look at Dante and focus on his pain. "Wanna tell me what happened?"

He looks more in control than he was a few minutes ago. Shaking his head, he counters, "Want to tell me why you're feeling guilty?"

My eyes widen in surprise. I haven't said a word to him about my conflicted feelings and I thought I was doing a decent job at masking my own distress while trying to help him with his. "What?"

"What?" he mocks, before rolling his eyes. "Don't waste both our time with that bullshit. Tell me what's wrong."

I didn't expect him to call me on it. I have to fight the urge to roll away from him and shut him out. I'd prefer to turn the focus onto his thing. "Nothing new. Tell me what's up with you."

For a moment, he doesn't answer. He stares up at the high ceiling, pensive but quiet. "My dad's dead."

My eyes widen. "What? When?"

His lips curve down as he shrugs his shoulder. "Mateo didn't specify. Just told me he's dead and we have to plan a funeral."

"Was it his illness?" I ask gingerly, realizing I'm not even sure exactly what illness he had. Something terminal, maybe cancer?

"I don't know. I was caught off guard, I didn't even ask. He seemed good last time I saw him. Better than he has been, even. He seemed like things were looking up, you know?"

I nod my head sympathetically.

Dante shakes his head. "But now he's just… gone."

Wrapping my arms around him and snuggling up against his side, I tell him, "I'm so sorry, Dante. I don't even know what to say."

"My brother's dead, too. Family members are dropping like flies, apparently."

I blink in mild surprise, since none of Dante's brothers are old. Clearly he's not referring to Mateo since it was Mateo who delivered the news of his father's death. "Alec or Joey?"

"Joey. Apparently he was behind the shot taken at Mateo. That's what Mateo says, anyway."

"You don't believe him?"

"It doesn't make any sense," Dante states. "Joey didn't hate Mateo and he wasn't ambitious, so what did he have to gain by taking Mateo out? I take over the family, nothing changes for Joey."

"Who does it change for?"

"Well, me."

That's obvious, but somehow I didn't think of it until Dante spelled it out. Fear lances me at the thought of Mateo considering Dante a legitimate threat. "Mateo doesn't think *you* had anything to do with that, does he?"

"I don't fucking know," he says, tiredly. "I don't think so, but who knows what Mateo thinks. He was definitely holding something back, I could feel it. He's not a fucking moron, so he knows as well as I do that it doesn't make sense for Joey to try to get him killed. As paranoid as he is, I don't understand why he's so sure it was Joey and not Vince."

"Why would it be Vince? Why would he want Mateo dead?"

"Mateo fucked Mia a while back. Kid's resentful about it. He's always been a hot-head and he just so happens to be Joey's best friend, so you tell me how it makes sense that *Joey*—the biggest fucking slacker in the family—took it upon himself to get rid of Mateo, and *Vince*—the only one of us Mateo has been fucking with lately—wasn't even involved."

It doesn't. And Mateo is among the most intelligent men I've ever encountered, not to mention the most paranoid of threats around him, so it *doesn't* add up that he wouldn't notice. "Is something distracting him?" I ask Dante.

"That fucking girl," Dante says, shaking his head.

"Meg?"

"Mia. Meg's a smoke screen. I don't know what he's doing with her, but it's Mia he's interested in. I don't know if he's literally blinded by her and can't see what's right in front of his face, or..." His voice trails off with a hint of dread, like he doesn't want to consider it might be whatever else he's thinking.

"Or what?" I ask, curious as an ill-fated cat.

His voice hardens. "Or he does know, and he's letting it go *for* her."

"You hate that idea," I surmise.

"It's not good. Doesn't bode well. When Mateo's in control of himself he's fine, but when he falls in love, he can do some stupid shit. Look at Beth. That bitch could have knocked our whole family down like a line of dominos, and all because he fucking trusted her and didn't see what she was doing. I'm getting the impression he trusts Mia, and he knows better now.

He knows you can't fucking trust anyone but family in this life."

Those words surprisingly hurt, and it takes me a minute to understand why. Dante *always* trusted me, and to hear him say that now, to hear the cynicism in his voice, his disapproval at the idea of his brother falling in love again… I put it there.

Despite how wrong his response was, despite the chaos he has wrought and pain he has caused, I have to acknowledge that I caused some, too.

"I'm sorry you feel that way," I tell him, softly. "It's not always a mistake to trust someone, and it's hard to give your heart to someone you *don't* fully trust. If I damaged your ability to trust, I guess I can see why you didn't fall in love again after I left."

"I didn't fall in love again because I never fell *out* of love with you, and you can't be in love with two people at once. Well, I can't. I guess you managed it."

He doesn't bother hiding his disdain, but I can see right through to the hurt underneath. I'm sure I'll regret saying this as soon as it's out there, but whatever lapse in judgment I'm currently experiencing, I can't help telling the truth. "I wasn't… in love. I mean, I loved Declan, but it was nothing like what I felt for you. He was safe and comfortable and couldn't hurt me if he tried; it was nice to feel that way after the intensity of us. I didn't really *want* to find that again with anyone else. When I left, I was looking for something completely different. I never tried to replace you, Dante. I knew that would be impossible."

His eyes lock with mine and we just lie there for a moment, looking at one another. After a minute, he rolls onto his side so he can lean closer to me, then his massive hand cradles my face and he pulls me in for a kiss. This one isn't brutal or aggressive, it's not an act of jealousy or a stamp of possession. It's tender and soft, his lips caressing mine gently, lovingly. I get the impression if I pushed him away right now he'd let me, but I don't want to. Kisses like this one are rare from Dante, they were even back when we were together and things between us were magnificent.

Normally it's the hard, possessive kisses that get my heart pumping, the ones that convey without words that he owns me, body and soul. But this soft, sweet kiss gets my heart racing for another reason entirely; it feels like asking instead of demanding. It feels like he's coaxing my heart back into his hands. I don't have a choice in the matter, but it's not because he isn't giving me one this time. It's because I can't say no. It's because no matter how awful the things he has done are, some part of me doesn't want to. The temptation to sink back into him and let him obliterate every legitimate objection I have is strong, and although he's the one who started the kiss, I'm the one who rolls closer into his embrace. I'm the one who won't let go.

With his free hand, he reaches down and spreads my legs. I open them willingly, then lock them around him as he moves on top of me. He reaches down to guide himself inside me and I sigh with relief, closing my eyes and pulling him closer.

His sensual lips brush my cheeks, the tip of my nose, my eyelid, then he presses them against my forehead. "I don't want to fight with you anymore," he says quietly.

Neither do I. The words get stuck in my throat, though. I don't know if I'm not there yet or I just don't want to be. I don't want to desert Declan's memory or accept the horrible things Dante has done. I desperately want him, but I can't let myself have him. I just can't.

"Just forgive me," he says, causing my stomach to plummet and my eyes to open.

Looking directly into his dark eyes as he moves inside me, I ask, "Is that an apology?"

"No," he tells me, not breaking my gaze. "I'm not sorry for what I did. I'd do it again in a heartbeat. I'd kill him with my bare hands. I would never let you marry another man, Colette. You know that. I am sorry it hurt you, though. I'm sorry I let you leave in the first place."

Tilting my neck as he moves to start kissing it, I murmur, "That was a terrible apology."

"I can apologize for the things I'm actually sorry for, Colette, nothing more." He leaves a trail of aroused senses as he drags his lips up the sensitive column of my neck. "I'm sorry I hurt you. I'll always be sorry for that. But I'm not sorry I killed the asshole who took what was mine. I'll never be sorry for that, and if you need me to be, you're always gonna be disappointed."

I sigh, torn between loyalties. It's shameful, but I'm sorely tempted to give up my ground and come back to the dark side. What Dante did to Declan was terrible, particularly if I'm looking at it like an outsider, but if I look at things from his perspective, it looks much different. It's clear now that regardless of how crazily inaccurate it is, Dante views my relationship with Declan as a betrayal. To him, I may as well have cheated, because once I promised myself to Dante, it was a binding contract, whether I physically left the relationship or not. I know he never would have, but if Dante had ever cheated on me, I would have wanted blood, too, and I'm not even a violent person. If I looked at some strange woman and saw her as the obstacle between myself and Dante when we were together, I would have been able to stop looking at her like a person long enough to do something horrible to her. Not that I ever had a real reason to be, but Dante and I have always been intensely territorial over one another, and how dare anyone else touch what belonged to me.

I would have felt that way, and I grew up like a normal human being. Dante grew up in a crime family where they take what they want without apology. It's in his nature to do what he did, and if I had realized how deeply he loved me, how attached he really was even after I had left, I would have known that.

Maybe he's bad, but he's not entirely to blame in this. I should have known better.

"Can you at least promise you would never do anything like this again?"

Dante's lips drift away from my skin long enough for him to make eye contact. "Only if you never give me another reason to."

I swallow uneasily, holding his gaze. "That sounds an awful lot like you want a commitment."

Dante's lips curve up in faint amusement. "You're committed to me whether you want to be or not, beautiful. All you gotta do is accept it and no one else has to get hurt."

I shake my head as I snake a hand up to caress the strong curve of his jaw. "You're a bad man."

Dante shrugs, unconcerned.

"When I was younger, I didn't *really* think about what that meant, but now..."

He gives me a moment to finish my thought, and when I don't he prods, "Now, what?"

Meeting his gaze, I ask, "Does loving you make *me* a bad person, too?"

Dante catches my wrist, his long fingers curling around it like a shackle. "Better question. Who cares? Who do you have to answer to but me?"

A reluctant smile pulls at my lips. "I like how you added that in there."

"You're worrying about shit that's irrelevant to us, Colette. Who gives a fuck what anyone else thinks about it? This is our life, no one else's."

"I know, but…"

"But nothing." He drops tender kisses to my restrained hand, telling me, "I'm yours and you're mine. Nothing else matters."

Declan mattered. I'm tempted to utter the verboten words, but I don't want to rile Dante up again. Rather than stoke that fire, I keep my mouth shut and let myself enjoy this rare pocket of tenderness.

24

DANTE

"WELL, THIS IS MORBID."

I glance over at my brother in his black suit and crisp black dress shirt—outwardly, the picture of mourning, but we're standing here picking out our dead father's casket and his tone is fucking light as can be.

Making it worse, he adds, "If you wanted to spend more quality time together, you could've just joined us for a drink in my study."

"It's not fucking funny," I snap, glaring at him.

Our younger brother Alec attempts to intervene, pointing to a sleek brown and white casket open in front of us. Addressing the salesman lingering nearby rather than us, he asks, "We don't have to get this hokey embroidering on the interior part, do we?"

The old man looks perplexed at being told his ornate gold embroidering of a cross and a loving inscription is *hokey*. "Most people like the opportunity to share a few last words about their departed loved one."

"And I'm telling you we don't," Alec throws back easily. "Can you knock off a few dollars if we nix the embroidery?"

My jaw locks and my fists curl until my knuckles are surely white. "Who fucking cares about a few dollars?" I murmur. It's bad enough Mateo skipped the top of the line models and brought us to the middle of the road casket instead. More than any of us, Mateo has money to burn. It wouldn't kill him to at least put up a pretense of honoring our father by ensuring he has a burial appropriate for a man of his stature.

Alec shrugs. "We're just gonna bury it in the ground, why not save a few bucks?"

"I'd bury him in a cardboard box pissed on by a homeless man if I could get away with it," Mateo offers.

Losing my cool, I burst out with, "What the fuck is wrong with you two?"

The old, rotund salesman jumps at the sound of my raised voice. He quickly looks between the three of us, then tells us he's going to give us a minute to look and hauls ass away from where we're standing.

"He was our father," I remind them. "Regardless of anything else, the man was our *father*. Show a little fucking respect."

"We'd show respect if he deserved any," Mateo says, meeting my gaze.

"Yeah?" I ask, my eyebrows rising. "I think a lot of people will feel the same way about you when it's your turn. You want people to bury you in a fucking pissed on cardboard box? Or you want to be buried like a boss deserves to be?"

His brow flickers for just a split second before he clears it and resumes looking at the caskets, but I think he gets my point.

"All right, let's..." Alec trails off, sighs, then glances between us. "Fuck it. It doesn't matter. Let's just go look at the nice ones. What's another thousand dollars? I'll pay for it myself, if it's that big a deal. This isn't worth you two fighting."

I straighten my jacket and roll out my shoulders. I can feel the need to hit something moving through my veins, but this is neither the time or the place. Last thing we need is the cops called on us—not because we're fucking criminals, but because my brother and I can't even do one simple, civilian task without it ending in violence.

"I think he would've liked the gray one," I state, trying to keep cool as Mateo and I start to follow Alec over to the nicer caskets.

"It doesn't have any of that bullshit embroidery, either," Alec says with approval, as if the unimportant stitching is some kind of dealbreaker for him.

"You two can pick, I don't care what we get," Mateo states.

"Yeah, we know you don't," I tell him, making my opinion clear with the way I'm looking at him.

"Don't worry, I'll pay," he says with a faintly snide half-smile.

"Don't fucking hurt yourself," I mutter.

"This is fun. I don't know why we don't do this brother thing more often," Alec states sarcastically.

"At least we'll never have to do it again. We don't have any more parents to bury, thanks to the man Dante insists we should mourn," Mateo states.

Alec sighs. "That was rhetorical. All right, I'm calling it.

Let's go tell this guy we want the gray one so we can get the fuck out of here."

"Maybe on our way home, we should stop along the roadside and collect some dandelions to scatter across the casket," I say, scathingly.

Mateo's lips curve up faintly. "Your captive girlfriend is a florist. I assumed she would take care of the flowers."

"You paying for it?" I ask.

"Of course. I'm always happy to support Colette."

He says it just to piss me off, I know he does. My hands fist again and Alec steps between us this time, breaking our eye contact on the way to fetch the salesman.

"You two don't kill each other, all right? I'm not trying to shop for a second casket."

Once Alec walks away, I tell my older brother, "Watch it, Mateo. I'm not in the mood for your bullshit today."

At that, he laughs, like he finds me so fucking harmless. I'm ready to punch him in the goddamn face, but before I can, he knocks *me* for a loop, asking, "Why was Mia at your house?"

It's such a hard turn, he knocks the wind out of my sails. "What?" I ask, completely baffled.

Mateo sighs. "Don't make me repeat myself, Dante."

Even though I know exactly what he's talking about since Mia has only been at my house once, I ask my next question just to see how he responds. "Which time?"

His gaze sharpens ever so slightly. It's not always easy to tell when he's surprised, but I've been around long enough that I can get a better idea than most people. I've seen his poker face progress as he has aged, and what bothers the hell out of me is that every time this girl is brought up, for just a split second, he betrays more than he means to. Loss of control like that means his emotions are engaged on some level; when his head is level, his poker face is fucking perfect.

A pinch of satisfaction slightly soothes my frayed nerves. Let the bastard feel worried for a minute that I might be dipping into his favorite honey pot.

His tone just a little harder than it needs to be, he specifies, "The time you had her deliver stolen drugs to your fucking doorstep."

My gaze darts up to search for security cameras. I can't believe he'd say a thing like that in public where it could feasibly be overheard. A brief perusal turns up no cameras though, and he probably already checked or he wouldn't have said it. At least, I fucking hope so. The alternative is his possessiveness is rearing its head so hard, he didn't even think before he spoke, and that would be bad fucking news.

"They were Colette's pills and she brought them to Colette; that hardly counts as delivering stolen drugs."

Barely letting me finish, he says, "It doesn't matter. It's inappropriate. Mia doesn't work for us and I don't want her involved in any illegal activity. Next time you need an errand run, ask someone on our payroll, not her."

"She wasn't engaged in *illegal activity,* she delivered some fucking toiletries and a prescription to Colette. I don't know why it fucking matters, but if it bothers you that much, I suppose I won't ask her to bring me things anymore."

"I don't want her at your house at all. There's no reason Mia should be coming over by herself. If she's there with Vince for whatever reason, that's one thing, but she doesn't need to be alone with you, and I imagine Colette would agree."

My lips curve up faintly. With no small measure of cynicism,

I say, "Oh, yeah. Clearly it's *Colette's* feelings you're worried about."

"I'm not *worried* about anything," he says carefully. "I'm letting you know I don't appreciate something you've done in the past so you don't do it again. Like when Isabella misbehaves and I take away one of her toys."

That last scathing line rankles just like it's supposed to. I'm ready to snarl back at him, but before I can, Alec hustles over with the salesman in tow. The man looks decidedly less excited to deal with us now, but Alec starts talking before me or Mateo can get in any more jabs at one another.

I glare at him good, but Mateo lets the moment pass, turning his attention back to purchasing Dad's casket so we can all get the hell out of here.

AFTER SPENDING the afternoon with my pain in the ass brothers, I need to unwind. I don't know if it's the right thing to do at all with Colette just starting to warm up to me again, but I want to go to Luca's house and I don't want to leave her at home.

When I walk in, I offer a terse, "Get dressed, we're going out," and watch her little ass spring into action. She's more eager than I thought she'd be. She's probably tired of being cooped up in the house all the time. I should take her out more, I just don't think it's a great idea to be seen together in the city with the lawyer so recently dead. Might raise questions if we saw anyone she knows.

Tonight we won't be in public though, we'll be on my turf.

Since I'm not sure Luca has anything Colette will like, I grab a bottle of wine to bring with us.

Once Colette is dressed and ready, we head out. On my way to the car I get a phone call. It's my main contact from the police station getting back to me, so I have to take it.

Colette lingers, trying not to pay attention, while I take my call. I like it because it's a callback to how things used to be with us, back before this whole fucking mess. I can't say much to my contact on the phone anyway, but we agree on a meeting place and I tell her I'll see her there.

When I end my phone call and open Colette's door for her, she hesitates and meets my gaze. "Everything all right?" she asks.

"Yep," I assure her, my voice calm. "We just have to make a quick stop on our way. You can wait in the car, but I need to talk to someone."

I'm a little on the tense side driving to the meet-up. I don't feel great about bringing Colette along—wouldn't do it, under normal circumstances, but these aren't exactly anticipated work hours.

I also don't feel great about bringing Colette to meet Ceren because of our history, if you could call it that.

Ordinarily I'd never fuck around with anyone involved in any integral part of our business operations, but Ceren caught me on a bad night one time. I didn't feel like going home alone, she was aggressive enough that I said to hell with it, and a couple months later, somehow I still occasionally found myself waking up next to her in bed. Closest thing to a relationship I ever had when Colette and I were apart, and although Ceren might be aware that our guys at the station had orders to shut down any investigation into Declan's death, I never told her after it was done I wouldn't be around for the occasional fuck anymore.

I also don't think it's very fucking respectful to bring Colette around another woman I fucked, even if we weren't together at the time.

Lot of reasons I'm not crazy about it, but I've gotta find out what she knows about this investigation into Rob's house. I don't care what Mateo says, I should be looped in on this.

As we approach the meeting spot, I think about giving Colette some kind of warning, but I don't exactly know what to tell her. I can't come up with anything that makes sense, so I keep my mouth shut. As I put the car in park, then kill the engine, I look over at Colette.

"I'll be right back, okay? You hang tight."

Colette nods her understanding and fidgets with the clutch in her lap. I linger for just another second, then I close the door, slide my keys into the pocket of my slacks, and approach the slate gray car parked across the lot. Normally I'd park closer, but I don't want her to look over and see Colette, and vice versa.

Her instincts tell her I'm approaching before I make it to her car. Her gaze snaps to mine and then her brown eyes warm, her plump lips curving up in an affectionate smile.

Ah, shit.

I shake off the split second of worry. Ceren is too busy with her work for a relationship anyway so she never seemed disappointed that I didn't want anything beyond the occasional physical encounter. That's why it happened past the first time, which admittedly was just a mistake. A twinkle in her eye doesn't mean shit. She can still be fond of me and not want to marry me. I don't know why I'm being paranoid about it now.

I open her car door and slide into the passenger side, then pull the door shut behind me. “Hey.”

“How have you been?” she asks, offering me a little smile as she looks over at me. Her dark hair is styled and she’s wearing a face full of make-up, but I can’t tell if it’s her work-day make-up or “I wanna fuck” make-up. A lot of things I can read, but the intent behind a woman’s make-up routine sure as shit isn’t one of them.

“I’ve been good,” I tell her, nodding faintly.

“Good, I’m glad.”

Her voice is so warm. Has her voice always been this warm when she was talking to me? I guess I never noticed.

Clearing my throat and trying to shuck the weirdness that’s probably all in my head, I reach into my jacket pocket and draw out an envelope. Passing it to her, I tell her, “This is for you.”

“Ah, another payment on my student loans,” she says brightly, but with a wry smile as she takes it. “Thank you.”

“Student loans are fucking stupid,” I grumble, unable to help myself. I’ll never understand why people want to throw their money away like that, paying to have some stuffy academic tell them to read books.

“Yes, well, we can’t all be born into the Morelli family,” she teases. “Some of us have to work for a living.”

“I work my ass off, thank you very much.”

“Mm hmm,” she murmurs, still with affection in her tone I never fucking noticed before.

I need to kill it, so I cut off the small talk and tell her, “So, not to rush you, but I was on my way out when you called.”

“Sorry, I would’ve called you back sooner but I’ve been swamped. I wasn’t sure if you were calling for business or pleasure, and I didn’t have time for the latter.”

"It was the former," I assure her. "I need to know what's going on with a complaint that was filed about that property I mentioned before. I need to know if there's an investigation already started. If not, if it looks like one will be, and I need to know what kind of timeline I'm looking at. When my brother told me about it, he wasn't exactly generous with the gritty details."

Now she frowns, bending over to retrieve her briefcase from the floorboard by my legs. "Yeah, so, the thing is, I couldn't find what you were asking about. There were no inquiries, no notes, no complaints—there's no record that anybody had anything to say about... well, anything regarding this property." Withdrawing her small laptop and opening it up, she glances over at me, "Do you have a name I can look up instead of a place? Maybe the address got typed in wrong."

I give her Rob's name and have her check, but he comes up clean as a whistle. I sit there scowling while she looks through file after file, asking question after question trying to help me find what I'm looking for, but there's nothing. Not a damn thing.

When she finally exhausts every last place she can look, I lean my head back against the headrest and stare out the front windshield. Lot of thoughts run through my head, but despite the excuses I'm tempted to make for my damned brother, there's only one conclusion I can draw: Mateo fucking lied to me.

A bit hesitantly, she says, "It's not possible it was a federal investigation, right? I wouldn't have access to that."

I shake my head half-heartedly. "I don't know. I think he'd mention if the fucking feds were sniffing around."

Shrugging apologetically before closing her laptop and

tucking it back into her briefcase, Ceren tells me, "I can poke around tomorrow and see if maybe it just hasn't been filed yet. Maybe someone who's friendly with your family intercepted the file and stopped it from being put in the system."

"Maybe."

Maybe not, though. I hate to even think it. Why the fuck else would Mateo want to shut down such a profitable arm of our operations? Not only that, but to fucking fabricate a police investigation—

"Mm, you smell so good."

My heart jumps as Ceren catches me unaware, running her hand over my chest and leaning across the console. I catch her wrist and drag her hand away. She gasps in surprise, but then a devilish smile crosses her face. "You caught me. What are you gonna do with me now?"

"Nothing," I state, releasing her hand now that it's not on me anymore. "I told you, I was just about to head out."

"Where you heading?" she inquires, pleasantly enough. "Want some company?"

"To a friend's, and no." I hesitate for a split second, then figure this is probably a good time to let her know I'm back off the market. "I actually already have company."

"Oh." She sounds faintly surprised, but not overly concerned. "All right. Well, maybe we could get together one night this weekend. All work and no play makes—"

"No, not this weekend either," I interrupt. "We need to shift this back to a strictly professional arrangement. I give you envelopes, you give me information, no more orgasms included for either of us."

Wrinkling her nose up, she asks, "Why? Your company? Is it serious?"

Normally I wouldn't hesitate to be an asshole when I'm ending something I don't give a shit about, but given Ceren is a cop, I don't want to risk making her vengeful. I try to be as nice as I fucking can, but to say it doesn't come natural to me is a colossal understatement. "Yeah, it is. It's, uh, actually my ex-girlfriend. We're back together."

Her brown eyes dim and her tone loses a little something, too. "The one who hurt you?"

I frown, not appreciating that she's speaking against Colette, even if what she's saying is true. My irritation makes it harder to be nice—and it wasn't exactly easy to begin with. "We're not gonna talk about her," I inform her succinctly, so she knows how it's gonna be between us now. "This is strictly business now, got it?"

Faint disappointment clings to her tone, even though I can tell she's trying not to let it. "Not even casual friendship, huh?"

I shake my head briefly. "Wouldn't be right."

She presses her plump lips together regretfully. "You're a good man, Dante Morelli."

"You're cracked for thinking that," I inform her.

A little of the sparkle returns to her dark eyes and she smiles. "Maybe. I still do, though."

"Well, I suppose you can afford to be wrong every once in a while," I offer.

"I'm not wrong," she insists. "She's a lucky woman."

Ha, someone should tell her that. Instead of saying anything else, I reach for the latch to let myself out of her car. "Let me know if you kick up anything tomorrow that wasn't in the computer."

"Will do, boss," she tosses back.

25

COLETTE

WE'RE ONLY at Dante's friend's house for about twenty minutes before I become intensely uncomfortable. Back in my day when we socialized, it was mostly with Mateo and Beth. I've gathered since returning that he and Dante aren't as close as they were back then and obviously Dante wants me to keep a distance from anyone I could grow close to who might not stick around, so I guess now he has a new crowd.

I'm not going to lie, I don't approve. Like, at all. Within ten minutes, three different girlfriends of Delmonico's pop up. At least, that's what my initial thought is because why else would he live with these women he's clearly very familiar with? One is even pregnant, and judging from the way she looks at him, he's the father. But then I see the way he treats them and I begin to question whether or not they're here by choice. Surely no woman in her right mind would stand for this kind of treatment and stick around, right? Let alone *multiple* women.

Pulling me from my thoughts, Dante's friend Luca snaps his

fingers. My gaze jerks to his and he almost smiles at me, but it doesn't reach his eyes.

"I'm sorry, were you speaking to me?" I ask, although I want to tell him I don't respond to a snap of his fucking fingers.

"That depends. Do you answer to 'whore'?"

My eyes widen. "Excuse me?"

There's a trace of warning in Dante's tone. "Luca..."

Luca's deep gaze dulls like he's bored by the prospect of interacting with me on a leash, then drifts to the woman approaching me with a bottle of water. She has bruises on her arms and a defeated look in her eyes. I don't feel like I should take a drink from her, I feel like I should bundle her up in a soft blanket and get her the hell out of this awful place.

"Faster next time," Luca snaps.

The girl's fearful gaze jumps to his and she nods fervently, then drops her gaze, swallowing hard as if worried she offended him by making eye contact.

I feel like I'm going to crawl right out of my skin. I have to get away from this man. Shaking my head at the girl offering me the beverage, I hurriedly stand and go to move past her.

"Where are you going?" Dante asks.

"I need air."

I feel as if I'm holding my breath until I get outside the house. Only then can I breathe, grabbing a post holding up the awning on the porch. My mind races in a confused attempt to both process where I just was and ignore it as hard as possible.

I'm only outside by myself for a moment before I hear the door close behind me. I feel Dante's presence so I don't turn to make sure it's not the monster he calls a friend approaching.

I don't know what to do with that. If *that's* the sort of man Dante considers a friend, what the hell does that say about

Dante? I've always known he dirtied his hands at work, but I never had my face rubbed right in the filth. Rather than feeling excluded by his family's "keep the women out of business" rule, I'm starting to feel grateful for the practice if this is the kind of dirty shit *business* entails.

Is it even business, or does Dante just enjoy the company of sociopaths? I'm so confused.

"You didn't bring your Valium, did you?" Dante finally asks.

I slowly shake my head, crossing my arms as a shiver runs through me.

"Do you need one? I'm sure Luca has some here."

"I don't want anything from that man," I tell him, not bothering to try to hide my distaste.

"I know he's a little rough around the edges," he begins.

Pivoting on my heel, I stare up at Dante with wide eyes. "Rough around the edges? That man gives me the creeps. There's something horrifying about him, and I'm a little horrified that you don't agree."

"I know him better than you do," Dante tells me. The way he says it, like I should just give the nice psychopath a chance, blows my mind.

"I don't *want* to know him. He's awful to those women in there."

"It's work," he says dismissively. "They're not..."

He stops, but I think he stops *just* short of saying they're not women. Trying not to look at him like he, too, is a monster, I shake my head. "I don't think I can stay here. Can you call Xander to give me a ride home? If you want to be here, fine, but I—"

Stepping closer and grabbing my arm, pulling me close to

him, Dante says with gentle authority, "*You* are going to stay wherever I am."

Narrowing my eyes and looking up at him, I tell him, "I realize this doesn't mean much to you, but I don't *want* to be here with you. I don't like that man, I'm not comfortable being around young women that look like they're desperately in need of help... If this is the alternative to hanging out with Mateo and whoever the hell he likes now, let's just take that risk. I'd prefer his company to Luca's any day of the week."

Nodding slightly, Dante runs his hands down my arms and says, "Unfortunately, that's not an option."

"Why not?"

"Because I said it isn't. Because I don't spend time with my brother anymore unless it's work-related. Luca is my friend. I know he'll never be your favorite person, but he'll grow on you once you get over the initial shock."

Laughing in light horror, I tell him, "I do not *want* to get over the shock, Dante. If I can ever walk into an environment like that and *not* feel horrified? I don't even want to know what would have to happen in life to make me that callous and uncaring."

Dante's jaw locks, but he doesn't let me go. "You've always known the kind of shit my family's into, Colette."

"Yeah, maybe," I say, shaking my head and shrugging, at a loss. "But I didn't know details, and I never had to *see* it. Maybe I don't *want* to see it. I don't *like* what I'm seeing, and I don't *want* to like it, either. This is who I am, Dante. I always accepted you for who you were, but you have to do the same. I have no interest in becoming the sort of woman who could see other women in that much trouble and not feel compelled to do something to stop it. I know I can't help them because I have a feeling *you're* the one hurting them, so just let me go home. I don't want to become desensitized to this kind of horror; I just don't want to be around it. Being here makes me feel terrible and I don't want to feel terrible."

"You're acting like—" He cuts himself off, but I can feel irritation radiating off him.

"Like what?" I ask, without humor.

Dante sighs, then looks out across the lawn instead of at me. "You're being naïve, that's all."

"I am *not* being naïve," I state, offended.

"You are. The world's an ugly place, Colette. People do shitty things to get ahead, especially fucking gangsters. I'm sorry if this is news to you."

"I want to hit you right now," I inform him.

His lips curve up faintly and warmth dances in his dark eyes. "Please do."

I sigh heavily, rolling my eyes as he tugs me against his chest. "I wasn't trying to be sexy."

"I guess you just can't help it," he states.

"Stop trying to butter me up."

"Would I do that?" he asks in a ridiculous tone of innocence, as he bends his head and kisses the bare ball of my shoulder.

"Yes, you would, and it won't work," I tell him, even though, shamefully, I can *feel* it beginning to work.

"Why not?" he murmurs, bringing his lips to the shell of my ear.

"Everything you do is horrible," I inform him.

"Not *everything*," he disagrees. To prove his claim, he runs his palm over my ass before giving it a firm squeeze. "I can think of a few things I do that you like."

"You can't buy me with sex, Dante," I say, struggling to ignore the stir of desire brought on by his touch.

"What about with money?"

That's so absurd, I almost laugh. "Wow, how crass."

Uncaring of whether or not he's crass, Dante kisses his way along my jawline. "I'm gonna send you shopping tomorrow."

"For Bibles? It'll have to be for Bibles to make me feel less dirty about tonight."

Dante rolls his eyes, then kisses me hard on the mouth. "No, not for Bibles. For clothes. Shoes. Purses. Make-up. Whatever you want. You've been cooped up in the house like a prisoner for long enough. It's time for you to go out and enjoy yourself a little. You'll have to take Xander along to make sure you're safe, but I'll give you your new credit card and you can go wild."

"That's not going to make me feel better. And it's not even fun to go shopping alone. I want a shopping buddy."

"I'll find you one," he promises me. "I'll make you a lunch reservation at that place you like in the city. After shopping you can gab away, get the scoop on all my family's new dirty laundry. It'll be fun to blow off some steam. You always liked doing shit like that."

"With Beth," I say softly. "It's not as fun without my friend."

Dante's quiet for a moment. I don't know how that will land. I know at the end Beth was disloyal and I wouldn't have defended what she did, but long before she hit her breaking point and did that desperate thing, Beth was my friend. Through ups and downs, good days and bad, when she annoyed me and when we had fun, we were *friends*. I still lost someone I was close to regardless of the circumstances, but I know Dante isn't sympathetic and last time I expressed my feeling of loss to Dante, he was offended.

In his world, once someone shows disloyalty to the family, they're cut off. It doesn't matter who you are, that's it. And I get it. I know his lifestyle makes loyalty much more crucial than it usually is. Families like his can fall if they have one disloyal member, and I get that... but I wasn't born into a family like his, so it doesn't come naturally to me.

"I know," he finally says. "I'm sorry."

Since he sounds more understanding than defensive, I look up at him. "I know she's gone, but I need to be able to make a new friend, Dante. This life is hard enough, moments like *these* are hard enough when everything else is solid, but... we're not there yet, at least I'm not, and I don't have any friends here anymore. I don't know where to turn for support. I don't know how you expect me to do this alone."

Pulling me against his chest and wrapping his arms around me protectively, Dante assures me, "I'll figure something out."

"Can we go home?" I request.

He's still hugging me, so I can feel him tense a little when I ask. "No, we can't. Not right now. I told Luca we'd be here for a while. He has Ivan coming over. I've gotta talk to Luca about some business, too. We have to stay for a little bit."

"Why do *I* have to be here?"

Tugging me back and tipping my chin up to look at him, he asks me, "How would that look, Colette? What would Luca think if his first impression of us together is you dragging me around by the short hairs?"

"To be perfectly honest, I couldn't give fewer fucks about how anything looks to Luca," I inform him. "I feel like I need to call in the Red Cross to rescue every girl he's ever touched."

Looking almost pained, he says, "Don't say shit like that, please."

I roll my eyes. "You know I'm not *really* going to call anyone," I mutter, a bit resentfully.

"I know, that's not the problem."

"What's the problem?"

"You remind me of another pain in my ass when you say shit like that."

A scowl transforms my face. "Who?"

Dante sighs, then shakes his head. "Forget it, it doesn't matter." As soon as the words leave his mouth, he stiffens and his gaze sharpens, but it's not on me. "Son of a fucking bitch."

I rear back. "Excuse me?"

"Not you. Motherfucker," he curses, letting me go and taking a step away.

"What?" I ask, mildly alarmed. "What's wrong?"

"I think I know why my fucking brother lied to me," he says, gripping his head between both hands, then raking his hands through his hair. "*Shit*. That fucking—" He shakes his head and I can tell I'm losing him even before he takes a step back toward the house. "I've gotta go back inside. Don't stay out here too long, I don't like you being out here all alone."

26

DANTE

AFTER A LONG ASS night and a silent ride home, I'm ready for this day to be over. Since I made her stay with me at Luca's place, Colette is in a sour mood. After Ivan showed up, we needed a fresh round of drinks. The pregnant chick went to grab them, but she dropped Luca's water bottle cap on the floor and couldn't bend over to pick it up for him. She had a fucking emotional meltdown, and while I thought it was a ridiculous overreaction, I could practically see her overwrought tears washing away any chance of Colette ever liking Luca. Colette rushed to pick up the dropped cap and insisted on helping her fetch our drinks, then she refused to so much as look at me or Luca for the rest of the visit.

I don't like that Colette is pouting and I *especially* don't like *why* she's pouting. I didn't expect her to love Luca, but I thought they'd be able to be around each other on a casual social basis.

What a fucking day. I'm so ready for bed, I don't bother turning on the light when we step inside the bedroom.

Colette moves quietly as she undresses in the dark. She's down to a pair of black panties and a matching bra when I look over at her. Her hair's pulled up off her neck, but a few wispy locks have escaped. I can't resist the urge to touch her and I don't try to. I cross the room, catching her attention. She straightens as I approach, but my gaze isn't on her face, it's on that perfect neck and those wispy locks of dark hair. I bring my hand up and cradle the back of her neck in my hand. I'm fascinated by her fragility. I know she doesn't think she's built to break, but as I lazily run my fingertips up and down that sensitive area of her body, it's all I can think about.

"Did you miss having a man in your bed?"

Her eyes narrow slightly with annoyance. "You know I *had* a man in my bed."

My grip on her neck tightens in warning and she tips her little chin up defiantly. I smile at her silent protest, then kiss the corner of her mouth. "Nah, that wasn't a man."

"Maybe we have different definitions of the word," she tells me, bending her head to try to get away from me. "You didn't think those girls tonight were women, maybe I don't think you're a man."

"Don't bring that here," I tell her, shaking my head. "That's business."

"It's not to them. You're ruining people's lives, Dante, and for what? Money?"

The disdainful way she says that perfectly illustrates how little she truly understands my world. To her, money means paying bills and buying shit she doesn't need, but that's not what money is to me. It's security, power, independence. More money means more safety, it means people might want what we have, but they know better than to fuck with us because we can obliterate them. More money is how I can keep her safe, sleeping soundly each night without knowing about the danger that waits for us outside these walls. If I have to choose between keeping my family safe or letting random fucking strangers be safe, I'll pick my family every single time.

"I won't apologize for wanting more for us, Colette. Everybody does, I just do what it takes to get it."

Shaking her head, she turns away from me and hugs herself. "It's too far. What I saw tonight is *too far*. Maybe you're desensitized because you've been around it for longer, but I bet the first time you were shocked like I was."

Turning my attention back to undressing myself, I tell her casually, "No, the first time I encountered a trafficked woman she was making me breakfast and telling me not to drip oatmeal on my trousers or I'd be late for school. Wasn't what you'd call traumatizing."

She turns back and frowns at me. "You were just a child?"

"You've met Maria," I remind her. "She's been with my family forever."

"Well, yeah... but... that's not what that was tonight, Dante. Maria works for your family; maybe she didn't choose to be there, but she's valued and well taken care of. Those girls I saw tonight—"

"You don't need to think about them," I tell her, shucking my jacket and starting on the buttons of my dress shirt.

She looks at me for a moment, still appearing discontent, then she shakes her head. "I do though. You may be able to control a lot, Dante, but you can't control my thoughts. I wouldn't be the person you claim to love if what I saw tonight didn't upset me."

I watch as she reaches behind her back and unsnaps her bra. I draw off my belt and drop it on the ground, then cross the room in just my slacks and socks. "No, beautiful. That is part of you, but it's like a blemish on an otherwise beautiful face—something I can look past, not something I'm excited about."

Laughing shortly, she says, "Only you would consider a conscience a flaw."

"It is when you're married to someone like me."

Her eyes widen slightly, then she shakes her head. "You and I are *not* married."

"We will be." I walk up behind her, bringing my arms around to her front and capturing her newly freed breasts in the palms of my hand. She inhales sharply and closes her eyes, then she lets her head fall back to rest against my shoulder.

"Why would I marry someone like you?" she asks, her voice soft with arousal.

"Because you love me." I place a gentle kiss to the curve of her neck as I tease her heavy breasts. "Because you know no one else could ever love you the way I do."

"I'm not sure that's a bad thing," she says faintly. "Your love is… a little terrifying."

Running my thumbs across her hardened nipples, I tell her, "You don't feel very terrified."

Her eyes are still closed, but her lips curve up in faint amusement. "I'm not afraid of you."

"I know. I don't want you to be."

"I'm a little afraid of the things you're capable of though," she admits.

"That's all right," I tell her. Dropping one of her breasts, I snake a hand down her taut stomach, then lower until my palm covers her pussy. "It's good for you to know what I'm capable of. Good for you to remember, in case you get too comfortable. In case you get bored and restless, as pampered wives sometimes do." I temper my words with a kiss to her cheek, then plunge a finger inside her. "It's good for you to always know who you belong to, and better for you to know the consequences if you ever forget."

"You're terrible," she tells me, not for the first time.

"Maybe," I allow. "But I'm yours."

Still leaning back against me, she brings an arm up to loop around my neck while I finger her. "I can make your life hell, too, you know," she informs me, her breath hitching when my finger brushes her clit. "If I wanted to."

My lips curve upward. "Oh, I know. And you know the price you'll pay if you make that choice."

"Mass destruction?" she says a little dryly.

"Mm hmm." I kiss the curve of her ear, the side of her face, the curve of her jaw. "Nothing comes for free, beautiful, most especially not my pain."

I hear her swallow, then she reaches down and grasps my forearm. Her hand drops to my hand, then she pushes it away until I withdraw my finger. Once I do, she turns in my arms and looks up at me. "I never wanted to hurt you, you know. That was never my intention. It kills me that I hurt you as much as I did. I honestly didn't think..." She drops my gaze, shaking her head. Then she looks back up at me and says, "Despite everything, I'm sorry for that. I took no pleasure in causing you pain."

I bring a hand up and push the loose tendrils off her face,

moving my thumb along her jawline in a tender caress. "I know. We don't have to talk about it anymore. It's in the past. I'm over it. I want to focus on our future now."

"I'm still sorry," she says.

"I'm glad," I tell her, offering a tender smile. "You shouldn't want to hurt your man."

Now she rolls her eyes at me, but it's good-natured, all things considered. "I never even said you were my man."

"Your pussy did," I inform her, bringing the finger I had inside her to my lips and tasting her arousal on my fingertip.

"She doesn't know what she's talking about," she informs me. "She's dumb. She'll say anything for an orgasm."

"Nah, she knows who her master is." Colette groans, and I outright grin. "You do, too, you're wasting your breath denying it." Since I have her so close, I haul her against my bare torso, slide my hand down the smooth curve of her back, and grab her ass. "Now, enough talking. Get your pretty little ass on the bed."

"Maybe I don't feel like it," she says, but her tone is light.

Even though I know her denial isn't real, my body responds like it is. Aggression surges through me and I squeeze her ass harder, pulling her more tightly against me and grinding my hard cock against her panties. "Maybe I don't care." Her breath catches and she swallows, but she doesn't bother really trying to pull away. "Maybe I've been thinking about your tight little pussy gripping my cock all night long, and I don't feel like waiting for it any longer."

The peaceful, pleasant noise that emanates from her throat is more purr than moan. If that weren't enough, I know she likes what she's hearing because rather than keep up her feeble pretense of protest, she slides her hand into the tight space between us and wraps her hand around my cock. She strokes me softly, lovingly. I feel her giving herself over to the moment and giving up the good fight even before she sinks to her knees without prompting and takes me into her mouth.

I fist a hand in her hair and let my head fall back. Colette gives the best head, so even though I was eager to get in bed with her, I allow the delay and thrust my hips deeper into her throat. She groans, her nails digging into my hips, and readjusts. It's not the wet heat of her mouth that feels best, not the eager strokes of her tongue, it's just the all around sense I get as she sucks my cock that my pleasure is everything to her in that moment, that she's on fire because she's pleasuring me.

Especially now when her stubborn little ass won't admit she's still in love with me, it helps soothe my impatience. She may not be ready to say it, but she's ready to show it, just so long as I don't call her on it.

I don't want to come in her throat, so as much as I enjoy the good work she's doing, I pull her off after a couple minutes. My blood heats as she climbs back to her feet, looking up at me with heat in her eyes and swollen lips from paying my dick so much attention.

I grab the back of her neck, yank her close, and kiss her hard. Her body melts against mine and she wraps her arms around my neck, pulling herself up so she's closer to my height. I already have one arm wrapped around her back, so I only need to move the other one under her legs, then I scoop her right up and carry her over to the bed. It reminds me of the day I took her, only this time, she wants me to hold her.

I deposit her onto the bed, then climb on top of her. She

starts to push her panties down, but I brush her hand away and take them off myself.

"Don't rip them," she murmurs.

"I'll be gentle," I assure her.

"Just with the panties," she adds.

Smirking at her, I say, "Obviously."

Relieved, she nods her head. Once the panties are off and safely tossed onto the floor beside the bed, she spreads her legs to make room for me. Since she's so eager for me, I tease her a bit. Rather than shove inside her like I want to, I rub the head of my cock up and down her slick entrance. Colette groans and licks her lips, but after a few seconds, she catches onto what I'm doing and looks up at me with narrowed eyes.

"What?" I ask innocently.

"Fuck me, don't tease me."

"I'll fuck you when I'm good and ready to," I inform her.

Her eyes narrow and she shoves me. It catches me off guard so I fall back a little—just enough for her to slide out from under me and push me back on the bed, climbing on top.

Normally I like things on my terms and it'd be easy enough to shove her back down on the bed and show her who's boss, but I let her have her moment of victory as she slides my cock inside her needy pussy and grabs onto my shoulders. Her up-do has gone to hell and now her dark hair falls in messy sections around her shoulders. The view from down here is nice while she starts bouncing up and down on my cock, hungry for an orgasm.

The novelty starts to fade after about a minute. I start to feel the strain in the ligaments of my muscles, imploring me to take my natural position on top. Colette and I have had some very good rounds in our time with her on top. Once, she came three times and nearly cried, so obliterated by the pleasure of riding my cock, but even then, it was hard for me.

When she pushes herself up this time, I grab her around the waist and keep her from coming back down on my cock. I throw her down on the bed and plant myself between her spread legs. I reach behind her head and tug her hair free because it's bothering me, then when her long, dark hair falls all around her on the pillow with nothing left to hold it up, I bring my hand up and caress her face. Her blue eyes twinkle with pleasure, then close as I lean down and brush my lips against hers.

"I love you, Colette."

She grabs onto my wrist and sort of hugs it, but she doesn't say it back. Aggravation propels my hips forward a little more brutally than I intended and Colette lets go to brace herself on the bed. She shifts in slight discomfort as I shove my bare cock into her—she's wet, but I'm thick and her channel wasn't entirely prepared. Once I'm all the way inside her, she wraps her arms around me to pull me close, offering up her soft lips as a repentant compromise. I don't do fucking compromises, but I take her offering anyway, devouring her mouth, then demanding more and more from her until she's struggling to keep up.

"Dante," she gasps against my lips as I pound into her.

I break the kiss and pull back to look down at her. Without word, I shake my head, letting her know I don't want to talk.

"It's just..."

Cutting her off, I wrap my hand around her throat and squeeze. Her blue eyes widen with alarm, her hands instinctively grabbing mine to stop the threat, but it's just her body's natural reaction. She doesn't put any oomph behind it. She knows I'd never really hurt her—not like that.

I tighten my hand around her throat, cutting off just enough of her air supply that her eyes roll back with pleasure. "Oh, God, Dante."

I don't say a word, just keep a firm hold on her throat and thrust into her with harder, more deliberate thrusts. Her small hands around my wrist tighten and her breaths become shorter and more desperate. When I can tell she's almost there, I press my fingers harder against her jugular. Colette clutches my arm more desperately, trying a little more earnestly to break my grip, but I ignore it and keep my grip firm.

I watch her pleasure overtake her as she explodes, feel the tight, vice-like grip of her pussy convulsing around my cock. I finally loosen my hold on her throat, letting her suck air into her lungs, listening to her cry of ecstasy as I continue to fuck her into oblivion.

A tear forms in the corner of her eye. I frown, starting to worry I pushed her too far for the first time doing that again in so long. As soon as I let go of her throat, Colette grabs onto me, plastering herself against me and holding on for dear life.

"Thank you," she whispers, squeezing me with her pussy. "Thank you, thank you, thank you."

Her desperate gratitude sends fire coursing through my veins. I catch her stray tear on my thumb and then hold her against me as I continue to pound into her. I love the way she clings to me, fucking crave it. Feeling her need me, feeling her grateful for me like this, it brings back the best feelings she ever gave me. None of the shitty ones matter right now, as long as we can still have this together.

When my pleasure finally overtakes me, Colette holds me tight while I empty myself inside her. She wraps her whole body around me in the aftermath when I collapse against her, too tired to move.

After a few minutes, when I finally do haul myself off her, she doesn't want even those few inches of distance. She scoots right up against me, skin to skin, and wraps her arm around my waist. I wrap my arms around her too, repositioning her until we're comfortable, because I doubt she's going anywhere the rest of the night.

I let her cuddle in peace for a minute, but then I shift her enough to get her attention. When she looks up to see what I want, I caress her jaw and demand, "Tell me you love me."

Her brow furrows ever so slightly, her blue-eyed gaze drifting away from mine. "Dante…"

A little harder, I command, "Tell me."

"You can't just order me to love you," she tells me, scowling.

"I don't have to order you to love me, you already do. I want you to say it."

"You're being unreason—"

I cut her off, wrapping my hand around her throat again. "Tell me you love me, or I *will* make you. I'll spend the rest of the night fucking you, Colette. I'll fuck you until you've come so many times, you feel like you're losing your goddamn mind, and I guarantee you'll tell me you love me then."

I've done similar things to her before, so there's a knowing wariness in her gaze as it meets mine. I feel her neck move beneath my hand as she swallows.

"Now, do you want to tell me while you still have all your faculties, or do you want me to drive you fucking crazy first?"

She holds my gaze, still a little wary, but she grabs my hand and pulls on it to signal she's ready to speak. Slowly, I release her throat and bring my arm back down to drape over her waist.

Colette swallows, still appearing conflicted. I know she doesn't want to say it, but I don't fucking care at the moment. I want to hear the words, I want to watch them leave her lips, and I'll get what I want one way or the other.

Knowing that, after a moment's hesitation, Colette curls close to me. Without meeting my gaze, while snuggled up in the safety of my arms, she quietly admits defeat.

"I love you, Dante."

27

COLETTE

RUNNING my hand down the front of a soft, forest green top hanging from the rack I'm currently perusing, I look back over my shoulder and ask my shopping mate, "What do you think of this one?"

Alec Morelli is leaning against a display of jewelry and purses, his eyes on his phone instead of me. He glances up when I ask for his attention, his dark gaze flickering to the blouse.

"Pretty," he remarks, unhelpfully.

I roll my eyes and sigh heavily. "You're useless. You're supposed to be helping me shop, not playing on your phone."

Pushing off the display, he slides his phone into the pocket of his slacks and approaches me. "Look, I'm sorry. I don't shop with girls I don't at least get to fuck afterward. I don't understand why I'm here."

"You like to shop," I say in my own defense. When Dante

gave me his younger brother for a shopping buddy today, he assured me Alec was on board.

I'm beginning to think he lied.

"Not for women's clothing," Alec states, lifting an eyebrow. "You wanna go buy me a new suit? We can stop and check out some sports cars on the way home, maybe buy some good liquor to indulge in." Turning and grabbing the very first thing he sees, he picks up a pink, stemless wine glass that says in gold, girly script *Wine makes everything better.* "Why the fuck would I want to look at *this*?"

My shoulders droop. "I don't know. I used to have Beth for stuff like this," I tell him despondently. "I don't have anyone to shop with now. Even if I could shop with any of the friends I've made or found again since leaving Dante, they would think I'm a monster to be out shopping for clothes to wear with someone else when I just lost my fiancé."

"So why not bring Meg or Mia? They know the score, they're not gonna judge you. Bring Meg *and* Mia, make it a girls' day. Hell, if you bring them, you can probably even get Mateo to foot the bill."

"Dante won't let me hang out with them."

Alec frowns in confusion. "Why not?"

I shrug, glancing around to make sure no one is within earshot. No one is, but I still lower my voice. "He doesn't seem to think they're long for the world, and he doesn't want a repeat Beth experience."

Now Alec's eyebrows rise in surprise, like that's nowhere near his understanding of the situation. "I'm pretty sure they'll both be around for a while."

"Dante doesn't agree," I state. "Do *you* have a girlfriend I could shop with? Preferably one I don't have to worry about going the way of Beth."

Alec shakes his head, stuffing his hands into his pockets. "Nah, I prefer the single life. No attachments. Plus, it seems like the males in my family have a sleeper cell of insanity that unlocks when they fall in love, and I'm not trying to turn into a raging fucking lunatic."

Smiling, I abandon the green top and drift closer to him. "I love you, Alec. I should've fallen for you instead."

Alec smirks faintly. "I'm not really into older women, sorry."

Swatting him in the arm, I shoot him a scowl. "I am not *old*."

"Older than me though," he points out. "Not my style."

"Rude."

Alec continues to smile. "I'd bore you anyway. You may not want to admit it, but you like those crazy fuckers. You don't want someone cool-headed who will lug around your shopping bags, you want the unhinged psycho who will ruin your life."

"Amen to that," I mutter. "Why do I love those life-ruiners so much more than the good guys?"

Alec shrugs. "Beats the hell out of me. Someone's gotta love 'em, I guess."

I take that and run with it. "That's it. I'm taking one for the team."

"It's noble, really," he adds, playing along. "The world appreciates your sacrifice."

Sighing, I try to ignore the tickle of real conflict this all still causes. I don't want to think about it right now. I certainly don't want to burden Alec with my moral dilemmas.

Then again, maybe Alec is exactly the right person to talk to about it with. Despite being a criminal—and a *Morelli*—Alec seems like he manages to remain a pretty decent person. He's not stuck in the moralistic struggle I'm locked in, but he's not one of the really bad guys, either.

"Can I ask you a question?" I ask him.

Shoving his hands into the pockets of his slacks, Alec looks over at me. "Sure."

"How do you do it? How do you manage to accept your family for everything they are and not feel badly about it? I mean they're—*you're*—so bad. They—you guys do unforgiveable things. I can't sleep at night if I think about all you guys are responsible for. When I was younger I didn't see all of it, but now… now, I can see the damage. Dante brought it right to my doorstep, and I can't unsee it. And I don't… I don't know how to move past it and be with him without feeling like a horrible person."

"That's part of the problem, right there. You can't take the weight of the whole world onto your shoulders. You can't focus on all the bad and think of it as your responsibility to stop it or control the damage. Not to be an asshole, but no one designated you as the morality police, right? I know this life's harder for better people, you have to *really* love us to look past the things we do, but limiting your responsibility to what you can control is the best place to start." Meeting my gaze, he tells me, "You cannot control Dante. This probably wasn't a problem before because you didn't try to. I know it's not fair what he did, I know you didn't get a choice in all this, but if you *want* it to work with him, you have to start there. I accepted a long time ago I'd never be able to control my brothers or stop their destruction. I still try when I think I might be able to make a difference, but if I can't, oh well. It's not my responsibility. I do the best I can. You do the best *you* can and that's it. That's all you can do. You can't try to change him, Colette. I know he's a far cry from perfect, but he is who he is, and that's not gonna change. Either love him for who he is, or…"

He trails off there, seeming to realize there is no "or" for me. My options are more or less be happy with Dante or be miserable with Dante. Any other option would pit me against him, and there's just no chance I would win. I don't even want to *win.* I don't want to be Dante's opponent. I've never wanted that. Back when we were together and in love, we were a team, and that's the way I liked it. We each had our role and together we were perfect. I'm not the same person I was back then, but he is pretty much the same man he was.

I felt like we were making fun when I said Dante ruined my life, but I'm beginning to realize I wasn't. He *did* ruin the life I had created for myself, and it's not fair that he just expects me to fall into the replacement life he had lined up for me.

"You know what he did," I state, since I can't be too specific in public.

Nodding once, Alec verifies, "I do."

"And you know every day he does things that are just as bad."

"Yes," he agrees.

"So, knowing that, how do I not feel like the worst person in the world if I just… love him anyway?"

Alec sighs, glancing off to the side and seeming to mull that one over. After a moment, his gaze returns to me and he says, "I don't think I'm the right person to talk to about all this, Colette. I'm no angel, either. I was born into this lifestyle as much as Dante was."

"I know that, but you're not… You know right from wrong. To some extent, you must understand why I'm horrified by the things he's capable of."

"I do," he admits. "Believe me, I practically begged Dante not to go through with what he did to you, but once it happened, I washed my hands of it. I knew it wasn't my job to stop him, I know the things my brothers do—right or wrong—aren't my responsibility. More often than not, I just stay out of their way, and I don't lose a wink of sleep over it. I don't struggle with accepting my stupid brothers for who they are, I don't think much about the bad shit they do. You need an expert on forgiveness, and that's not me. You need to talk to Mia."

"Does she know what Dante did?"

Alec shrugs. "I doubt it, but it doesn't really matter. You don't have to share the gory details, just your emotional predicament. She's an outsider too, so she would probably be able to relate more to where you're coming from. She has forgiven Vince and Mateo for some seriously fucked up shit. She manages to love them no matter how horrible they are, and her morality remains pretty much intact, too. I don't think she cares as much about that as you do, she's not as straitlaced as you, she's just very empathetic and not as self-centered as most of us; nurturing monsters seems to come second nature to her. Anyway, Mia's a trouper; she might be able to give you some pointers on getting over your moral quibbles and moving past it. She accepts all of us for who we are without trying to impose her own morality on us and she doesn't seem to compromise who she is to do it, either; maybe she could help you get there, too. Only thing I can tell you is, if you want to be happy here, you've gotta stop thinking about how to change other people and focus on shifting the way *you* look at things. You only have control over yourself, no one else."

"Would you give that advice to your sister?" I ask him wryly.

"Well, no, I'd just tell her to stop trying to date one of our brothers. That's weird."

I crack a smile. Despite the harshness of what he just said, I know Alec means well. "You know what I mean."

He shakes his head. "You've gotta get out of your own head. Get over this morality roadblock. Morality is relative to the culture you live in, and you know our culture isn't like everyone else's. You couldn't have possibly forgotten *everything* while you were away."

"I was young and dumb back then," I tell him, reaching out and touching another soft-looking fabric.

"But you were happy," he states. "Now you're old and stuck on yourself, and I'll tell you now, that'll never serve you here. If anything, Dante will eventually get sick of it, and where will that leave you?"

My jaw drops and I shoot him a look. "You just called me old *again*. You're the worst shopping buddy ever. Keep saying mean shit to me and I'm not gonna buy you lunch when we're finished."

"That's okay," he says. "We can just head back to your assisted living facility. I'm sure they've got food there, right?"

"Just applesauce," I offer back. "Sometimes we get Jell-o cups for a treat."

"Do you think we'll even have time to eat?" he asks, checking his watch. "Don't old people go to bed at like 5 o'clock?"

For that one, I swing my handbag and hit him in the arm with it. "Shut your stupid mouth, Alec."

He grins at me. "What?"

I roll my eyes and walk ahead of him. "I changed my mind, I don't love you. You're like the younger brother I never wanted."

"Aw, don't be mad," he says, falling into step beside me and slinging an arm across my shoulders. "You know I'm just messing with you. You're still young and hot. My brother probably wouldn't have kidnapped you if you weren't."

"That's terrible. You're all terrible."

Alec nods with mock solemnity. "Yeah." He barely misses a beat, then says just as casually, "Now, let's go find you a pretty dress to wear to my dad's funeral."

28

DANTE

OUR CONFLICT with the Castellanos family comes to a quick and jolting halt when Adrian finds our missing sister holed up in some suburban house with none other than Salvatore Castellanos. His dad, the boss, was shot dead in the scuffle, apparently; I don't have all the details yet, but I know that Salvatore Castellanos is the next boss of their family, and given my little sister has apparently been warming his bed behind all our backs, he's as interested in peace as Mateo is.

There are still a lot of unanswered questions, but a ceasefire brings a measure of relief to all of us. It means we can finally rest a little easier, not worrying there's some fucker with a gun around every corner, poised to take us out. It's too soon to tell if there will be any ripples from other syndicates who might be waiting in the wings, watching the conflict and hoping for a show of weakness so they can attack. Just in case, I tell Xander I still want him to cover Colette's first day back at work—but I don't tell Colette about it. I trust that we're in a good enough place she wouldn't try anything fucking stupid as soon as she gets out of my sight, but it doesn't hurt to keep an eye on her just in case I'm wrong.

For the first time in far too long, Colette stands beside me at the bathroom vanity as we both go about our morning routines. Her side of the sink is cluttered with all sorts of shit as she gets ready for work—new makeup and hair products and mysterious female shit I can't even put a fucking name to. Thank God Alec was the one who had to go shopping with her and not me.

As Colette winds her hair around a hot iron, she glances over at me in the mirror and says, "I hate to bring this up, but I have a lot of paperwork to catch up on today and I was hoping to get the invoice together for the flowers for your father's funeral. Should I bring it home or email it to Mateo, or...?"

"You can bring it home. I'll give it to Mateo myself."

Colette nods, releasing the lock of her hair. It falls in a long, dark curl beside her face. "I think you'll like the casket spray I designed. I did a lot of research and went all out. Imported these really delicate, beautiful flowers from a supplier I've worked with before in Italy. They're purple, but keep an open mind; purple is a color associated with royalty, not girls. That's what I was thinking when I ordered them for your father. Like, a fallen king. Anyway, they'll complement the white roses and chrysanthemums really well. It's a beautiful arrangement, I'm pretty proud of it."

"I'm sure it is," I tell her, like I give a damn about flowers.

"I figured I could bill him a little extra for the imported flowers, too," she adds with a sly little smile. "I thought it would make you happy to overcharge Mateo."

At that, I crack a smile. "You know me so well. If there's an asshole tax, make sure you give him that, too."

Colette grins, putting the hot iron down and mussing her carefully curled hair with her fingers. "I'll see what I can do."

We fall quiet for a couple minutes while I comb my hair and she does her thing. When she spritzes perfume on her wrists, I know she's about finished with her routine. "Speaking of things we don't want to talk about," I begin, glancing over at her.

Colette sighs, her shoulders drooping. "Let me put my perfume away first."

"Can't you just keep it on the sink?"

She shakes her head. "The steam from the shower isn't good for the fragrance."

"Well, God forbid we make the perfume uncomfortable," I remark as she ignores me and heads toward the walk-in closet.

When she comes back to the bathroom, she shoots back, "Hey, you care about how your alcohol is stored, I care about my perfume. Now, what dreadful thing do we need to talk about?"

"This is your first day back in the outside world alone," I point out.

"Are you worried I'm not adequately dickmatized to send out into the wild by myself?" she inquires. "I'm not an idiot; I won't run screaming to the police station, I promise."

"It's not you I'm worried about," I tell her. "Since you *will* be in the outside world, that means the people from your old life will have access to you again."

"Uh huh."

"That can mean complications," I state. "You fell off the face of the planet and no one knows why."

"Well, my fiancé died in a tragic 'car accident' on the day we were supposed to get married," she points out, her gaze hardening slightly. "It probably would've been stranger if I had been out painting the town red. I don't think it's odd that I've disappeared for a little while to mourn."

"It's not, but it probably *is* strange that you didn't attend his funeral or visit his family or… whatever the fuck. I don't know what your relationship with them was like, I don't want to know, but knowing you the way I do, I assume you had attachments there."

Since I said I don't want to know, she crosses her arms over her chest and mean mugs me, but doesn't confirm or deny.

I never wanted to see this fucking thing again, but I open the unused bottom drawer on the right-hand side of my vanity and draw out the engagement ring I took off Colette's hand the first night I brought her here. She loses a shade of color at the sight of it and my jaw locks. I have to work to unlock it so I don't sound angry when I tell her, "You might want to return this."

Colette stares at the ring for a long time. A *long* fucking time. The rock I hate looking at just sits there in the palm of my hand and she doesn't touch it. I notice her taking her breaths more deliberately, like she's having a hard time. Finally, she turns away, bracing her hands on the vanity and tells me, "Put that away."

I close my hand to cover it up so she doesn't have to look at it. "His family might—"

"Then we'll mail it to them," she snaps. "I don't want to see it, Dante. Don't show that to me ever again."

Her response is enough that I put the damned thing back in the drawer. "All right. I'll handle it," I tell her.

"I can't believe you kept that thing in our bathroom," she states, still not looking at me.

Cocking an eyebrow, I ask, "Do you not want it in the house? It's just a ring."

"It's *not* just a ring, it's..." Trailing off, she shakes her head. Finally, she regains enough composure to tell me, "I'll buy a nice sympathy card on the way home today. I'll fill it out for his mom with an apology for disappearing and everything and I'll drop it off when she's not home."

"Do you know when she'll be out of the house?"

Colette shakes her head.

"All right. I'll get someone on it. When she leaves the house tomorrow, I'll have someone drop it off. You don't need to deal with it yourself. I like the idea of a card better than you actually being around those people, anyway."

Sighing heavily, Colette shakes her head again, I think this time at herself. "Jesus. How am I supposed to refrain from thinking about this when it keeps coming up?"

"It's just for now," I promise her. "Once we deal with this initial bullshit it'll be over and you won't have to think about it anymore."

"She will," Colette states. "Her son is dead, Dante. She'll never stop thinking about that."

"Don't take that road, Colette," I warn her. "Don't think about that shit."

"How? When it's my fault he's dead, how am I not supposed to think about it? I didn't merely break his heart, I cost him his life. I'm the nightmare girlfriend that every mother fears her son will encounter someday."

"Well, I don't have a mother, so it doesn't matter now that you're with me," I tell her, lightly, considering what I'm saying.

Meeting her own gaze in the mirror, she states, "I'm going to Hell."

"A week ago you thought you were already there, so I guess we're making good progress," I tell her.

She slides me an unamused look in the mirror. Our business here is pretty much concluded. I still need to coach her on what to say in case anyone stops in to the flower shop wanting to ask her questions, but now's not the time. Sonja is cooking us breakfast, so we can finish talking while we eat. Since she didn't have a full blown panic attack and she seems more or less okay for now, I leave her there to finish collecting herself and head to the closet to retrieve my jacket.

My father was a polarizing man, so I guess it was inevitable that his funeral would be uncomfortable. I was in a preemptively pissy mood on the way to the funeral home because I know all of my siblings agree with Mateo on this one, but the joke of a service only made me surlier. Normally, it would go without saying that Mateo would give the eulogy. Not only because he's Dad's heir and the head of this family now that he's gone, but because Mateo is the best talker. He can spin bullshit effortlessly, so we all know he could've put together a nice speech for Dad in no more than a few minutes.

That makes it doubly fucking insulting that he refused to. He told me I could do the eulogy since I'm the only one who liked the guy, but he knows I'm not a talker. There's no chance I'm going to stand behind a podium like some kind of stuffed suit and address a room full of people with a heartfelt fucking speech.

Alec ends up doing it, just to keep the peace. It's a generic eulogy that could've been about anyone and all it does is piss me off. No one but me even cares that Dad is gone, and they're not willing to pretend otherwise.

When we get to the gravesite, I case the place to see where I want to stand. The funeral director bows his head respectfully and gestures for me to join my siblings on the left side of Dad's coffin. Alec, Francesca and Mateo are already gathered on one side of Dad's coffin. Our Uncle Ben flew out from Vegas and he stands on that side with the family. Consequently, his son Vince has defected from the family side of the coffin and he stands with Mia on the opposite side of Dad's coffin.

Colette's hand gently grips my bicep and I glance back at her to see what she wants.

"We should probably walk, we're holding up the line," she whispers.

I flick one last glance at the family side, then grab Colette's hand and haul her over to the side where Vince and Mia are instead. Vince flicks me a brief look of surprise that I'm standing with him instead of my brother, but it's crowded over there anyway.

Salvatore Castellanos lacks no fucking audacity, so he stands beside my sister on the family side of the casket. I still can't believe this shit. A Castellanos should never be present at a Morelli funeral. It's a fucking travesty. I might like the additional money my brother brings in, but I'm not wild about this aspect of his leadership.

We're the stronger family; we should take advantage of their weakened state and eliminate our competition, not invite them to join forces with us. Sal was next in line, but he hadn't taken over his family the way Mateo has ours. Our dad dying does nothing to weaken our empire because Mateo was already the one running things, but it's not the same for the Castellanos family. Antonio was the boss in every respect, so his death leaves them vulnerable until the new leader establishes himself.

Now would be the perfect time to pounce and take the rest of them out, but instead Mateo gives their new boss his blessing to marry our fucking sister.

Misreading my general grumpiness, Colette leans her head against my shoulder and caresses my arm in a comforting gesture. My gaze remains steady on Sal until he feels my stare. Finally, his gray eyes meet mine across the casket. It's not the time or place for a stare-down, but once we lock gazes neither of us looks away until the pastor starts speaking and asks everybody to bow their head in prayer. I'm compelled by respect for my father, and Sal is compelled by being a good Catholic boy, so we both give up our ground for the moment and bow our heads.

29

DANTE

AFTER THE BURIAL, everybody heads back to Morelli mansion to eat and commiserate. There are far too many people to fit at the formal dining room table, so Mateo had tables set up in one of the drawing rooms and the maids are bringing out food to serve buffet-style.

"Should I help?" Colette inquires, watching Maria and her daughter Cherie bring out dish after dish for the assembled mourners.

I like the idea of her assuming the wifely role and pitching in to play hostess since no one who lives here is bothering to do the job. Francesca won't leave Salvatore's side, like she's afraid if she does one of us will kick him out. Alec is single so he doesn't have a girlfriend to play hostess. Mateo doesn't care about this, so his live-in girlfriend is treating my father's funeral like a fucking social event instead of a funeral she should be hosting. It's a load of bullshit. Same way the women take care of dinner on Sunday nights to make family dinner more loving and personal, they should be the ones serving the food and playing hostess at our father's funeral.

"Yeah," I tell her, glad that she's volunteering. "Someone in our family should be doing it. Doesn't seem like anyone else plans to step up."

Colette nods, smoothes down the front of her modest black dress, and follows after Maria and Cherie to see what they need help with.

Once she's gone, I look around for some adequate alcohol to make dealing with my family a little easier. I only have to circulate around the room once to realize that while my brother has a few cater waiters circulating with alcohol, none of them have the good stuff.

I know he has the good stuff in his study, so I slip out to get myself a real drink. There's a bathroom just outside the drawing room for guests, and just as I'm walking past, as luck would have it, I run into someone I've been meaning to talk to anyway.

Mia Mitchell isn't paying attention as she exits the bathroom. Her head is down as she rummages through her small handbag. Since she's not looking where she's going, she's moving slowly, so there's no urgency in deciding what I want to do. As I saunter closer, I take a moment to look her over while she digs around in her bag.

She's all dolled up for my dad's funeral, her blonde hair curled and falling around her shoulders. Colette has worn a dress in a similar style to the one she's wearing before, but not to a dignified event like a funeral. It has a skimpy black slip underneath and a sheer overlay so it can pretend to be modest, but the shape of her body makes that impossible. The material clings to every dangerous curve and I can't help wondering how many times my brother has stolen glances at her already when he was supposed to be mourning the loss of our father. Given the way this dress looks on her, I'm betting a lot.

Vince is fucking stupid. He should take away her make-up and make her wear flannels and sweatpants around Mateo, not let her doll up like this. The fucking kid knows Mateo was already attracted to the girl when she came to the mansion dressed like the help on a day off.

Then again, I bet her ass looks good in sweats, too. That probably wouldn't work.

Since she hasn't looked up and noticed me in the hall yet, I go ahead and announce myself, offering a slow, dark smile. "Elle. What a nice surprise."

Mia's gaze snaps to mine at the sound of my voice. Her blue eyes widen in alarm and she takes an intuitive step back. "Dante. Hello."

"I'm glad to see you," I state.

"You are?" she asks, sounding incredibly confused.

"Mm hmm." I grab her arm and haul her back toward the bathroom.

Her instincts for self-preservation kick in a few seconds too late and she grabs for the door frame as I haul her ass back into the bathroom. "What are you doing?" she asks, trying—and failing—to hide her panic.

"Cameras," I state simply, jerking my head toward the hallway. It's common knowledge within the family that my paranoid brother has every room and every hallway under careful surveillance—everything but the bathrooms. "I want to talk to you alone."

"I don't think—" she begins uncertainly.

I cut her off. "We don't keep you around to think, sweetheart."

She's still gaping at me when I haul her back against the wall and lean over to lock the closed door. "You are so rude," she informs me.

I move in on her and bring the palm of my hand down hard against the wall beside her head. She jumps, fear leaping to her blue eyes as she looks up at me.

"What do you want?" she asks warily, holding my gaze.

I don't know why it's so fucking exhilarating to scare the shit out of her. Scaring women for shits and giggles isn't really my thing, but there's something so vulnerable about this one. It's like she has a natural perfume that wordlessly invites the predators closest to her to sink their teeth into her. I can kinda see why my brother enjoyed fucking with her to begin with, he just should've stopped before he got addicted.

"I have a friend who would love you, you know. Well, not love *you*, but he'd love finding creative ways to extinguish the light dancing in those pretty blue eyes. If I keep finding you in my way, I might introduce you two."

"I don't know what you're talking about, Dante. I barely know you; when have I ever been in your way?"

The little pain in the ass doesn't even know how much she's in my way. Telling her the extent of her damage would infuriate Mateo, though, so I'll stick to the things she *does* know about.

Reaching up with my free hand to wind one of her blonde curls around my finger, I tell her, "Like I said, we need to talk."

She swallows hard, the fear wafting off her in hot waves. I've never felt more like a predator; not in a house full of girls I'm going to sell like cattle, not standing in front a man I'm about to kill—never.

"About what?" she asks warily.

"About rats, and how much I don't fucking like them." I give her hair a sharp tug and she gasps, but she doesn't swat my hand away. Maybe because the way I have her cornered, if she did, she'd have to bring her hands up between our bodies and she doesn't want to touch me.

"What does that have to do with me?" she asks, looking genuinely confused beneath her fear.

"Think back to last time we saw each other, when you came to my house. Do you remember what I told you *not* to do?"

"You asked me not to tell Mateo."

"I *told* you not to tell Mateo," I correct her. "Maybe that's why you got confused, Elle. It was a demand, not a request. When I make a demand, I expect it to be obeyed."

Narrowing her eyes at me, she says, "Whatever you want to call it, I didn't say anything, so I'm not sure why you're bringing it up."

"Bullshit."

Her eyes widen in legitimate surprise. "No?"

I scowl at her now. "What the fuck do you mean, no?"

"It's not bullshit. I never mentioned that day to Mateo—he had enough on his plate already. I didn't think Vince would much appreciate it, either, and I didn't want him to find out because he tends to accuse me of things first and ask questions later. I never mentioned it to *anyone* because I didn't want to cause trouble between you and *any* of your relatives. Sure, you were mean to me, but nothing *actually* happened, so why would I mention it to anyone?"

Denial isn't all that surprising, but she looks so goddamn earnest. She's not just denying telling on me, she's offering plausible reasons she wouldn't do it in the first place. None of it sounds like a lie, but it can't be the truth, either.

"Did you tell Meg?" Mateo's girlfriend has a big fucking

mouth, maybe Mia mentioned it to her and that's how it got back to my brother.

"No. Like I said, I didn't tell anybody," she states.

Okay, maybe she didn't tell him I intimidated her, but she must have at least mentioned stopping by. "Don't fucking lie to me, Mia. Even if you didn't tell him I was an asshole, I know you must have mentioned coming over. If you slipped up by accident, just tell me that, don't lie and try to cover your ass."

"I didn't slip up and I'm not lying. Trust me, you'd know if I tried to lie. I'm a terrible liar," she states.

"You're a terrible liar and you expect me to believe you lied to *Mateo*?"

Cocking an eyebrow, she says, "I didn't have to lie to him, because *I never brought it up in the first place*."

"*He* never brought it up to you?"

Mia shakes her head no.

I narrow my eyes and try to glare her into submission, but either she's telling the truth and she's got nothing to tell me, or the girl is a million times more clever than I give her credit for. Time to find out.

"My brother has a thing for you, doesn't he?"

Her eyes widen in shock, then she breaks eye contact and tries to inch away from me. I drop the lock of her hair and put my arm on the other side of her to stop her from going anywhere.

"Your brother has a girlfriend and I have a boyfriend," she states, almost tonelessly. "Now, if you'll excuse me, I need to get back to the drawing room before that boyfriend notices me missing and comes to investigate. Literally the last thing I need is to get caught locked in a bathroom with you."

"That would probably expedite your imminent death sentence, wouldn't it?" I murmur.

Mia rolls her eyes. "Yep, and if I die, who will you harass?"

"I'm sure I could find someone," I offer back.

She finally brings a hand up and lightly pushes at my chest to get me away from her. "Maybe someone whose name you can remember," she mutters.

I take a step back. "I remember your name just fine."

"Then why do you keep calling me Elle?" she inquires, cracking open her purse and drawing out her cell phone. Predictably, it has a sparkly pink case and I almost laugh at how fitting it is.

"Elle Woods."

Her gaze jumps back to mine like that's more shocking than anything else I've said or done to her. "Elle Woods?"

"From *Legally Blonde*. Don't tell me you've never seen it. Ditzy blonde who likes pink and thinks the world is made of rainbows and sunshine."

Biting back laughter, she says, "You mean clever, Harvard-educated lawyer who can kick ass in the courtroom and make her way in the world without being an asshole? Yeah, *I* know who Elle Woods is; I just can't believe you do."

"Colette loves that stupid fucking movie," I explain, though I'm not quite sure why.

"Mm, she has good taste. In movies, at least," Mia adds with a touch of snark.

"Not in men though, huh?"

"Shit taste in men," she agrees, but lightly, all things considered.

"You're one to talk," I tell her. As I watch her fiddle with her cell phone, I cock my head, a sudden thought occurring to me. "Did my brother buy you that phone?"

Her gaze snaps away from the phone and right back to mine. Guardedly, she answers, "Yes. Why?"

There it is. That actually makes a lot of fucking sense. I couldn't make sense of why she would tell him she came to my house, but not tell him how I treated her. If he knew where she was but she didn't tell him, I'd bet my fucking house it's because she's unwittingly carrying around a tracking device—the goddamn cell phone he gave her.

If he didn't trust her I might think he's just using it to keep an eye on her whereabouts to make sure she's not making trouble, but I know that's not the case. Since she passed his test, I know he has all the faith in the world in this girl's loyalty. He was tempted to believe in her even before she passed the loyalty test until I knocked some fucking sense into him.

That can only mean he's so fucking besotted, he has to know where she is at all times. Jesus Christ. This is worse than I thought it was. That's not the mark of a minor infatuation, that's... he didn't even track Beth like that.

Maybe this girl *isn't* going anywhere.

Shaking my head, I tell her, "No reason."

"No reason?" she asks, suspiciously.

"I figured if you can't afford groceries, you probably couldn't afford the latest model iPhone," I offer, since I apparently have to give her something.

Her cheeks flush with faint embarrassment. "Oh. We can afford groceries," she mumbles.

I don't care. The mystery is solved and I never did get that drink, so I'm done here. Without a word I make for the door, but I stop before opening it. I feel Mia behind me, ready to make a beeline out of here. It should go without saying, but just in case, I glance back and tell her, "Don't tell anyone about this time, either."

"Don't worry." Then, with a mischievous smile, she adds, "My hair is full of secrets."

I cock an eyebrow and automatically look at her hair. "Okay?"

Her smile droops. "*Mean Girls*? You don't know that one? Now I'm disappointed. I liked the idea that after a long, grueling day of torturing innocents, you go home every night, kick back on your couch, and watch chick-flicks."

"That definitely does not happen," I deadpan.

She shrugs. "You could have let me have my fantasy."

"No."

"You should watch it. I mean, *Colette* should watch it," she says with an exaggerated wink, like she's in on my dirty secret.

Shaking my head, I open the door and back up against it. "And you should get your little ass back to the drawing room before I text Vince myself and tell him you lured me into a bathroom with you."

"That's not funny," she informs me as she scoots past me.

I shrug my shoulders, watching her. "I don't know, I think it'd be pretty funny."

"I've never done anything to warrant you wishing for my death," she informs me.

Now that I have a handle on the crisis she has caused with her well-meaning bullshit, I can agree with that. I know my brother is off-track right now, but I also know I was able to straighten him out and make him see things clearly last time he tried to do something stupid for this girl. Now that I understand what I'm dealing with, I feel a lot better about the whole thing. My brother is a reasonable man; all he needs is a good talking to.

Hell, even if this girl *did* find out about his involvement in trafficking, I don't think it would be enough to alienate her. I've treated her like garbage on two occasions now, and I still get a friendly vibe off her like she's willing to sweep it all under the rug and start fresh. And she hasn't slept with *me*—surely Mateo has an advantage there.

Maybe I *should* let her and Colette be friends.

I bring my attention back to Mia at the sound of her voice. She's flashing me a friendly smile, saying, "Well, I'm gonna head back. I'm sure I'll see you in there."

"I'm sure you will."

"Oh, and... I'm sorry for your loss," she offers.

I nod my head once. "Thanks."

With another faint smile, she turns and heads back toward the drawing room.

I turn in the opposite direction and head to Mateo's study to grab a drink.

30

COLETTE

ALL THE FOOD has been put out for the mourners, but as the first few come up to fill their plates, I realize there's something missing.

"I'll be right back, I'm going to run and grab some napkins," I tell Maria.

She nods her head at me but doesn't speak. She's not normally *this* surly, but I know she has some kind of unpleasant history with Vince's dad, and I think his presence here is making her crabby.

Without another word, I go to head out of the drawing room, but I stop dead in the archway at the sight before me in the hall. *Dante* has just opened the bathroom door to come out, but he backs up against the door like he's holding it for someone. Dante doesn't even hold doors, but why the fuck would someone be in the bathroom with him? Then my stomach bottoms out as I see a pretty blonde girl look up at him as she walks out of the bathroom.

Mia.

For a couple seconds, I can't process everything I'm feeling, but then it hits me all at once. Rage turns my blood to fire, jealousy ignites and melts all my bones. My legs feel shaky so I step back into the drawing room and plaster myself against the wall for support.

Dante *never* lied to be about other women before, not once. I already caught him in the lie about her coming over while I was asleep that one day when he said it was Vince, and despite his claims that he definitely never slept with her, my instincts told me there was something there. I believed him because of his spotless track record, and why the hell would he go to all this trouble to bring me back if some other girl made a big enough impression on him that he's willing to *lie to me* to... to what? Divert my suspicion? To protect her? He swore he hadn't slept with anyone I would have to continue seeing once I came back, but what if that was a lie, too?

Why was he locked inside a *bathroom* with her? I try to give him the benefit of the doubt. Maybe she was inside using the restroom and she forgot to lock the door. Dante had to use the restroom so he opened the door on her by accident, but... that scenario is implausible, because once he realized she was inside, why would he have gone inside with her? These are residential bathrooms, not public restrooms with stalls for multiple people. And Dante *opened* the door from the inside, so he was most definitely inside that bathroom with her.

Something *has* to be going on between them. Or something went on between them while I was away, and now Dante is trying to mitigate the damage. Maybe he's lying to me about that because he knows I would hold that grudge forever, I would always hate her if she slept with Dante, even if it was when I was engaged to another man. It doesn't matter if it's fair; Dante could have never endured Declan's presence, and I would never be able trust that whatever was between him and this girl had completely fizzled, could never endure her presence at family events knowing Dante's hands had once traveled her naked body, knowing she might have curled up beside him in my spot on our bed. Dante keeps telling me she's not going to be around much longer, but no one else seems to agree with him. Maybe it's wishful thinking. Maybe he's *hoping* she goes away soon because as long as he can keep a lid on their involvement until she's gone, I will never know it happened.

At the end of the day, I don't know if it matters if he's lying to try to protect me from pain and jealousy I don't need to feel. I don't want him lying to me for any reason, period.

Just as that thought blows through my mind, the scent of coconut wafts my way and Mia comes breezing into the drawing room.

Without much thought, my hand shoots out and I grab her by the arm.

She gasps in surprise and whirls around to see who is accosting her, but her alarm softens when she sees it's only me. "Oh, hi, Colette."

I'm so tightly wound, the mere sound of her voice shatters my self-control. My hand on her bicep tightens and I head toward a quieter corner of the room. "Come with me. We're going to have a little talk."

Since I don't really know her, I don't know whether she'll whip her arm out of my grasp and tell me to fuck off, call for Mateo since apparently she holds some sway with him, or perhaps follow me, watch me with amusement dancing in her eyes as she relives all the times she's fucked my man.

My own thoughts make me so angry, it takes me a minute to process that she has let me haul her across the room to a quiet spot, and now she's waiting—confused, but patient—to see what I want with her.

Now that we're here, I don't even know what to say. I've never been in this situation before. I did have a high school boyfriend cheat on me, but I didn't say shit to the girl he cheated with, I just reamed the bastard I was dating. This is different, though. Dante didn't cheat on me, he just maybe sparked up a relationship with someone else when I abandoned him and left him all by himself.

I fucking suck.

I'm so confused, so angry, but I still want to bash this girl's head against the ground if he ever touched her. I'm so overwhelmed with emotion, I could almost cry.

I shake it off and channel the rage, trying to keep it in check enough to get a confession out of her. I don't know what I'll do once I get one, but—

"How have you been doing?" she inquires, regarding me like this is a social interaction and not a confrontation.

"I've been great," I snap. "Back in Dante's bed where I belong."

Her eyebrows rise and fall in momentary surprise, but once she recovers, she offers a smile. "Oh. Well, good. I'm glad to hear that."

Sure she fucking is. I narrow my eyes at her and she frowns.

"Is something the matter?" she asks me.

"I like your shoes," I say, but my tone is still aggressive. I can't seem to help it.

Mia glances down at her shoes, then over to mine. "Thanks. I like yours, too."

"Yeah?" I ask, pouncing. "They look familiar?"

Now she cocks her head, looking back at the shoes, then slowly to my face. "No? Those aren't the ones you wore to family dinner."

"Did you and Dante fuck while I was gone?"

Her jaw drops, her cheeks pinken, and her eyes widen in shock. "What? No! Of course not."

"Don't lie to me."

Sighing with exasperation, Mia brings a hand to her forehead and shakes her head. "Jesus Christ, you two were made for each other."

"What does *that* mean?" I ask sharply.

Before she can answer, Mateo's voice suddenly cuts through my rage fog as he approaches me from behind.

"What's going on over here?"

Mia answers tiredly, "I don't know, your whole family seems to be on a collective mission to get me in trouble with Vince today."

Mateo catches my gaze, holds it for a couple seconds, then lets his gaze drift to Mia. I felt sternness in his gaze when he looked at me, a silent warning to let him cut in and handle this, but when he looks back at Mia, it's gone. "Only I'm allowed to do that," he jokes.

Mia shoots him a look.

"Go on, head back to Vince before he gets pissy," he tells her.

I attempt to stop her departure. "But I need to—"

Mateo lightly grabs my upper arm and shakes his head. "No, you don't." He nods at her again, "Go on, Mia."

I grit my teeth and glare at him, but I don't say another word to Mia as she cautiously regards me, then walks away.

Once she's gone, rather than talk to me, Mateo nods toward the exit to the hallway. "Outside. Let's go have a chat."

Despite the knowledge that he can't actually hurt me—Dante would never allow it—a faint wave of concern moves through me at the curtness of his tone. I let him haul me out into the hallway since there's no point in putting up a fight and making a scene. I'm tempted to, since I'm not supposed to be alone with Mateo, but given I think he's about to reprimand me, I'm not even remotely concerned he has romantic intentions.

Once we're alone in the hallway, Mateo releases my arm and moves to stand in front of me. "Now, what was that all about?"

"There's something going on between her and Dante," I state.

"There isn't," Mateo replies without even a trace of doubt.

"Then there was. Maybe while I was away, but there's... there's still something."

"Nothing happened between them while you were away, and nothing is happening now. Mia never even formally *met* Dante until he brought you to dinner. He doesn't socialize with us much anymore."

"You're wrong. I can feel it. And there's this little stuff, these little instincts. Like, I don't know, I had this thought when I opened my walk-in closet at Dante's house and saw the clothes and shoes he bought for me. You know Dante, he doesn't know shit about women's fashion, but there were these stylish outfits in the closet and I just had this *feeling* that he had some girlfriend to waste time with while I was gone, and he must have made her pick out some things for me so I would have some stuff to wear when I first got there." Jabbing an accusing finger back toward the drawing room, I tell him, "And they're *her* style."

Smiling faintly, Mateo tucks his hands into his pockets. "Colette, Mia makes $8 an hour. Her style is whatever happens to be on sale at Target."

Frowning at the mental image of the expensive outfits I've seen her in, I open my mouth to object, but he speaks again before I can.

"Anything Mia has that's high-quality, I bought for her. The reason the clothes in your closet were the same style as Mia's is because *my* personal shopper is the one who picked them out for you. As you said, Dante can't shop for shit. I already had someone trained to shop for Mia and Meg. I remembered you wearing the same style of outfits before you left, so I told her to pick out a few things for you and then Dante bought them."

My temper falls a few notches. "You…?"

"Me," he verifies.

Well, okay, that explains that. "There's other stuff, too," I tell him, shaking my head. "It's not just that, it was… Like, she made a point to come over when I was sleeping one day to visit Dante when she had to drop things off for me."

"You're attributing false motives to Mia's actions based on your own insecurities. It's not true," Mateo states. "Mia *did* bring your medication over because Vince asked her to, but she was simply doing her boyfriend a favor. She'd never even been to Dante's house before that; she had to call me to ask for directions."

That knocks more wind out of my sails. "She did?"

He nods his head. "This great love affair is all in your head. You're inventing reasons to believe it and you have to stop. Mia hasn't done anything to you, and you would like her if you got to know her. That will never happen if you keep casting her in this role she doesn't deserve. Mia has nothing to do with Dante. Any interaction they have had hasn't been because she was initiating it."

Because I'm so deep inside my cocoon of crazy, all I process is the last part. "You're saying *he's* initiating?"

Mateo pauses briefly, like he needs to figure out which path to take through the maze of my irrationality. "No, I'm saying there *is* no interaction between them—not enough to remark on, anyway."

Crossing my arms over my chest, I tell him, "You're wrong. Right before you intervened, the whole reason I pulled her aside was because I *saw* them walk out of the bathroom together. Why are two people who have nothing to do with each other locked inside a bathroom together?"

Mateo is a tall man and he always uses that height to his advantage, but as he receives this new information, he puffs up and seems to grow even larger. He doesn't have an immediate response for that one, so rather than answer me, he takes me by the arm again and proceeds to lead me down the hall away from the drawing room.

"I'm not sure about that one, but I'll find out. The point is, I'm not guessing or assuming or giving the benefit of the doubt here. I am telling you, without question, there is nothing between Mia and Dante; there never has been, and obviously there never will be. He hasn't gone to all this trouble to get you back so he can pursue someone else. Think it over, Colette. That doesn't make any sense."

"Coming back hasn't been easy," I tell him. "Maybe… I don't

know. Maybe Dante's tired of fighting for me. Maybe he can't get over the fact that I almost married someone else and some part of him wants to get back at me. Maybe whatever new thing he feels for her is easier than fixing things with me. You said he only really met her after I came back, so maybe his attraction to her is new."

"He is not attracted to her," Mateo states, but so firmly, I don't think it's for me as much as for him. He wants to believe that as much as I do, maybe more.

"I think he is," I tell him, miserably.

Mateo's gaze is sharp, sharper than I've seen it in a long time. "What's going on with you two? You seemed cozy at the gravesite. I thought everything was moving along nicely."

"It… it is, but it's far from perfect. I have these blocks that I can't seem to get past, and sometimes I can tell Dante is tired of trying to push past them. Sometimes I make him so mad, he doesn't even come home because he doesn't want to be around me."

Stopping short, Mateo whips around to shoot me a dirty look. "Well, why the fuck are you doing that?"

"Because he's a terrible person! And he won't let me ignore it like he did before. He took me to Luca's house, Mateo. Do you know what that was like?"

Mateo stops walking, so I slow to a stop behind him. He runs a hand through his hair and appears to be grabbing for patience he can't find. "Why the fuck would he do that?"

"I don't know. That's what I'm saying, what if he's testing me like that to *try* to push me away? He may not even realize it's what he's doing, but… why else show me something so ugly? I can't forget it now. I can't go to sleep at night and not know… he's out there every day doing horrifying things, things more horrifying than I ever imagined. And I feel awful loving someone who is out there doing that kind of thing to people—and he's not just capable of it, he's remorseless about it."

"Jesus fucking Christ," he mutters under his breath. He's only exasperated for a second or two, then he collects himself and looks back at me. "All right. Look, I'm going to tell you something to help you, but this is for your ears only. You can't tell Dante. I will tell him when the time is right, but it has to come from me. You can't squeal on me if I tell you first."

"I won't," I promise.

"Luca won't be working for us much longer. That whole operation, everything you saw there, that's going away. We're getting out of that business entirely. We won't be doing anything that dirty anymore; we're in the process of shutting it all down right now."

I don't even realize we have stopped walking just outside Mateo's study until the door drifts open and Dante leans against the door frame, holding a glass of amber-colored alcohol and staring intently at his brother.

"Is that so?" Dante asks, cocking his head. "Well, that's news to me."

Mateo cuts a look at Dante. Without looking back in my direction, he orders, "Go back to the drawing room, Colette. My brother and I need to have a little talk."

"Damn right we do," Dante agrees. "But I don't think it's your place to order around *my* woman."

"I don't think you want to talk to me about that right now," Mateo informs him, his dark eyes flashing with annoyance.

Holding up my hand to intervene, I inform them, "I'm going

back to the drawing room. Should I send Adrian to play mediator?"

"No," Mateo says, still holding Dante's gaze. "I've got it under control."

I'm not entirely sure that's true, but after a moment's hesitation, I turn around and leave them to it.

31

DANTE

COLETTE ISN'T EVEN out of sight yet, but I can't hold back. "We're in the process of shutting down the entire trafficking operation, huh? When did that happen?"

Instead of answering my question, Mateo brushes past me and walks deeper into the study, approaching his alcohol cart and pouring himself a stiff drink. Once he's taken a couple sips, he turns around, meets my gaze, and asks, "What exactly were you doing locked inside a bathroom with Mia?"

"Playing truth or dare," I deadpan. "What the fuck are you thinking, Mateo? I know the investigation into Rob's house is bullshit. I talked to my contact at the police department and she said there's no fucking investigation and you're just full of shit."

"It doesn't matter if there's an investigation or not," he snaps. "There could be, easily, and it's not a risk we need to take anymore. I'm the head of this family now, I make the decisions about the kinds of business we do, and I have decided we're going to pull out of trafficking. End of fucking story."

"The fuck it is," I argue, slamming his study door shut and stalking across the room toward him. "That is my *main* fucking revenue stream, Mateo. You shut that down, you cost me literally *millions* each fucking year."

"Damn," Mateo states, like he doesn't give a single fuck.

My temper stirs. "Are you fucking shitting me right now? Damn? As much as I put into this fucking family, 'damn' is all you have to say?"

"All *you* put into this family? What about what *I* put into this family? I've invested and sacrificed more than any-fucking-body else, Dante. I've bled for this family, same as you. Just because I'm at the top now doesn't mean you get to forget that."

"You're the one who seems to be forgetting that," I tell him. "I'm not a fucking idiot, Mateo. I know exactly why you want to shut this arm of operations down all of a sudden, and it doesn't have a damn thing to do with the kind of heat it could bring down on us. It has *everything* to do with Vince's fucking do-gooder girlfriend. You didn't have any moral qualms about it until that fucking girl crashed our business meeting and told you to read some bullshit 'stop the trafficking' book. Are you the boss of this family now, or is she?"

"Maybe instead of worrying about my love life, you should focus on your own," he shoots back. "You have a second chance with Colette and you're blowing it."

"Oh, fuck you," I fling back. "You're the last person alive I'm gonna go to for relationship advice right now. You're shacked up with one bitch, half in love with another. Get your own fucking house in order before you start talking to me about mine."

The accusation that he doesn't have his personal life

together doesn't infuriate him like I hoped it might, but it does remind him that I never gave him a real answer to his question.

"You never explained why you were locked inside a bathroom with Mia," he states.

"I'm not going to, either. Fuck you. I'd say you can ask *her*, but she won't tell you." Meeting his gaze, I offer a dark smile and something I know will bait him. "Know why she won't tell you, Mateo? Because *I* told her not to."

His hands clench into fists. His nostrils flare as he breathes, his body's natural instincts preparing him to engage in a physical altercation. He makes no attempt whatsoever to mask his fury with a poker face, and that... I haven't seen that since we were kids.

If his openly emotional response hadn't been enough of a warning, the loathing in his gaze would tip me off that I might've pushed him too far. After a couple of seconds, his next words obliterate any doubt. "I'm giving Luca to Salvatore as a wedding present."

All the satisfaction I felt over getting a good dig in drains right out of me. My face falls since he caught me off-guard and I stare at him. "What the fuck are you talking about?"

"Luca abused our sister. We were assholes to let it slide. He's gone, as soon as all the houses are shut down."

Rage explodes inside my chest. I feel like I should burst open and kill my bastard brother with all the shrapnel. "Bullshit. *Bull-fucking-shit* this is about Francesca."

"Believe me or don't. Doesn't matter." Mateo smiles slightly, but there's still nothing but aggression in his eyes. "I'd tell you to say your goodbyes, but obviously you can't do that. Besides me, you and Colette are the only two people who know he's on his way out—Salvatore doesn't even know yet. Obviously *your* loyalty can't be questioned and *you're* not going to say anything, so if it somehow gets back to Luca and he runs before Sal can get to him, I'll have to kill Colette for ratting me out."

So much rage fills my body, everything locks up and I can't even move. "So it's like that."

Nodding once, he says, "It's like that."

I can't fucking believe he's putting me in this position. It's bad enough he's going to feed my only friend to the fucking wolves, but to tell me beforehand and then tie my hands like this... it's fucking cruel. "He's my best friend, Mateo."

"Guess you'll need to find a new one," he tells me, calmly.

Slowly, I shake my head. "You son of a bitch."

"Son of a sadistic monster, actually," he corrects. "And *thankfully,* he's fucking dead."

I guess he's twisted enough knives in my chest for the moment, because after refreshing his drink, Mateo walks past me without another word, leaving me to rage alone in his study while he returns to the party.

IT TAKES a while before I'm civil enough to walk back to the drawing room. I put a good dent in the best Scotch Mateo's alcohol cart has to offer and try to think of some way to get Luca out of Mateo's crosshairs, but I think it's too late.

I fucked up letting my temper get the best of me. I shouldn't have baited him with the girl. I know she makes him fucking crazy. He's already completely destroyed his relationship with Vince over her, and since Beth died, he and I aren't much closer. Mateo might still care more about Adrian than Mia, but not me.

And if he *did* go back to the party and press her about what happened in that bathroom, it's a lose-lose for me. If she obeys me and keeps her mouth shut, there won't be words for how pissed he'll be. If she spills her guts and tells him everything I said to her, all she'll have to repeat is the empty threat I made about feeding her to Luca—he'll know who I meant, based on what I said to her—and I may as well be the one loading Salvatore's fucking gun myself.

Fucking Salvatore Castellanos.

He's not the most accurate target for my anger, but he is the only one I can shoot at right now. It hits me how much of that Scotch I've consumed when I stand up and I'm unsteady on my feet. I shake it off, pull my shit together, and head back to the drawing room.

As soon as I get there, I search the room for Castellanos. I find him camped out in a corner looking cozy with Francesca. Seeing her even pisses me off, since she's the reason Mateo gave for deciding to kill Luca. I don't fucking believe that he's ready to kill Luca now over shit that happened years ago, but regardless of his real reasons, the result will be the same.

Salvatore catches my eye as I head in their direction. He must be able to tell I'm not coming over for anything pleasant, because he tugs away from my sister and pulls himself to his full height—still significantly shorter than me, the little fucker.

I'm just about to them when Mateo's words from the study break through the alcohol fog and I remember that he said Salvatore doesn't even know about Luca yet. I can't be the one to tell him. Mateo lies when he needs to, but he sure as shit doesn't bluff. He knows I'd never let him harm Colette, but that only means if he went after her to punish me for standing up to him, he'd kill me, too.

He might be willing to rip our fucking world apart over that girl, but I'm not.

By the time I stop in front of Salvatore, he's already sending my sister off to fetch him a drink. I can tell he anticipates this isn't gonna be a friendly, "welcome to the family" type interaction.

Francesca looks between us uncertainly, but she heads off anyway.

"Dante," Salvatore acknowledges with a nod once she's gone.

"Fancy seeing you here, at my father's funeral," I say, my words barbed.

Nodding once more, he says, "I'd invite you to *my* father's funeral, but we ran out of *My Little Pony* invitations. I know you were looking forward to it," he adds, slapping me on the arm. "Sorry, bud."

"Don't touch me," I tell him. "Mateo may welcome an alliance with your family, but me? I'm not convinced it's such a good idea."

"Yeah, well, it's not up to you, is it?" he tosses back rather casually, for such an irking fucking remark.

"Your boss is dead. Your family's weak," I state.

"Well, with me in charge and your sister by my side, I have a hunch we'll strengthen right back up," he tells me, mistakenly thinking I might be protective of my little sister.

Shrugging noncommittally, I toss back, "Oh, I don't know about that. Francesca's not that strong."

Up until I said that, he seemed unconcerned, like we were exchanging friendly barbs. Now his gray-eyed gaze turns icy and he takes a step closer to me. "Don't fucking talk about your sister that way. She's stronger than you'll ever be, you sick, selfish fuck."

Seeing that I've hit my mark, I offer him a dark smile. "Funny, Luca didn't think so."

Fury leaps beneath the surface of his icy gaze. I can feel the rage coming off him like it was coming off me just a few minutes ago. "I think you need to get the fuck away from me before I make my first Morelli family event a little too memorable and punch you right in the fucking face."

Turning my cheek, I point right to it. "Go ahead. First one's free."

I can tell he wants to. He takes another step toward me, his fists clenched so tightly, his knuckles are white. Rather than throw the punch he's dying to throw, though, he looks around the room and sees my sister walking back in our direction already. She must have been really worried about this talk to have retrieved the drinks so hastily.

"You're not worth it, you fucking scumbag," Sal tells me, shaking his head and taking a step back.

"Not worth skinning a few knuckles?" I question. "Funny, I think *you're* worth it."

"No, Dante. You're not worth upsetting your sister," he says, shaking his head like he's disgusted I didn't know what he meant.

Francesca hurries back to his side, offering him a drink and keeping one for herself. Her gaze jumps from him to me. We exchange pointless greetings, but she's the last person I want to talk to right now, so I make an excuse about going to find Colette and go to find more alcohol instead.

Doesn't much matter at this point that the cater waiters are serving sub-par shit. I take two to make up the difference in quality.

Eventually, Colette finds me sitting in a wing chair, alone in a corner.

"Hey, you," she says softly, her hand coming to rest on my shoulder.

I lean my head back against the chair and look over at her. "Hey, yourself."

Grimacing, she gingerly sits on the edge of the chair. "You want me to get you some water?"

"I'd rather you got the keys so we can get the fuck out of here," I tell her.

"We can't leave yet," she says apologetically. "They're reading the will after everyone leaves, the heirs have to stay for it."

"Fuck the will," I mutter.

"It's just a little longer," she assures me. For a few seconds, she looks at my thighs as if debating, then she slides off the arm of the chair and into my lap.

That's more fucking like it. I rest my hands on her hips and look up into her face.

She secures her arms around my neck and leans in close. I think she's going to kiss my neck, but instead she whispers, "I have to ask you something."

"What's that?" I murmur back.

She keeps her tone low to keep the cameras from catching what she says, but I can hear the anxiety in her voice. "Are you attracted to Mia?"

Just the sound of her name brings rage roaring through my veins. "Fuck that little cunt. No, I'm not fucking attracted to her. Why would you ask a stupid thing like that?"

"I saw you together in the hall. You were in the bathroom together. Why were you locked in the bathroom with her?"

"I don't fucking remember," I mutter, grabbing Colette around the back of the neck and pulling her closer so I can kiss her neck. "I don't want to talk about her anymore."

"I just… I'm obviously not comfortable with you sneaking off to be alone with other women."

"I wasn't sneaking off to—"

Colette brings her hand up to cover my mouth and she shakes my head. "We don't have to talk about it. You say you're not into her, I believe you. You say it won't happen again, I believe you. But don't lie to me, because if you start doing that, I can't believe you anymore."

I hold her gaze for a moment. Because I'm a little drunk, it takes longer than it should to recognize the hurt in her eyes. That pierces the fog and I grab her hand, bringing it to my mouth and kissing her knuckles in the tenderest of pledges. "Colette, there's no one for me but you. I said that and I meant it. I'm a lot of things, but I'm not a fucking liar."

Her gaze is a little less guarded now. "I know you're not."

"It wasn't anything like you're thinking," I assure her.

"I feel… I feel like there's a vibe between you two," she tells me, clearly uncomfortable saying it.

"There is a vibe," I tell her. Just as her face starts to fall, I add, "It's hatred. That bitch controls my fucking brother and I feel a passionate loathing toward her because of it; I'm not surprised you can feel it."

Colette sighs with relief, then melts against me. "That makes me feel better."

I shake my head, letting my hand come to rest at the small of her back. "You never have to worry about me with other women, Colette. You know that. I might have to deal with women sometimes when it comes to business, but there's only one I want, only one I give a fuck about, and that's you. Never doubt that."

Snuggling into the curve of my neck, she starts kissing me. Between kisses, she tells me quietly, "I think I got a taste of how you felt about Declan today."

"No, you didn't," I disagree. "When I felt that way about you and Declan, it was real. I was never fucking with Mia, that was all in your head. I had damn good reason to feel like a fucking maniac."

"I know," she assures me, pulling back to meet my gaze. "And I'm so sorry. I never should have left. Not just because then he'd be alive, I just..." She looks away, swallows, then looks back at me. "I shouldn't have left you when things got hard. I should have trusted you. I should have waited and made you talk to me when the time was right and everything wasn't so fresh. I shouldn't have left."

How fucking long have I been waiting to hear those words? They wash over my soul, pulling away the pain and anger from today. "Yeah?" I ask, a bit leadingly. "Why's that?"

"Because you're my man and I love you," she answers sweetly, kissing each corner of my mouth. "And you're not supposed to hurt your man."

The first real smile of the day spreads across my face. I grab the back of her neck again, yank her close, and kiss her hard on the mouth. "Damn right, you're not."

32

COLETTE

THE REAL WORLD doesn't find me as quickly as Dante feared it might, but eventually, the inevitable happens and my past does come knocking at my door.

It's a slow day at the flower shop and I'm the only one up front. The bell above the door jingles, letting me know I have a customer. My heart sinks when I recognize Declan's brother, Russ, walking toward me.

I don't know exactly what to say. He doesn't look friendly, but he doesn't look aggressive, either. I guess he still looks kind of sad. I guess that's reasonable. The people who truly loved Declan will be sad for a lot longer.

Guilt wraps itself around me like a vine, but I snip my way out of its suffocating grasp and stand tall behind the counter.

I'm still immensely regretful for what Dante did to Declan, but nothing I say or do now can fix it. If I had realized Dante would take it that far, I would have stopped it, but I didn't. No measure of miserable guilt or wretched unhappiness now will resurrect him, and I choose to believe Declan would want me to be happy. I may have been the reason he died, but it's not like I wanted it. I did care for Declan, but now I realize I never actually loved him. And Declan cared for me, but he still dismissed my rational fears about Dante coming back for me and told me I had anxiety issues.

I would've been just as miserable—and just as much to blame—if Declan had died saving me, pushing me out of the way of a train or a car that I didn't see coming. But he would have done it. Even knowing the risk to himself, Declan would have tried to save me—in fact, he did, it's just that the unstoppable force he tried to rescue me from was Dante, and he failed.

At the end of the day, I did warn Declan about Dante being dangerous, and he chose to take the risk of being with me anyway. I didn't make him. He's the one who pursued me, he's the one who stayed even after finding out I had belonged to Dante Morelli before he met me. Declan knows the players in Chicago's underworld; he should have known once something belongs to Dante Morelli, it always belongs to him.

Alec was right; I can't take all of that blame onto my shoulders anymore. It was my responsibility to make Declan aware of the risk, but it wasn't my responsibility to live my whole life cloistered away, not even living, to make sure Dante didn't hurt anyone.

It wasn't easy to get to this place mentally, but this is where I had to get if I wanted to be with Dante. Realizing he might want someone other than me made me see that I still do, I always will, and it's not worth risking what I have with him to protect the memory of someone who is gone.

I haven't become heartless, I've just had to be more selective about who gets space there, and Declan and Dante can't both reside in the same space.

"Hi," I say, since Russ hasn't spoken.

"Colette," he acknowledges, his gaze falling automatically to my empty ring finger. Bringing his gaze back to my face, he says, "You look well."

"I am, yeah," I say awkwardly, shifting my weight, unsure where to look. Just because I'm in a different headspace now is no reason to be callous. I'm not actively mourning his brother anymore, but it would probably be easier for Russ to swallow if he thought I was. "As well as can be expected, anyway."

His lips curve upward, but the smile doesn't reach his eyes. "Yeah. Seems like you're really suffering from the loss." He barely misses a beat, definitely doesn't give me time to respond. "Mom got the package you dropped off on her doorstep. Thought it was a little cold. You could've at least called; she would've made sure she was home to receive you."

"I just..." I trail off, then go with the simple truth. "I didn't know what to say to her."

He presses his lips together and nods. "I bet. If I got someone killed, I wouldn't know what to say to his mother, either."

My blood runs cold and my gaze jumps to his. "What are you talking about?"

"I never liked you, you know," he states, the gloves apparently coming off now that his brother's dead. "I told Declan not to get involved with you. You were filthy, but he thought you were perfect."

More than a little offended, I say, "Ex*cuse* me? Who do you think you are, coming into *my* flower shop, saying this shit to me?"

"I think I'm the one who lost a brother, and you're the one already warming the bed of your mobster ex-boyfriend," he shoots back. "Didn't take you very fucking long to grieve, did it, Colette? Did you care about my brother at all?"

Panic hasn't hit me in a while, but as I stand here across from this man, I can feel it starting to claw its way along my insides. "You need to leave, Russ."

"Or what? You'll sic your boyfriend on me?"

"Maybe," I snap, my eyes flashing. "Maybe I fucking will. Get out of my goddamn shop!"

"I thought you'd break his heart, hell, maybe even ruin his life, but I didn't think you'd get him killed," he states, shaking his head as he backs toward the door. "You're an evil bitch, I hope you know that."

"Get out!"

I'M calm by the time I close up shop and head home, but I still feel the inky remnants of dread clinging to me until I pull into the driveway. With each step toward the door, I'm filled with more peace, my sense of safety affirmed. Dante shouldn't be home yet, but I saw his car in the garage, so I know as soon as I'm through the door, he'll be there to melt away the stress of the day.

I hang my keys on the hook, drop my purse on the small table nearby, and kick the heels off my aching feet. Contentment washes over me as I pad through the house, then my heart practically explodes, affection running out of my chest cavity and coating all of my insides at the sight before me on the couch.

Dante is lying on the couch with the kitten he bought me sleeping soundly on his chest. Daisy is curled in a tiny ball with her little eyes closed while Dante absently runs his massive hand along her tiny back. She's so fragile and he's so strong, but his touch is so gentle when he pets her, it melts my insides.

My big brute can be tender when he needs to be.

With a warm smile I can't suppress all over my face, I walk over to the couch and kneel down in front of them since he's taking up the whole thing. If he moves, he'll wake Daisy, and I don't know how long she's been asleep.

"What are you doing home already?" I ask him quietly.

Less concerned about Daisy's naptime and more concerned about my comfort, Dante scoops her up in one hand and sits up to make room for me on the couch beside him. "Decided to beg off early," he tells me. "Luca's house is finally empty, so this is his last night there. Mateo told me if I want to see him one last time, I needed to go early."

Taking a seat beside him and curling my legs up behind me, I ask, "Did you?"

Dante shakes his head no, looking down at Daisy as she yawns and climbs onto his chest. "No. Wouldn't feel right, knowing what I know and not telling him."

Sighing, I pull on his shoulder to move him, then climb on my knees behind him so I can give him a back rub. "I'm sorry, baby. I know how it feels to lose a friend. I can't imagine knowing about it beforehand and not being able to stop it."

"After all the good work Luca has done for us, all the loyalty he's shown this family, he doesn't fucking deserve this."

I hold my tongue, kneading his tense muscles. While Dante

and I are very happy together, we're obviously very different people. Consequently, we don't always agree on everything.

He and I *definitely* don't agree about this. On this, I'm on Mateo's side. I think Luca Delmonico is the kind of monster that desperately needs to be vanquished, and I'm glad Mateo's going to kill him. There would be no benefit in saying that to Dante though, so instead I nod my head, massage his shoulders, and lend my support. "I know. It's hard."

"He's a bastard," he states.

"He's your brother," I remind him, gently. "I know it won't be easy to get past this, but you will in time. You have to. Carrying resentment over things you can't change will only hurt you, not him."

"When did you become the expert?" he murmurs.

"When the love of my life murdered my fiancé and I had to get over it," I offer back.

"Stupid fucking Declan," he mutters. "I put out the hit, but Luca was actually the one who killed him."

All the more reason I feel no remorse over the monster's death. "Life goes on, that's the point. I know Luca was important to you while I was gone, but I don't think you were as important to him, and now that I'm back home... we can fill any empty spaces we find in each other. We don't need other people so much anymore."

"I can't argue with that," he tells me, catching my hand on his shoulder and dragging it in toward his chest. As soon as Daisy catches sight of my hand, she climbs over and flops on her back, grabbing my finger between her little paws and playfully nipping me with her pointy kitten teeth.

I grin, reaching over his shoulder with my other hand and scooping her up. I bring her against my chest and lean back into the couch cushion. "Hello, little girl. Did you miss me while I was at work? I sure missed you."

She meows at me and closes her eyes, rubbing the top of her head against my hand.

"Did Daddy feed you?" I ask her, as if she can answer me.

"Sonja took care of it before I got here," he answers.

I screw my nose up and make a face at Daisy. "Did mean old Sonja feed you yummy kitty food?"

Dante cracks a smile and flicks a gaze toward the kitchen. "Better be quiet or she'll hear you."

No longer talking in my sweet kitten mom voice, I tell him, "Let her hear me. I've had it up to here with people giving me shit today. I don't care who doesn't like me anymore. Fuck 'em all."

Scowling, Dante asks, "Who else doesn't like you?"

I've been dreading telling him all day, but it would be foolish not to. "Declan's brother paid me a visit today."

Dante sits up a little straighter, more alert. "What did he have to say?"

I tease Daisy with my finger as I tell him, "He knows we're back together. I'm not sure how. He wasn't there for long. He started hurling insults and I kicked him out."

"Hurling insults?" he asks, sharply. "You should've called me."

"I handled it myself. He didn't put up a fight or anything. Anyway, it pissed me off, but he was just venting. I get it, but it's still damned aggravating when someone's being rude to you. I didn't handle it very compassionately, I told him to leave and he asked if I'd sic my boyfriend on him if I didn't. I might have shouted back 'maybe' but I don't think he took me seriously."

Dante harrumphs and rolls his eyes. "Boyfriend. Sounds so insignificant."

"Next time I'll make sure to tell my ex-fiancé's grieving brother he better address you as my man, not my boyfriend like we're in high school."

"Damn right," he mutters, reaching over and rubbing Daisy's head with the tip of his index finger. "Come here, you."

I let him take her, then watch as he rises off the couch. "Where are you going?"

"She's gonna help me find something. Why don't you go ask Sonja how much longer on dinner? Grab us some drinks while you're in there."

I sigh as he takes my kitty and disappears into the other room. I don't feel like dealing with Sonja, but maybe she'll sense it on me and be cool. I push up off the couch and head to the kitchen. She's busy wiping down the counter when I come in. She looks at my arms for the kitten, since more often than not that's where she is. Apparently disappointed that it's only me, she turns back to wiping down the counter.

"How much longer until dinner's done, Sonja?"

"Twenty minutes or so." She looks back over her shoulder at me as I grab a wine bottle and open a drawer to dig out the corkscrew. "You'll ruin your appetite."

"I can manage my own appetite, thank you," I assure her, feeling a little rebellious as I pop it off and grab two wine glasses from the cupboard above me. I pour some of the white wine into a glass for Dante while she mutters under her breath. On second thought, I put the cap back on and go to the fridge, grabbing an unopened bottle of water and pouring that into my glass instead. "There? Feel better."

With a satisfied huff, she mutters, "I slave away all day to make your favorite meal, least you can do is eat it."

I roll my eyes at her and grab the wine glasses, heading back to the couch to wait for Dante. A minute or so later, he sinks back into the couch, puts Daisy on his chest, and puts one of her toys down on his chest for her to play with. She doesn't play with her toys much, probably because the colorful rat toy beside her is the size of her whole head. She still tries to tackle it, though, and it's adorable to watch her attempts to best the little plushy mouse.

Sighing, I lean my head on his arm and watch Daisy play. "She's so cute. I can't handle it."

"She is pretty cute," he acknowledges. "Do I win the 'best boyfriend' award for picking out such a cute kitten?"

I elbow him for the tone of his voice as he ridicules the term boyfriend. I know he's not a fan, I never call him that myself, but it *is* the conventional term for what he is, so he shouldn't be so salty Declan's brother used it.

"What would you prefer I call you, then?" I ask, lightly teasing.

"How about husband?" he suggests.

My stomach drops at the mere idea of referring to him as my husband. I lean forward to grab my wine glass and take a sip, then I put it down and lean back on the couch. "Maybe someday."

"How about next weekend?" he asks.

I stare at him, my tummy turning over and over. "What are you talking about?"

"I told Mateo I need to take a week or so off after everything goes down." Reaching past Daisy and into his jacket pocket, he draws out a box I recognize from the day I rummaged through the junk drawer.

"Dante..." I breathe, staring at the ring box. "It's... it's so soon. I haven't even been back for that long..."

"Doesn't matter," he states, lazily popping it open to show me the gorgeous diamond ring nestled there. "I've wanted you since before I even knew your name, Colette. I think it's time you finally took mine."

My heart pounds like a drum and my stomach is a mess. My hands tremble as I draw the ring out of the box and slide it on my empty finger to see how it looks. "It's so beautiful, Dante."

Daisy catches sight of something shiny and abandons her mouse, crawling across Dante to get to me. She watches my ring, then flops down on my hand and rolls around on top of it. I laugh at her, surprised at the faint burn of tears behind my eyes. I don't know why I'm crying, but before I can even think about it, big, dumb tears well up in my eyes.

"Is that a yes?" Dante asks, faintly amused. "Daisy thinks you should say yes."

"Do I even get a say?" I ask, only halfway joking.

"Of course. Unless you say no," he replies, also only halfway joking.

I laugh and push him in the arm, then I scoop up Daisy so I don't crush her and lean in to kiss him. "Yes. Of course I'll marry you, you crazy man."

"Good. I already have us booked for a honeymoon suite in Santorini, so I would've had to kidnap you again if you'd have said no."

"Well, we wouldn't want that, now would we? I've been your captive girlfriend, no need to make me your captive bride, too."

"Now no one can ever call me your fucking boyfriend again," he states, satisfied.

"Are we inviting your family to the wedding?" I inquire.

"Nope," he states. "It'll be me, you, and Daisy."

I grin at him. "We're bringing Daisy?"

"Of course we are. She's part of the family, isn't she?"

Grinning bigger, I lean in and kiss him again. "I love you."

"I love you, too."

33

COLETTE

AFTER A GORGEOUS DAY spent sailing the clear blue sea on a chartered yacht, the sun is down and we have made our way back to the hotel to rest up before the big day tomorrow. We already had a delicious dinner prepared for us by the chef on the staffed yacht, but when Dante comes out to join me on our private balcony overlooking the water, he brings a plate of fresh fruit.

"Mm, my hero," I tell him, snuggling back against him and taking the plate.

"If my bride is hungry, it's my job to make sure she has a snack," he tells me, wrapping his arms around me snugly.

Biting into a juicy strawberry, I sigh with contentment and rest my head back against his shoulder. "This is nice. I'm glad we came a few days early. I haven't been on a vacation in forever."

"Your lawyer didn't take you anywhere?" he asks, but without any heat.

I shake my head and take another bite of my strawberry. "Wouldn't have been the same without you. You're my favorite travel buddy."

Squeezing my side and wordlessly threatening to tickle me, he says, "Buddy. That's worse than boyfriend."

"My favorite travel person," I offer, tipping my head back to look up at his beautiful face. "How's that?"

He bends to kiss my forehead. "Better."

"Greece is as beautiful as I remember it," I tell him, looking back out at the ocean of blue under the dark evening sky.

His arms tighten around me. "Yes, it is."

Inside our room, a beautiful white dress hangs on the outside of the closet door. Tomorrow, I'll wear it on the beach at sunset, at my wedding. It won't be quite the way I always imagined it—none of our loved ones will be there, not even my future husband's family. It will be us, an officiant, and a photographer—no one else. It still feels more like my perfect wedding than the one I planned with Declan, because this one has the right groom. The night before my wedding to Declan, I couldn't stop looking at my bridal gown and obsessing over the details, but tonight, everything else is an afterthought. The details don't matter, only the end result. After the longest of roads, tomorrow I will finally marry the man my heart belongs to.

"I have a wedding gift for you," I tell him, grabbing another delicious strawberry. "Do you want it tonight, or would you rather wait until after we're actually married?"

"You didn't have to get me a gift," he states, rather surly for a man about to receive a present. "Spending the rest of your life with me is your gift. It's good for birthdays," he says, kissing the ball of my shoulder, "Christmases," he adds, kissing his way in toward my neck. "All the gift-giving holidays."

"That doesn't seem fair. You get me gifts all the time," I tell him.

"You like getting gifts. I don't."

Sighing, I shoot him a grumpy look back over my shoulder. "Well, you'll like this one, you big ingrate. Now, do you want it tonight or tomorrow?"

"Up to you."

I shake my head. "You're such a pain in the ass."

"So are you," he informs me.

"I'm your favorite pain in the ass," I tell him, leaning back to shoot him a cheeky grin.

"My very favorite," he agrees.

I smile and pucker up my lips for a kiss. He leans down and gives me one, so I murmur against his lips, "Don't worry, you're my favorite, too."

"I wasn't worried," he states.

"Ugh." I grab a pillow from the couch we're lounging on and hit him with it. "Forget it, no gift for you, you arrogant man."

"Oh, come on," he says, taking the pillow from me and tossing it to the other end of the cushion. "I'm looking forward to it now."

"You are not," I say, sullenly.

"I am. I've never been so excited in my life," he insists.

"Don't you lie to me, Dante Morelli."

"I would never," he promises.

"Well, it's too late now," I tell him, cheekily. "No present for you."

He lets me finish my strawberry, but as soon as I deposit the top on the plate, he snatches it out of my hand.

"Hey," I object, as he sits up and forces me forward. "You're my comfy cushion, what are you doing?"

"Taking my present." He puts the fruit plate down and lifts me into his arms. I wrap my arm around his neck and he carries me inside, past the couch and Daisy's kitten bed where she's curled up, soundly sleeping. He carries me all the way to the bedroom, but before he can toss me down like he usually does, I lock my arms around his neck.

"Gently, please."

He cocks an eyebrow at my unnatural request, but puts me down softly anyway.

As soon as he climbs on top of me, my hands slide under the crisp white fabric of his T-shirt. "I'll never get used to you in casual wear," I tell him.

Smirking and nodding at the bikini top I'm wearing, he says, "Funny, your casual wear is my favorite part of vacations."

Inexpertly, I yank his shirt off and fling it off the bed. Biting down on my lip, I look over his sun-bronzed skin, running my fingers over the chiseled muscles along his abdomen. "God, you're hot."

That startles a little laugh out of him. "Oh yeah?" he asks, leadingly, lowering himself to eliminate the distance between our bodies.

"That's my opinion, anyway," I tease, snaking my hands down between us and unbuttoning his charcoal grey shorts.

"Your opinion's the only one that counts," he assures me.

Sighing with contentment, I bring my arms up and wrap them around his neck, looking into his dark eyes. "I love you."

His lips curve up only a little, but I can see his happiness in his eyes. My heart fills up because I know I'm the one who put it there.

His gaze leaves mine and rakes over my body beneath him, then he unfastens my sarong and spreads it open. Next, he slides his hands down the front of my bathing suit bottoms. I gasp and hold onto him tighter, but all of a sudden, I can't keep in my surprise any longer.

"Wait," I tell him, closing my legs on his hand. "I changed my mind. I don't want to wait. I want to give you your wedding present now."

Clearly unimpressed with my timing, he asks, "*Right* now?"

"Right this very moment."

"You want me to let you off the bed, *right now?*"

I shake my head, barely biting back a grin. "I don't have to get off the bed, I have it right here with me."

His eyes narrow with suspicion. "Must be a tiny gift."

I nod my agreement. "Very tiny."

"Where is this tiny, mysterious present?"

Silently thanking him for the perfect set-up, I grab his big hand and flatten it over my tummy.

His gaze sharpens, his playfulness dissipating. "You're pregnant?"

Nodding my head, I tell him, "You're gonna be a daddy."

"I'm gonna be a daddy," he repeats, in mild disbelief.

Biting down on my bottom lip, I nod more vigorously. "Are you… excited?"

For a moment that drags on long enough for me to get nervous, he doesn't respond. I can't quite read his face, so I'm not sure what he's feeling. A couple more seconds pass and I start to panic, wondering if his messed up childhood has shaped him differently, given him a skewed view of what it means to become a father. I know he wanted to get me pregnant, but the panic clouds my thinking and I can't be sure if it was because he felt ready to start a family, or just because he wanted to mark me.

Before I have time to work myself up into a full-blown panic, Dante envelops me in the tightest hug he's ever given me. "We're gonna have a baby."

Relief sets in and reignites my excitement. Squeezing him back, I tell him, "We sure are."

"I can't believe it." Pulling back, he asks, "How long have you known?"

"Not long," I assure him. "I held onto it instead of telling you right away because I wanted it to be special. I figured holed up in a honeymoon cave in Greece, the night before we get married? Probably the right time."

"Christ. You've outdone me; this is a better gift than a kitten."

Grinning up at him, I lightly shove him in his well-muscled chest. "Hey, Daisy is delightful."

Grabbing the back of my neck, he kisses me and murmurs against my lips, "You're delightful."

I can't resist teasing him just one more time, so I break away from the kiss and ask innocently, "Best girlfriend ever?"

Dante rolls his eyes at me. "Best *wife* ever."

EPILOGUE

DANTE

IF THERE'S one thing you can always count on at a party my brother is paying for, it's that he will spare no expense and go completely overboard.

Today, we're here for my niece Rosalie's sixth birthday party. I know Rosalie is crazy for princesses, so I guess I shouldn't be surprised when we stroll through the archway into the back yard and it looks like a fucking carnival is in town. Disney princesses have their own zones—Elsa is passing out snow cones, Belle is reading to a small group of children under a rose-adorned canopy, Tiana is hosting some kind of cooking class, and Ariel is set up by the pool showing a little girl a fork and inexplicably using it to brush a lock of her long red hair. Cinderella is all decked out in a ball gown, but she's running around cleaning up after everyone, affecting a painfully cute voice and saying things like, "Oh, my, how did this mess get here? Better clean it up before Gus Gus finds it. He'll get a tummy ache if he eats all this food."

It is utterly ridiculous.

Beside me, I hear a gasp and a small hand clutches mine tightly. I look down at my daughter and see her eyes wide with wonder. "Daddy, look at all the princesses!" Tugging desperately on my hand, she attempts to drag me across the lawn. "Come on, come on!"

"Look, there's a bounce house, too," Colette points out, adjusting our fussy son on her shoulder and gently patting his back.

"And a unicorn!" Gia shrieks, releasing my hand and dashing toward a white pony decked out in purple flowers with a horn on its head. She stops after only a few feet though, looking around as if she can't decide where to go first.

A familiar voice rings out, drawing my attention to the French doors leading out of the house and into the back yard. Mia approaches with a big smile on her face and a veggie tray in her hands. "You made it. We waited a few minutes, but the princesses—" She stops, looking down at Gia, then decides not to say whatever she had been planning to say. "Oh, look at this, we have another princess in attendance. I love your dress, Gia."

Gia puffs up with pride and smiles. "Thanks! I picked it out myself."

"You have excellent taste," Mia assures her, bending down to match her height. "Would you like a carrot stick to munch on?"

"She doesn't eat carrots," I tell Mia, just before my daughter runs over and snatches a carrot stick off the tray like it's a chocolate bar.

Mia smirks up at me. "She does for me."

I shake my head at her. "Witch."

"Thanks, Aunt Mia." Gia takes a bite of the carrot stick, then looks around. "There's so many princesses, I don't know what one to pick."

"Well, you don't have to pick. They're here all day, so you'll have plenty of time to do everything. Tiana's teaching us how to make her famous beignets, but the powdered sugar can be a little messy, so if you head there first, make sure to grab an apron so you don't ruin your pretty dress, okay? Did you bring a swimsuit?"

Gia nods and points back at Colette. "My mommy has it."

"Oh, good. You might get wet playing with Ariel, so maybe save that one for a little later since you're dressed so nicely right now. Rapunzel is painting faces over by her tower, how about you start over there?"

"Yeah! Can I pet the unicorn, too?"

"Of course you can," Mia says, glancing over at the unicorn. "Her name is Glimmer, she's from Rosalie's favorite book series. A little bit later, Glimmer is going to take kids on princess carriage rides around the driveway. Won't that be fun?"

"Yeah, yeah!"

"Do unicorns usually pull carriages?" I inquire, earning a hard nudge and a dirty look from my wife.

"Let them enjoy the magic, you meanie."

"You realize now the next party we throw her is going to be a massive disappointment, right?" I point out.

Smiling faintly as she surveys the massive back yard that Mia has transformed into a child's wonderland, Colette tells me, "Maybe we should ask Mia to plan it."

"Maybe I should stab myself in the eye with a hot poker."

Colette shrugs. "You could pull off an eye patch. Like a hot pirate. Mmmm."

Despite myself, I feel a smile tugging at the corners of my

lips. I stifle it and wrap an arm around my wife's waist, absently leaning over and kissing her temple.

Apparently furious that Colette and I are enjoying ourselves for a moment, our grumpy, teething son smacks me right in the head. I turn my head slowly and meet his gaze, a move that would make grown men shit themselves, but Marco just drools all over the offending fist. "Da da!"

"Aw, he didn't mean it," Colette lies, affectionately kissing the side of his head.

Marco grins at me victoriously, then bobs and turns his attention to his mom, starting to whine again.

"What's wrong, baby?" she asks, swaying and kissing his head again. "Do your gums hurt?"

"Aunt Mia, come on," my daughter prods. I look over to see her tugging on Mia's free hand impatiently, eager to get her face painted.

"Just one second, honey, I want to say hi to your brother."

Gia sighs and releases Mia's hand, crossing her arms and scowling. Mia wanders over to Colette, who turns so Marco can see her.

"Hello there, you handsome little man," Mia says, offering her finger for him to grab. "I haven't seen you in a while. Boy, you got big!"

"He's a little grump today," Colette says apologetically.

"He must take after his daddy," Mia jokes.

"He likes you; he certainly doesn't get *that* from me," I offer, dryly.

"Daddy, that's not nice at all," Gia informs me, arching her dark eyebrows in disapproval.

"Oh, he's just kidding," Mia assures Gia. Shaking her head, she tells Marco, "Your daddy's so silly, isn't he?"

No longer fussing, Marco grins at Mia and reaches for her.

"Do you mind?" she asks Colette quickly.

"God, no. He's been fussy all day, please take my baby."

Mia chuckles and unceremoniously shoves the veggie tray into my hand. I let go of Colette to steady it with my other one, narrowing my eyes at her as she takes my son in her arms.

Mia is referred to as the baby whisperer in our family because all babies—and children, but it's more obvious with the babies—love her. As soon as Marco gets close enough to his favorite aunt, he squeezes her neck in his version of a hug and leaves an open-mouthed slobber kiss right on her cheek.

"Aw, I'm happy to see you, too," she says, hugging him back. "You want to go see your uncles? Give Mommy a break for a few minutes?"

"Are you sure?" Colette asks. "You're hosting a party; you shouldn't have to babysit, too."

Mia waves her off. "Please, I have tons of help with the party and I'm accustomed to juggling babies. Go, enjoy yourselves. Are you hungry? I'll show you to the food table."

"You'll have to, since apparently I'm in charge of the veggie tray," I tell her.

Mia kisses Marco's head in the same motherly way Colette does, then reaches down, reclaiming Gia's hand, and beckons us to follow after her. Colette takes advantage of her free arms and wraps one around my waist, leaning into me as we walk.

"I think this party's going to be fun," she tells me.

"Mm hmm," I remark, unconvinced.

"I can't stop picturing you as a sexy pirate now," she adds, her tone a little lower. "I want to sneak off and do naughty things with you."

I change my hold on the veggie tray and sling an arm around

her shoulders. "Well, this house does have a ton of spare rooms."

"I didn't bring a spare blouse, though," she teases.

"Take one of Mia's. She'll never notice it missing."

Once we reach the food table, I add the veggie tray to the impressive array of snacks already assembled. No matter how picky the eater, there's something for every kid to devour on this table.

Nodding her head toward the poolside patio, she tells us, "There's a bartender serving adult beverages over there." Glancing down at Gia, she asks, "Are you thirsty? Should we stop and get some pink lemonade on the way to Rapunzel's tower?"

Gia nods her head, but her eyes are glued to the unicorn. "Can I meet Glimmer on the way?"

"Sure," Mia says easily, leading us over to the white pony.

Tugging on Colette's waist to slow her down, I ask, "Why are we still following her?"

Colette's dark eyebrows rise. "You think I'm *not* going to take a picture of Gia with a *unicorn*? Have you met me?"

I roll my eyes. "For Christ's sake, it's a pony in a costume."

She swats me in the stomach again for trying to ruin the magic and we continue over to the damned unicorn. Rosalie is over there right now, brushing the pony and talking to it. Her gaze drifts to us as we approach and she slowly stops grooming the animal.

"Hi Uncle Dante, hi Aunt Colette. Thanks for coming to my birthday party."

Not even giving us a chance to respond, Gia breaks away from Mia and approaches the pony, gazing up at it like it really is a magical creature. "I can't believe you got a unicorn at your house. Is it yours?"

Rosalie shakes her head. "No, she belongs to Princess Bella. Mama said she was just letting Glimmer visit today for a surprise for my birthday."

"Who's Princess Bella? You mean your big sister?"

"No, not her." Rosalie hops down off her stepping stool and lifts her floor-length, giant, poofy purple dress. She makes her way over to a basket full of books and grabs one. Bringing it back to Gia, she says, "Here you go, you can meet her in this book. We ordered a lot of copies of book one to give away so other kids can read about Glimmer now that they've met her."

Gia flips over the book, inspecting the back. "Thanks." She makes a beeline over to Colette and holds up the thin paperback. "Can you hold this for me?"

"Of course," Colette says, taking the book and bending to stuff it in Marco's diaper bag. She extracts a package wrapped in pink gift wrap while she's at it and holds it up, looking at Mia. "Where should we put Rosalie's gift?"

I have no idea what Colette got her. It's hard as hell to shop for Mateo's kids. They already have everything imaginable, and some things no sane person would *ever* imagine.

Mia holds out her free hand. "I'll drop it off on the way to the tower."

Things that can only be said at my brother's house. Colette makes me hold the diaper bag while she takes a dozen pictures of the girls in various poses around the unicorn. A brunette woman with a big camera hanging around her neck comes over and snaps a couple photos of them. Mia assures me it's the photographer, like that's a normal thing to have at a children's birthday party, then she and Colette talk about the birthday scrapbook Mia's going to make.

After promising to send Colette copies of the photographs with Gia in them, Mia hauls both of my children away to the newly erected gray tower my brother had built in his back yard. I love the hell out of my little family, but I still think it's crazy how much Mateo does to please his wife and kids. A far cry from our childhood, that's for fucking sure.

As we walk away, Colette hugs my waist again and murmurs, "I can't believe he built her a *tower* for her birthday. I mean, plenty of kids get a tree house or a play house in the back yard, but Rapunzel's *tower?*"

"He's fucking crazy. He had to bribe the chairman of the zoning board to get special approval just to build that fucking thing." I look around until I find the bloated bastard I spotted a minute ago. "Right there at that table, that's the chairman and his wife. Their three kids are probably running around here somewhere. Bet he really thinks he's something now, being invited to Mateo Morelli's house like they're friends."

"Oh, stop. I think it's sweet Mateo went to all that trouble just to make his girls happy. I like seeing him finally settled and happy. You're right, though, the bar has definitely been raised. Gia's going to think we're the worst parents ever if we don't get her something really good this year. It might be time for a puppy."

"Goddamn Mateo," I mutter.

AFTER A LONG DAY and way too much sugar, Gia crashes on the couch curled up beside me. It was supposed to be my night to put Marco to bed, but Colette didn't want to wake Gia up, so she took him up instead.

When she comes back, she curls up on my other side and rests her head against my chest. "What a long day. I'm beat."

"That was entirely too long to spend with that many children," I agree. My brother has enough children to fill a party all by himself, but adding in all the guests they had, it was a fucking tiny human zoo.

Colette nods, absently rubbing my thigh. "I think when we have Gia's birthday party, we'll keep it at four hours." Tilting her head to look up at me, she says, "Unless of course you're planning to surprise her with a tower."

"Definitely not."

"A life-sized pirate ship? She's very into pirates right now."

"I think you're confused about which Morelli you married. I'm Dante, not Mateo. I might buy her a puppy, but I'm not going to commission part of a castle."

With mock disappointment, she says, "Clearly you just don't love us enough."

I squeeze her in the side right where I know she's ticklish. She laughs and squirms to get away from me. I stop when I feel Gia stirring. Colette claps a hand over her mouth, but Gia just snuggles up, puts her hands under her face, and stays asleep.

"Oops," Colette whispers.

"That's what you get for saying ridiculous things," I state.

"Well, while I'm saying things you won't like, I might as well tell you: I did ask Mia to help me plan Gia's birthday party."

I blink at her. "You're kidding."

She shakes her head. "I'm not. I know she's not your favorite person—"

"That is a *massive* understatement. Want me to crunch the numbers and tell you how much her existence in our lives has cost me? I *could* build a fucking castle with that much money."

Holding up a hand to stop me, she says, "But I don't care. You saw the party she threw for Rosalie, you've seen all the parties she has planned over the years; she's good at it. Your quibbles with her in the past aside, there's no reason not to let her make Gia's birthday as much fun as Rosalie's was. I even told Mia we don't have her budget to blow on a party, and she told me if we go over budget, she'll pay for it. She's *throwing* the party, she's even helping foot the bill, so… there's no acceptable reason for you to say no."

"I strongly disagree."

She shrugs. "It's happening anyway. Suck it up, buttercup."

"I can't believe this. You're selling me down the river for some fucking snow cones."

"Mm." She rests her head on my shoulder and bats her eyelashes at me. "They were *really* good snow cones."

"This is some bullshit. You're gonna have to work pretty hard to make this up to me, Mrs. Morelli."

"Oh, yeah?" she asks, with interest. "What'd you have in mind?"

"Nothing I can put into words with our daughter in the room," I tell her. "Seems to me you need a reminder of who the boss is in this family."

Playfully tapping her finger against her chin, she looks up at me and pokes the fucking beast. "Mateo?"

I know she's just fucking with me, but my hackles rise, regardless. "Oh, all right. I see how it is."

"Do you? Do you see how it is?"

Fisting a hand in my wife's hair and tugging her head back

to force her gaze to mine, I tell her, "Seems to me, you're looking to get your little ass beat."

Her blue eyes heat with unrestrained desire. "Among other things."

I pull her close for a crushing, brutal kiss. Her mouth softens and she kisses me back hungrily, twisting and turning until she's on her knees with her arms wound around my neck, trying to pull me closer.

I need both hands to take this any further, so regretfully, I break away from my wife's hungry kiss. "I'm gonna carry Gia up to bed, then we're gonna continue this."

Settling back against the couch with a soft smile, she says, "I'll be waiting."

I carefully move away from my daughter, scooping her up in my arms and catching her heavy, sleepy head against my chest. Her long, dark curls bounce gently as I carry her up the stairs, but she's so worn out from the party that she stays asleep.

Her room is dark and despite being told to several times, she didn't clean up her toys before we left for my brother's house this afternoon. I have to walk carefully to get to her bed without tripping over any of her shit, but I make it. Shifting her in my arms and cradling her against my chest, I pull back her blankets so I can tuck her underneath them.

I had to move her too much, so when I pull the blankets up to tuck her in, she's stretching her little arms over her head, looking up at me with her big, brown eyes.

"Hi, Daddy," she murmurs, sleepily.

"Hi, baby," I say, leaning forward and kissing her on the forehead. "You fell asleep on the couch, I was just bringing you up to bed. Go back to sleep."

"But what about my bedtime story?" she asks.

"You're sleepy. How about two bedtime stories tomorrow night instead?"

She shakes her head at me. "I'm not too tired for a bedtime story."

I cast a glance back at the door, thinking of my horny wife waiting downstairs. Then I look back at my daughter, and she gives me her biggest, most innocent puppy dog eyes.

Sighing heavily, I stand and stalk over to turn on her light. "Fine. A quick one," I stipulate.

"Yay!" she says, clapping her hands together. "I wanna read the unicorn book Rosalie gave me at the party."

"I said a quick one. That's a chapter book," I tell her.

Utilizing the knack for getting her way with me that she clearly inherited from her mother, she tells me, "You're smart, Daddy, I bet you can read really fast."

"Oh, you little manipulator, you."

Cocking her head in confusion, she says, "I don't know that word."

"Yes, you do," I say wryly, walking over to her dresser. I grab the chapter book Colette put there and make my way back to Gia's bed, taking a seat on the edge. "Only one chapter," I tell her, sternly.

Gia nods her head obediently. "Yes, Daddy. Only one chapter."

Two chapters later, Gia is tuckered out and struggling to hold her eyes open, so she is too exhausted to beg me for a third. I put the book down on her nightstand and lean down to give her another kiss.

"You get some sleep," I tell her.

"Mm, night night, Daddy," she mumbles, rolling over and

tossing an arm around the stuffed puppy toy she sleeps with each night.

I turn out Gia's light and check on Marco real quick to make sure he's asleep. Last thing I need is the baby monitor interrupting all the filthy shit I plan to do to my wife as soon as I get back downstairs.

Marco is passed out, his pacifier on the bed beside him, his chubby fingers clutching the soft, crunchy spider toy he likes to squeeze when he's trying to fall asleep. A wave of contentment washes over me and I reach into the crib, lightly running the backs of my fingers along the side of his face.

"G'night, buddy," I whisper, even though he can't hear me.

Now that the kids are both settled, I can finally go back downstairs and enjoy the woman who made my life what it is. I lick my bottom lip, still tasting her. I envision her surprising me by already being naked when I get back to the living room, saving me a little work and having that beautiful body of hers on display as soon as I walk in.

Instead, I walk into the living room and find her fully dressed, passed out on the arm of the couch, holding onto a decorative pillow.

I sigh loudly, hoping she's barely asleep and that'll be enough to rouse her.

It's not.

I stand there and watch her for another minute, hoping she'll wake up, but she's completely out. Finally, I give up. I do my bedtime routine and check all the locks to make sure the house is secure, then I shut off the lights. I hit the living room light last, then I approach my drowsy wife and pry the pillow away from her.

She mutters at me incoherently, something about sheep. She

says the weirdest shit when she's half-asleep. I shake my head at her and pick her up, pulling her against me and carrying her up the stairs to our bedroom. I kick the door shut on the way in, but don't bother turning on the lights. I put her down on the bed and undress her in the dark. I give this woman every chance in the world to wake up, but she doesn't.

Resigned to going to sleep with a case of blue balls, I undress myself and then climb into bed. Colette is sleeping on her side with her back to me, so I reach over and drag her back against me. A soft, sleepy, contented sigh slips out of her and brings a little smile to my face.

"Are you awake, beautiful?"

No response. I wait another few seconds and when she doesn't answer, I finally close my eyes. It *has* been a long day, and I've got an early morning tomorrow, so it doesn't take long until I've just about joined my wife in sleep.

That's when her hand snakes back and brushes my hip. That's when she wiggles her little ass against my cock and whispers, "Thought you were gonna teach me a lesson."

Oh, this woman.

I'm gonna teach her a lesson, all right.

I know she expects me to grab her and handle her roughly, so instead, I lean forward and tenderly kiss my way along the back of her neck. A faint noise of surprise slips out of her, then she leans her head forward to give me more space to work. I move her hair aside, letting it tickle her skin as I do. I run the blunt tip of my finger lightly along the curve of her neck. I drag my lips lower, kissing my way across her bare shoulder, then I finally take a fistful of her dark hair in my hand and tug her head to the side. She's so soft and pliant, so aroused she's willing to be my puppet, if that's what I'm in the mood for. As I kiss my way up the side of her neck, I murmur lowly, "Who's your king, Colette?"

Already breathless from my sensual assault, she sighs and whispers, "You are, Dante."

"Damn right, I am." I yank my beautiful wife underneath me, climbing on top of her and looking down into her perfectly flushed face. "And don't you forget it."

Smiling softly, all the love in the world right there in her eyes, she reaches up and cradles my face in her hand. "Never."

THE END

ACKNOWLEDGMENTS

There are so many members of this wonderful community I want to thank for all sorts of things, but I'll try to keep it short so I can hit publish on this damned book!

Obviously first and foremost, I want to thank you, the reader! I'm so glad my whacky characters and their messed up stories entertain you. Thank you for buying/borrowing my books! Thanks for you for reviewing and recommending them to your friends! Thank you for all those wonderful things you do. My job would not be possible without you.

An enormous thank you also goes out to my alpha and beta readers for lending their time and their eyeballs to help me catch things I missed! Kate, Jen, Sara, Vivian, and Azalia, you ladies rock! Your messages were so much fun to read while you were reading!

I hope everyone enjoyed Dante's story! If you have the time to leave a review, however short or long, hey, guess what? I'd appreciate that, too! ;)

There are still a couple more Morelli world spin-offs coming before the second generation's series launches, so stay tuned! :)

ABOUT THE AUTHOR

Sam Mariano loves to write edgy, twisty reads with complicated characters you're left thinking about long after you turn the last page. Her favorite thing about indie publishing is the ability to play by your own rules! If she isn't reading one of the thousands of books on her to-read list, writing her next book, or playing with her adorable preschooler... actually, that's about all she has time for these days.

Feel free to find Sam on Facebook, Goodreads, Twitter, or her blog—she loves hearing from readers! She's also available on Instagram now @sammarianobooks, and you can sign up for her totally-not-spammy newsletter HERE

If you have the time and inclination to leave a review, however short or long, she would greatly appreciate it! :)

Made in the USA
Las Vegas, NV
28 December 2022